ALICE – LOST

by

SURREAL

This book is sold subject to the condition that it shall not, by way of trade or otherwise, be lent, resold, hired out or otherwise circulated without the publisher's prior consent in any form of binding or cover other than that in which it is published and without a similar condition including this condition being imposed on the subsequent purchaser.

The characters and situations in this book are entirely imaginary and bear no relation to any real person or actual happening.

CHIMERA

Alice – Lost Soul first published in 2005 by
Chimera Publishing Ltd
PO Box 152
Waterlooville
Hants
PO8 9FS

Printed and bound in Great Britain by
Cox & Wyman, Reading.

ALICE – LOST SOUL

Surreal

This novel is fiction – in real life practice safe sex

Disconcerted pitched headlong into utter confusion, Alice not understanding a word of his accusations. Her right buttock smarting aggressively, her ear feeling as if it was being torn off, she finally gave thought to the injustice of her predicament. Hughes whipped her backside as if she were a child, or worse, a slave. And what did she do in return? She meekly accepted his rough handout. Did she subconsciously seek such abuse? Did she deliberately provoke those most likely to respond with physical indignity? She wasn't sure. But she *was* decided about her immediate susceptibility.

Humiliation and embarrassment tickled an elusive core, Hughes spanking her bare bottom, his complete dominance and her utter subservience adding their pennyworth.

Prologue

Hear no evil. See no evil. Speak no evil. That could well have been Alice Hussey's precept. Forever affording the benefit of doubt she succumbed repeatedly to the wiles and demands of others.

Ignorant of an intrinsic allure, she was bludgeoned by life's fickle passing. Infatuated with a man more than twice her age, fate continuously frustrated consummation of that relationship. Confused by irregular sexual desires, beaten by a conscience instilled by religious indoctrination, she battled constantly with the two sides of a naïve personality: animal lust and virtuous purity.

In *Shadows of Perdition* Alice naively pursued the idolised Jonathan. She prevaricated with the ever inquisitive and shrewd Jennifer. She pursued an intimate friendship with the eccentric Kate, and fell foul of the sadistic Harris.

Bent on facing the dreaded, volatile Uncle Richard, Alice plunged into a nether world of vilification, ignominy and terror. The pious erratic brute partook of the foulest liberties, and dealt a mental blow that lowered the girl into the abyss of despair.

Her world in tatters Alice ran from all, unable to face the world, her friends, her enemies. She briefly visited Howell House to change clothes, and write a short letter of explanation, to the effect she needed time on her own, and that she had borrowed money. The letter she handed to Odette to give to Jonathan on his return.

Harris took the letter, ignoring protests from the maid. After reading, he destroyed it.

Chapter One

Billowing steam, steel screaming on iron, a train pulled into Chester Station. A lost soul alighted and headed directly for the ladies' washroom. There the young woman scrutinised her reflection. Dejected green pools, eyelids bearing the mark of too many tears, stared mistily into space. Full lips tendering the spent remnants of subtle pink lipstick formed the demand, 'why?'

In an attempt to adopt insignificance she had donned a plain grey shirt, knee length, woollen charcoal skirt, long socks and a duffel coat. Alice brushed strands from a blotched complexion, examining the remaining make-up. Decision made, she scrubbed the pallid skin, eradicating all remnants of what she saw as a mask of decadence.

There were no cosmetics for a reconstruction; those along with her more exotic clothes had been deliberately left behind at Howell House. Alice wished to remain inconspicuous. She had suffered enough of the wiles and vagaries of men. There in that sterile atmosphere, amidst the gleaming white of sink bowls and ceramic tiles, a disparate Alice rose from the ashes. Determination, or perhaps desperation gripped, the crusade she had ruminated on became a sincere cause.

Mind in a state of flux, she had travelled from Chapel to Manchester, constantly churning over the events of that fateful day. She had courted the why and wherefore, delved for reason, searched her soul for answers. Confusion reigned supreme. The shock of disclosure, betrayal and equivocal intent erected an impenetrable wall, a barrier bolstered by possessive pangs of guilt.

At Manchester Central the girl had sat bewildered, pondering the imponderable. Life was impossible, her future as bleak as the Lancashire Moors in the grip of a desperate winter. Finally she reached the conclusion that her winter had come, but in turn, winter eventually gave to spring. Spring heralded the coming of summer where an abundance of blossom and fruit would be yielded. Without winter there could be no spring. If she permitted the abominable to jaundice her outlook, then the likes of Richard would win. She had to fight back. She had to forge her own path, resist outside influences, including those of the well-meant Jay.

That night she walked the grimy soot-stained streets of central Manchester, the cobbles glistening beneath penetrating drizzle. Alice had much to think about, and much to decide.

Early the next morning she purchased another ticket, a one way to Flint. There she would begin an arduous journey, the trek to finding her past and hopefully a future. She tugged the papers from their yellowed envelope, a small, tightly folded wad falling to the ground. Puzzled, curious she stooped and retrieved it. Edges worn and frayed she carefully unfolded what transpired to be two handwritten letters. The first bore barely legible black ink on letter headed paper. The correspondence was dated three months before Alice's birth.

Dear Reg,

With respect to your daughter, Rose. I have found her a place at The Ashby Priory, Halkyn Road, Flint. She will be held under the care of a Dr Compton, the resident psychiatrist. Please be assured that, as requested, all arrangements have been made using the utmost discretion.

You will be notified of the birth in due course. Please let me know your instructions should the infant be born 'in need'.

Regards,
Michael

Alice studied the print. Dr M. Yates. The Surgery, Knapp Road, Southport. The addressee would have been her grandfather,

Reginald senior. She had heard he was a man of connections, maybe even a Freemason. The letter certainly smacked of the 'Old Boys Club'.

Alice reacted with disbelief, anger and sheer repugnance. 'Utmost discretion,' she sighed, exasperated. 'Ashamed, in other words. Mortified by a medical disorder.' Alice let the new information settle, mulled it over, the second letter dangling, almost forgotten.

How much did her father have to do with this? How could he? The older brother, he stood idly by and let it happen. Poor Rose. Poor mother. Perhaps they weren't close, but if they were? That must have seemed like the worst kind of treachery. It might have broken her completely.

In need. What could he mean by in need? Hungry? No. Financial support, she supposed. So it looked like grandfather at least felt obliged to pay her keep.

She remembered the second letter, and placing that on top of the first, she read.

Dear Father,

There has been a terrible storm here in Flint. All the telephone lines are down with no word as to when they may be repaired. I am writing to say that should you wish to recognise her, there is an addition to the family. Alice Rose was born in hale and hearty at two minutes past ten this morning.

I have discussed at great length with 'your daughter' the child's future. Regardless of your bearing and influence, I have taken it upon myself to adopt Alice. Edith agrees and is very much enamoured with the baby. I do believe this is the best course for this family's plight.

Alice unfolded her birth certificate. She noted the place of birth. 'Going home,' she whispered, tears spilling freely.

Would fate be kind? Would the road end there? Could she resolve the inner conflict slowly ripping her to pieces? She could hope.

Aboard the train, a young man furtively assessed the young woman hunched in a corner, her face turned to the outside world. He studied the crossed legs, visible calves and skirt-cloaked thighs. Inquisitive eyes roamed higher, deliberating on the press of bosom, dress tight about prominent orbs. That interest detected by means of reflection, Alice ignored.

Tiredness gaining ground; she idly observed the rush and scurry of passengers, a contrast to the snails' pace of barrow pushing porters. Eyelids wavered, swept unperceived over pensive eyes, cloaking awareness, permitting serenity to dominate.

A shrill whistle sounded distant, the signal to all that the train was about to leave. The compartment door swung open, laboured breathing and shuffling feet announcing a late arrival.

Her name whispered loud confused, the familiar voice unsettling. 'Alice. Thank God I've found you.'

She sat upright, eyelids blinking, mind trying desperately to comprehend the absurdity.

'Shut the door please, sir,' offered a token of reality. 'The train is about to leave.'

'Two seconds,' Jonathan snapped in his usual abrupt manner. He turned to the other passenger. 'There's an empty compartment next door.'

'So?' the young man countered, hackles rising.

Jonathan rummaged in a pocket, pulling a ten-shilling note free. He held it up. 'Compensation. It's all I have on me. I need to talk to this young woman in private.' He held the money out, adding, 'Please.'

The lad rose, and snatching the note transferred to the next compartment.

Door shut and wheels rolling, Alice asked, dumbfounded, 'How, Jay? How the hell did you find me?'

'Questions. Is that all you have for me, Ali? Questions?'

Her heart ached fit to bust. Her mind swam dizzily. Tears of relief, sheer joy sprang to emerald eyes, spilling, cantering down flushed cheeks. She threw her arms about the man's neck, their

9

lips meeting, the kiss sensual and passionate. The train gathered speed.

Alice desisted, pulled away. Their eyes drank of one another, Jonathan tenderly wiping away her tears. 'Why run, Ali? And above all else, why run away from me?'

'I wasn't,' the girl assured. 'I wasn't running from you.'

'But you were running?'

'Not as such, Jay. Oh hell, it's so terribly complicated. Trust me, Jay. Just trust me.'

'We were worried. All of us. Jenny, Katy, and the staff.'

'Oh yes, I'm sure Harris was out of his mind.'

'He is concerned. I'm sure of that.'

'So Jay, how did you find me?'

'You should be getting ready for Heptonstall. I was looking forward to seeing you in that uniform.' He leant close, lips nuzzling her neck. 'There's something about you in a school uniform.'

'Something's come up, Jay…'

'Oh, and don't I know it.' He stifled her explanation, his mouth smothering hers, hands wandering intent.

Still nonplussed by the fortuity, the man, her lover avoiding explanation, Alice held back. Suspicions lurked, the impetuous Jay too precipitate.

He sensed her reluctance. 'Are you sure you weren't running away from me?' he asked.

She held his face, palms affectionately lain against his cheeks. 'Believe me, Jay. It's not you. I just need to sort my feelings, that's all.'

'And Richard? Does he have anything to do with this?'

Alice could not lie to the man she adored. 'Yes. But in an indirect way.'

'Has he said something? Hurt you?' Jay's dark eyes seemed to bore to her soul. The man stared, disbelieving. Anger creased his handsome features. He shook his head, rage and anguish consuming. Hands reached for that shock of dark hair, fingers clawing, fists grasping the locks. 'I'm going to kill him,' he

10

whispered. 'I'm going to break every fucking evil bone in his wretched body. He's dead,' he vowed.

'No, what are you thinking? Jay, he didn't…'

The man calmed, settled. 'Something's happened,' he surmised, suspicious. 'I wouldn't put it past the irksome scumbag, uncle or no uncle.'

'He, he has my best interests at heart.' She tossed the confused statement at Jay more to protect him than Richard.

Jonathan held out his hands in despair. 'This is more like a mad dream. Nothing is making sense. For Christ's sake, Ali, it's simple enough. I love you. I want you. I will do anything for you. Anything at all. Richard's a slimy toad. He's only concerned for himself, nobody else. If he has an interest in you, then you can bet it's because he stands to gain by it. Come home, Ali. Come back with me.'

She shook her head. 'I can't. Not yet.'

'Then make love to me. Give me something. Some token of how you really feel. At least do that.'

Alice looked shocked. Unsure, she lowered her eyes. 'We're on a moving train, Jay. A very public train.'

The man laughed. 'So innocent. Oh God, how different you are to Kate. We won't be interrupted, Ali. We have ten minutes or so before the next stop. But it's up to you.'

Part of her leapt to respond, doubt yielding to recklessness. Dilemma spun resolve, Alice losing sight of perspective. The combined effects of the last twenty-four hours pressed heavy on a belaboured conscience. Affection extended a merciful escape, Alice desperately in need of demonstrative love. Surrendering to Jay would eradicate her troubles, albeit temporarily. The man would become her protector, shielding her vulnerability. His strength would correct her weaknesses, his wealth resolve her parenthood. She had no doubt he could and would crush the despicable bully Richard.

Alice pulled aside the coat. Fingers effortlessly loosened blouse buttons, Jay hovering impatient, face expressive of his eagerness. She separated the cloth; pale breasts projected by her one emblem of independence, a black brassiere, half-cups heavily laced. Only she and chosen intimates would ever see it.

Spread fingers glided inside grey flannel, a rounded breast greeting a delicate exploration; his touch; sensual caress; the first whisper of sexual incitement. The knot of arousal formed, agreeable probes delving her groin. That delightful stirring invaded her abdomen, stomach adding its emotive cartwheels to the sweet feeling of euphoria.

She watched, thrilled as Jay impulsively sank his face in her luxurious cleavage, soft pillows stimulating his ardour. She sensed his lips kissing, teeth then nipping, tongue placating the sting. Fears and objections floated distant, an inner desire for unmitigated sexual intercourse gathering strength.

Jay gripped the retaining elastic, pulling and lifting the cups, breasts jerking free, their responsive quiver seductive. He drew her close, her torso angled forward, jutting breasts swaying tantalisingly. Mouth opened his tongue darted, a teat the recipient, the lick sending shivers through her body.

Alice severed the final strings of uncertainty. Lust replaced the horns of dilemma. She urged the duffel coat from her shoulders, the shirt quickly following. Unable to release the cuff buttons she watched instead her lover's animated contortions.

Her breasts rippled with the man's rough groping. Forceful fingers sank without finesse, comely orbs pressured beyond recognition. Simultaneously his tongue ran rampant, glistening with saliva. Nipples erect with expectation yielded to his lips and teeth, drawn deep into his attentive mouth.

Jonathan noticed her predicament, the tight cuffs pinning her arms. He grinned wickedly, hands disappearing beneath her skirt. Sleek thighs met that forage, Alice parting her legs, facilitating an easy path. His mouth busied with those consummate spheres, Jay wriggled searching fingers within the girl's panties. Alice could only indulge, her body energised with arousal.

She closed her eyes, wallowing in the tide of pre-orgasmic

flushes. Jay's intrusive fingers inflamed her further, tips prodding hirsute mound, nails clawing intimate knoll.

The man seized her panties, tugged them over those generous hips. Alice slid forward, balance undermined, control abandoned. She reeled to that wonderful sensation, guardian knickers in full flight, traversing smooth legs then torn from her feet. Shapely limbs surrendered to pressure, parting wide, vulnerability flooding her body.

Her panties landed in the far corner, Jay's head lost beneath her skirt. She lay, back to the seat, bottom supported by the man's hands, backs of her knees draped over his shoulders. A thumb rammed between her suckling lips, the fingers of her other hand tugging at auburn locks, she simmered.

That lithe torso tensed, hips jerking, his tongue raking her protrusive vulva. Fingers delved ample buttocks, probing, roaming free. He licked at her cunt, each pass spiralling her closer to nirvana. Her hips swayed, the gentle roll a response, her demonstrative accompaniment.

Sex lips gave, parted, meddlesome probe pushing inside. Alice surrendered in totality. 'Fuck me, Jay,' she whispered. 'Please fuck me.'

The tongue combed that fragile, sensitive pink inner. Alice moaned. 'Stuff me, Jay. Let me feel every inch of your excited cock.'

Turned, she laid the length of the seat, Jonathan climbing between her legs. She watched mesmerised the descent of zip, the uncloaking of that promising brute and its emergence into daylight. She hungered for it, ached to see it sink between her thighs, burned to feel it force an entry.

It hung massive, bigger than she recalled, the man's forefinger and thumb urging a retraction of foreskin. Cognisance snatched, enthralled, she followed the grudging surrender to glistening pink bulb, that singular eye seeming to wink suggestively. Jay's fist traced that solid shaft, to its root where he cupped full and impressive balls, lifted and draped outside his trousers they offered Alice a glimpse of the complete and capable poker.

Jay took hold of her ankles, lifting her calves. His member seemed to take on ever more significant proportions as he manoeuvred, his jerking glans advancing. Her feet offering company to her ears, her sex seemed unqualified to encompass the awesome proportions Jay offered. His swollen dome touched, kissed her fanny. Jonathan straightened, holding his erection vertical, that immense torpedo readied to plunge.

Alice gazed at him, at her lover, at her adored. Eyes lowered to watch, to drink of that carnal immersion. She felt the pressure, the push of eager penis, the press of hot, prodigious meat. Resilient folds surrendered to that goad, the stretch uncomfortable. The length glided in, vaginal walls facilitating, the spectacle a sensation.

Six inches crammed her fanny, two more posted proud, the thickness imposing. 'All of it, Jay,' Alice urged. 'I want it all.'

His hips lowered, driving the remaining shaft deep into her pussy, balls colliding, resting on her anus. The weight and touch compounded the feeling of depravity, the heady scent of promiscuousness. The lewdness opened a new and thrilling window, a portal to sexual utopia. Why? her mind cried. Why should she not enjoy it? Why should her body be only for the pleasure of others? Why was it such a sin when no harm was done? She felt deceived. She felt used. This was… this was wonderful!

That pole rose, drawn from the slick of her sex, wet and impressive. The precarious dome emerged, foreskin stretched about its neck, then plunged, the shock breathtaking. Fire seized her belly, frenzied bolts of energy loosed. She writhed, virtuous walls crumbling, a deeper purpose stealing ground. Unbridled pleasure had been procured by a natural use of *her* body.

Jonathan permitted Alice a more comfortable posture, her ankles resting on his shoulders, his hands about her knees. A steady rhythm adopted, Jay lunged repeatedly, impetus forceful. Her body jerked to each thrust, naked breasts trembling, sex primed for a second explosion.

The train slowed, brakes squealing. Heaven bound, Alice barely noticed, Jay impervious to everything except that spellbinding coitus. Numbed awareness warned, Alice looking toward the door. Jay increased momentum, his groin battering her buttocks, his cock shafting at speed. Her body jostled, jarred, his stroke was close to full bore.

Indistinct, a figure loomed, a grey, hazy blur. Rationality eluded, muscles heavy, Alice incapable of reason or reaction. With Jay's rigorous fucking growing distant she stared stupidly, unable to grasp the development. The spectre raised an arm, a finger pointed accusingly. Alice tried to make out the face, shrouded, unclear, fogged. A voice grated, slowed, unintelligible. She glanced up at Jay, the man fully absorbed, unaware of the arrival.

Her plight absurdly inconsequential, near naked with Jonathan's pace frenzied, Alice shook her head, indicating she didn't understand. She waited on enlightenment, endeavouring to penetrate the mists of confusion, and then clarity spread a nightmarish veil. No more the stranger, Richard stood over her, his face gnarled by rage, by disgust. 'Damnable whore!' he spat. 'See, as soon as my back is turned, the first opportunity and you're at it with *him*!'

The man bent, spittle flecked, bespectacled face inches from hers. With eyes bulging, manic, he mimicked sneering. 'Honestly uncle, we haven't had sex. I'm still a virgin. We've only petted.'

He grasped her breasts, one in each hand, fingers probing, thumbs massaging. 'Petted! Like this, Alice? And that's all, honestly uncle. Well, Alice, it looks like he's got his cock well and truly up your cunt. It seems to me, Mr Howell is fucking the arse off you. But you're not participating, are you girl? You're not enjoying his hard meat shafting your pussy. What is it? A service? An experiment? Or perhaps I'm seeing things. Perhaps the lecher isn't ramming it in to the hilt. Perhaps his bollocks aren't swinging in rhythm and slapping against your naked arse.'

Spasms of terror paralysed, lungs refusing air. Her heart seized, the shadow of eternity edging near.

'I warned you what would happen,' Richard snarled. 'Now are you ready, Alice? Are you ready for eternal damnation? Look.' He pointed toward the window. 'The fires of hell. Purgatory awaits.

'Sins of the flesh, Alice.' Richard cried with glee. 'I did my best to deter you. But you wouldn't listen, would you? I gambled my body, my soul to save you. I risked the wrath of God to expose the path you travelled. But you settled on condemnation. You refused to see, to open your ears to divine integrity. Your evil mind twisted the truth. Your devil body yearned for degradation and filthy liaison. Well, Alice, you have earned your place. Hell accepts you as a devil's disciple.' He lifted an arm toward Jonathan. 'See now your prize.'

Barely daring Alice turned her face, revulsion gripping, and stared disbelieving, the horror too much.

She screamed. Hands fell upon her, gripping, squeezing her wrists. Fingers grabbed, hurting her upper arms. She fought, arms thrashing. She begged, the pleas barely intelligible. 'She's 'avin' a fit,' penetrated the terror. 'Slap 'er face.'

Pain lashed a cheek, the girl's eyes jerking open. She stared uncomprehending, a large woman towering over her.

'I'm sorry, my dear,' the woman tendered, 'but we tried to wake you and you went for us. I had no choice but to slap you. Were you having a fit? Is that what it were?' Her face loomed close, eyes peering at Alice. 'Are you all right now?'

The girl struggled to her feet, legs shaking, and weak she leant on the doorframe. 'Here,' called the young man who had shared her compartment, 'your bag.'

Alice nodded her thanks, and aided by a porter managed to step from the carriage. Dizzy, disorientated she turned, bent and threw up. A hand pressed to the woodwork she tried to grip reality, but that dream, nightmare – dreadful premonition? – remained clear and sickening.

She sat a while mulling it over. Her witnesses departed, eyeing her as if she were mad. Perhaps she was. Perhaps her mother,

16

Rose Hussey, began her journey to the asylum that way. Did her dreams mingle with and overlap reality? Could Rose no longer differentiate between figments of the imagination and the kosher occurrence? Alice couldn't help wonder if that was how she came into the world, the product of a befuddled woman who'd lost her grip on reality.

Alice clasped her hands, head bowed. It was so vivid! It was only a dream, but Jay and Richard were so real! Her head lifted and she studied the sky, cotton wool balls drifting aimlessly against an azure saucer. Even in that depressed state she still held an admiration for the oak and elm that lined the station, their leaves giving to the red and gold of autumn. Where did the dream end? What was real? What was imagined? Was she awake or asleep? How could she know for sure? Did Jay really have sex with her while Richard rained abuse? Had she passed out and found this as a retreat? Was this where madness began?

Alice stood, her body lethargic. She'd assume this was reality. God, it was bleak enough. Maybe there was truth in what Richard spouted. Perhaps Jay wanted to eat his cake and she was the icing, Jenny the sponge and heaven knows who the jam filling was. Where was Jay when she needed him? He should have been there for her. He should have talked her out of leaving. If he felt the way he said he did, then why cling to the past? Why hang on to yesterday's clothes?

Alice strolled towards the barrier, ticket in hand. Was she gifted in body? Was that her appeal? The perfect arse? The consummate tits? Legs in a million? Was she man's desire, and was that devil driven? Was she the devil's disciple? Was she temptation? Was that her slot in life, to draw the loving husband from his doting wife? To seduce the devout Christian from the path of righteousness? *'Are you in there, Satan?'*

Alice unfastened the buttons of her shirt. She peered down; satin pillows snug in their black upholstery. *'Well, Satan, speak to me. Do you possess my tits? Are you tucked in my fanny ready to pounce? Will you infect any that trespass in my hole?'*

She reached the barrier, the porter frowning. Alice looked up

17

and smiled. 'What would you say?' she asked, pulling back the shirt. 'Are they temptation? Are they devil-made? Will you rot in hell if you touch them?'

Fifty-something, married forever and not having seen a girl like Alice before, the man nearly choked.

She handed him the ticket. 'Perhaps Richard has a point.'

Fists squeezed iron railings as dispirited eyes perused a board. *The Hope-Ashby Preparatory College*. Her heart hung heavy. Nothing in life would prove simple. Every attempt to improve her wretched existence was met by disappointment and frustration. Where was the sanatorium? Where was her mother? Too much to hope for. Too easy an answer. For her there would be no trouble-free path. Alice would have to fight for every inch of ground. Fate decreed a torturous route, and if she wanted happiness she would have to endure the long haul there.

The facility bore the hallmark of an asylum. Something about the Victorian structure cried misery. The building exuded anything but hope. Even the windows sported metal bars. Alice shivered. Just the thought of being incarcerated in that place oppressed, spiralled the prevailing gloom into a pit of darkness. Foreboding failed to convey the melancholy that edifice communicated. Knowing her mother may have spent years there intensified the misery she already suffered.

Forlorn, unsure of her next move, Alice wandered through imposing, intricately wrought gates. The possibility that someone there might recall the sanatorium, and a nagging curiosity about her birthplace urged her forward. The girl strolled towards the main doors, the strange sensation that she walked in her mother's footsteps chilling.

She was met by a restive soul, a woman in her early thirties who gave the impression her knickers were on fire. 'Ah, you must be… you're not a new student, are you?' She gave Alice no opportunity to reply. 'No, new students don't walk blithely in. They're usually escorted. So, perhaps you've come about the job. I do so hope you have. Mr Hughes. That's the headmaster. Though headmaster isn't actually his title. Principal, really. He's been giving me so much aggravation about the lack of interest. But what can I do? I can't make people apply, can I? I've done all I can. I've put an ad in the local paper. I've notified the National Assistance office. Please say you've come for the job.

'Oh, I'm Miss Jarvis, by the way.' She offered a hand.

Alice took advantage of the temporary silence. A job might prove the interim answer – an income, a roof over her head, a place to make further enquiries from. 'I might be interested,' she offered, smiling.

'Oh, wonderful! The wages aren't terrific, but it is live in, bed and board included. And Mr Hughes does have his charitable side. Oh, he barks, but that's mainly due to the pressure. He won't suffer fools, you see. A bit gruff on the surface. I think that's why the last help left. She couldn't see beneath the flinty exterior…'

Miss Jarvis faltered. She gazed imploringly at Alice. 'Oh, my mouth! It just runs away. I haven't put you off, have I? He does have a heart, I'm sure he does. After all, I'm still here after seven years.'

'No, Miss Jarvis, you haven't put me off. What's *your* position here?'

'Secretary. Mr Hughes' right arm.'

'And what does the job entail?'

'It's a sort of girl Friday, I suppose. Cook and clean for the principal. Help me in the office. And take on anything that might arise in an emergency.'

'And the wages?'

'I think about three pounds a week plus bed and board. But Mr Hughes will verify that.'

'And I'll live here, at the college?'

'Yes, your own room. Plus use of a bathroom, of course.'

The pair wandered inside, Mavis Jarvis blissful in locating a possibility, and Alice flush with questions.

'What was here before the college, Miss Jarvis?'

'Mavis, please. If you're to work with me then please call me Mavis.'

'Okay, Mavis.'

'This used to be a sort of hospital. Patients with mental troubles. Not the dangerously insane, oh no. Just those that couldn't cope.'

'Did you live in the area in those days?'

'I've lived in Flint all my life. The hospital was closed down in forty-seven. It was then renovated, and reopened as the Hope-Ashby in forty-eight. Part of the building had to be rebuilt. A bomb dropped by a damaged aircraft struck it in forty-two. It turned back from Liverpool after being hit by ack-ack. Several houses were destroyed and the hospital hit.'

Alice's heart missed a beat. 'Was anybody killed?'

'Dreadful business. The poor devils were locked in. They didn't stand a chance. Oh, the siren went off as they passed over on their way to Liverpool, but we'd become complacent. I mean, what's worth bombing in Flint? No one was aware of that lone plane coming back. Twenty-three patients were killed; another ten seriously wounded. I think that had a lot to do with them closing the place down. It was a terrible embarrassment to the establishment.'

'Where did the surviving patients go?'

'I don't know. I think those that couldn't be released were sent all over the country. Anywhere that had a bed spare.'

Alice chose not to further the questioning, not wishing to arouse suspicions.

'I'll go and tell the head, sorry, principal, that you're here. I'm sure he'll be only too pleased to interview you when he has a moment. I'm sure you'll get the job. You seem such a delightful young woman.'

Jarvis led Alice inside, the distinctive smell reminiscent of school. Shades of green decorated the long hallway stretching before them. Dismal polished ivy paint covered the lower half, an insipid avocado the upper. The mottled grey floor appeared recently buffed, an end window casting pools of reflected light.

A burly uniformed man stood waiting with a bunch of keys. He grunted as the pair strode by, closing the doors behind them. Alice frowned as she detected the click of a locking bolt.

'Oh, that's Mr Pierce, the custodian. We have to ensure the security of our girls. We can't have just anybody wandering in.'

'It's a girl's faculty then?' Alice enquired. 'No boys.'

Mavis smiled. 'Plenty of company for you. Oh, your name, I haven't even asked your name. How remiss.'

'Alice. Alice Hussey.'

'Not by nature, I trust.' The woman giggled nervously. 'Sorry, you must have heard that a million times.'

The young woman looked away, guilt needling, but a resonant mental whisper squeezed that remorse. *'Oh, how observant of the dithering drab. Hussey by name, hussy by nature. You'd part your legs at the dip of a hat, wouldn't you? Hussey. Not fussy, are you hussy?'*

'I didn't offend you, did I?' The woman's apology dragged her back.

Alice shook her head, and flustered, she assured Jarvis. 'No, I'm used to that one.'

Alice followed the secretary up several flights of stone steps. 'Mr Hughes' office is on the second floor. The top is reserved for living quarters. That's ground and first for classrooms. Second for offices and studies and the third for...' The woman panted. 'Ah, here we are. The head's office.'

She knocked, a baritone voice booming from beyond the heavy door. 'Come.'

Two girls loitering further down the passage engaged Alice's attention. Both appeared nervous, their stance and gestures indicating anxiety, but more to the point, and of particular interest, were the way the pair were dressed. In Alice's mind, college inferred informal, but the two restless souls she scrutinised wore pale blue pinafore dresses; attire that cried *school*. Heptonstall was different. The place was a public school that catered to further education, and as such its scholars were expected to adhere to a code of dress. Expected, not instructed. However it would be a courageous or foolish student who chose not to demonstrate their pride in Heptonstall.

The girls whispered to one another, voices hushed, lips imparting confidences inches from one another's ears. One habitually rubbed her backside, dress pleats rising and falling, swaying with her agitated movements. The other leaned sullenly against the wall, eyes staring into space, bottom lip sulkily pouting.

Their posture spoke troubled. Alice had witnessed the like before. At Carters, she recalled girls waiting for execution outside Miss Lake's office. The memory of her one caning there floated clear. Savage strokes administered by a reserved martinet. Gruelling cuts that sliced agonisingly into taut buttocks, the cheeks insubstantially covered by gossamer panties. And then whipped on the naked bottom. She had endured a good few thrashings since, but that one still haunted.

Miss Jarvis emerged, face coloured, hands shaking worse than ever. 'If you would like to go in, Alice, Mr Hughes will be with you in due course. Just take a seat.' The woman seemed embarrassed, unable to look Alice in the eye. She darted away, her footfalls echoing as she descended the stairs.

Alice nosed in, a musty smell assaulting the senses. The room proved typical study, lined with bookcases and volumes of tomes. Alice took a seat, a hard, stiff-backed chair. Before her stood the principal's desk, strewn with papers, the urge to nose irresistible. A large coat-stand filled a corner, four angular pieces rising from a base and braced at the top. A trilby, scarf and raincoat hung from a brass hook.

Another door lay ajar, Alice assuming the man left by that means. A pipe settled in an ashtray explained the peculiar odour. A large window beyond offered a panorama of rolling fields and faraway haze obscured hills.

A distant report and ensuing squeal startled her. Ears pricked, listened intently, lest they were mistaken. A second thwack, the categorical crack of cane on flesh unmistakable. Alice rose, almost tiptoed to the door. She listened. A third echoed far off. Her intuition had been proved right. Those two girls were hanging on tenterhooks. They were scheduled for a caning, and waited anxiously on the principal's appearance.

Horror mingled with ghoulish curiosity. Part of her urged departure, the remainder desirous of a more intimate view. Withering principles stabbed at her conscience, a prospering malignancy born from outrage gaining ground.

Alice edged the door wider and peered beyond. Another office devoid of furniture met her prying eyes. Another open door led onto the corridor, the punishment obviously being carried out further down the hall.

Six strokes at ten second intervals were dispensed. A lengthy three minutes dragged before the formidable thump of cane on backside resumed. By then Alice had been seduced as far as the corridor, where she concluded the rod whipped a bared behind. She recognised that distinctive splat only too well.

Another six volatile strokes dealt she detected the murmur of a man's voice, the words indistinct. She pushed the door to within an inch of the jam as the punished wretches emerged. They strode awkwardly towards her, their expressions discomforted, eyes red with tears. Alice withdrew, resettling her self in the principal's office. What misdemeanour had the pair committed to warrant six of the best? And what circumstances prevailed at Hope-Ashby to provide Hughes with the authority to beat girls of that age. They gave the appearance of being in their late teens, close to her own age.

Heptonstall stipulated the signing of a waiver, thereby giving the principal the option of using corporal punishment in extreme cases. The understanding was that for the famed and exacting level of discipline to be upheld, the ruling body had to command an ultimate deterrent besides expulsion. Heptonstall viewed sacking as failure.

The arrival of Hughes terminated that mental enquiry. Alice would be expected to answer rather than ask.

'Alice Hussey, I understand,' he said by way of an

introduction.

The young woman stood, offering her hand. 'That's right.'

'Geoffrey Hughes,' he advised, accepting the handshake. 'I am the principal in charge of this institution.' He smiled. 'Yes, institution rather than educational establishment. I will explain in due course.'

He took his seat and with pen and paper ready, asked, 'Your age, Alice?'

'Eighteen.'

'And your address?'

'I'm between. I lived with my uncle, but, um, let's say we didn't see eye to eye.'

'Not sleeping in the park I trust?'

'No. I left Southport this morning.'

'Southport? So why come to Flint?'

'Coincidence. I was seeking information about something that occurred some years ago. That brought me here. Your Miss Jarvis said you have a vacancy for a girl Friday. I'm not in work and looking for accommodation. I won't deny this would be most opportune, should you find me acceptable.'

'And experience?'

'I'm a female, sir; cooking and cleaning come naturally.'

Hughes chortled. 'You have a gleam to your eye, a sparkle that implies intelligence. You sound educated. So why apply for a menial's job?'

'May I be impudent and ask a question?'

'Of course.'

'Did you go straight into teaching?'

He shook his head. 'No, I joined the army.'

'But you had your sights on teaching?'

'No, I had my sights on Field Marshall.' He lit his pipe and puffing smoke continued. 'Along came the war, and this humble servant went where and did as he was instructed. The sights I witnessed disillusioned me, so I happily accepted my demobilisation. From there I joined the ranks of prison guard. Within five years I attained the position of Governor.'

He knocked the embers from the bowl. 'I tell you this as it has a direct bearing on this particular establishment. After the war many found it difficult to adjust. Some couldn't fit back into society. The crime rate soared and the prisons filled. And then there was the younger generation that were influenced by grievous loss. Many found themselves in orphanages until they reached their majority.

'I would like to be able to state that they matured with grace, that the homes were caring, that the staff did their best. Alas, I cannot. I witnessed many arrive in prison that without the war would probably have become model citizens. I think the government, the older generation and people like myself, owe those unrecognised casualties a little understanding and perhaps a second chance.

'This faculty is a last chance establishment for young women. We cater for girls up to the age of twenty-one. There is no definitive demarcation line. You will discover should you work here, that there are women of twenty-three or four. The criterion is that they can prove the war had a detrimental effect on their lives, and that they are younger than twenty-one when sent here.'

Geoffrey Hughes leaned back and spun the swivel chair full circle. 'Their crimes?' he barked, arm raised, finger pointing at the ceiling. 'We do not cater for the violent. Only the weak. Therefore our clientele, shall we say, are primarily prostitutes…'

'There's a place for you here, Hussey!'

'…petty thieves, defrauders and habitual drunks. A motley crew, I would say – some good, some bad, and some indifferent. It is my job to sort them, to show them the road to righteousness.' Hughes laughed. 'There I must fail, I'm afraid. Religious I am not. But fair? Strict? Idealistic? I would like to think so.'

He eyed Alice, gaze penetrating, seeming to read her. 'Any questions so far?'

Alice shook her head.

'The girls remain until either they are recommended for release, or written off and returned to prison.'

'What criteria do they have to meet to get parole?' Alice enquired, seeing their stay as interminable.

'Good question. Show's you're listening. We have several milestones. At the Hope they either learn a trade or study academically. There is no place for idlers. Should they fare well and pass the requisite exams then they are considered. But every inmate has to be given the green light by our resident psychiatrist, Dr Sheila Doodney. She is highly competent and quite able to root out the wolves.'

'Do many go back to their criminal ways?'

'So far, none. The Hope has been in operation for seven years now. We have been releasing remodelled young ladies for the last five. None have been rearrested. I believe our methods are effective and are therefore justifiable. When the girl is offered a place at the Hope she is made well aware of our practices and is asked to sign a waiver. She is also informed that should she accept and pass out with credit, then her criminal history will be erased. She will have a new start in life. That is an opportunity only the incorrigible would ruin. And believe me, Miss Hussey, we do not free the incorrigible.'

'My duties, sir? What would be expected of me?'

'This is an experimental institution. There are those in the administration that would have us closed tomorrow, and all our unfortunates locked away in borstal or prison. The job advertised is for a girl Friday. What that means in terms of involvement, remuneration and satisfaction will be very much down to you. But initially I would wish you to learn our ways by helping in the kitchen at mealtimes. Serving, not cooking. Aiding and abetting our industrious Miss Jarvis and odd jobs I might throw your way. How does that sound?'

'Fine. Is there anything you wish to ask me?'

'Can you provide two character referees?'

'Miss Lake of Carter's Academy at Stoke on Trent. Miss Lake is the headmistress. I had to leave when my parents were killed. I can't think of anybody else.'

'No matter. Miss Lake's word will suffice.

'Are you happy to live in? The wages take that into account. Though living in will mean your hours aren't nine to five, I'm afraid.'

'I'm not shy of hard work or long hours.'

'Excellent. You will be given one day per week off. Do with that as you please. I can offer you three pounds a week, your own room and free meals. I might even be able to extend that to a clothing allowance. Is that agreeable?'

Alice smiled and nodded.

'When would you like to start?'

'You mean I've got the job?'

'A month's probation and dependent on this Miss Lake writing an agreeable reference.'

'I can start immediately,' Alice tendered, ecstatic.

'Tomorrow will be fine. See if you can find Mavis. Tell her you are now a member of the team. She can sort your room and introduce you to the rest of the Hope fraternity. I'm sure you will be happy here, Alice.'

Hughes settled, leaning back in his chair. He lit his pipe, puffing cogitative, then jabbed a finger in her direction. 'I see something in you, Alice.' He chewed the stem. 'Promise. You emanate potential.'

Sweet-scented tobacco smoke billowed and curled. 'I sense empathy. You, I believe, will not only be able to relate to the endeavours of Hope, but contribute to its successful future.'

Hughes spun the chair and gazed out of the window, his back to the girl. 'I feel certain you will not disappoint, Alice.'

Chapter Two

The top floor offered a perfect view of Flint. The intrepid Miss Jarvis took immediate charge of what she construed as *her* girl Friday. Alice digested an impressive panorama stretching to the sea as Mavis laid the girl's clothes out. 'I don't know what you'll wear tomorrow, Alice,' she fussed. 'Is this all you have?'

'I thought I might travel light,' Alice offered as excuse. 'There *are* other clothes, but they are miles away in Chapel-en-Frith. I'd rather do without than send for them.'

Mavis threw her arms up. 'Well to be frank, this will not be enough. I could get you a Hope uniform to tide you over, but that might cause a bit of confusion. You could be taken as one of the pupils.'

'In the short-term, yes, but it would soon be sorted, wouldn't it?'

'Very well, I'll arrange a couple of blouses and two pinafores to be drawn from stores. And tomorrow I'll speak to Mr Hughes; see if we can't agree an advance.'

'You're very kind, Mavis.'

'Not at all.' Miss Jarvis blushed a little at the compliment. 'Now, are you hungry?'

'Starving.'

The pair descended towards the ground floor, a group of a half dozen girls blocking a landing. 'What's this, Miss Jarvis?' asked a slight blonde, her accent telling of East End London origins. 'Another lamb to the slaughter?'

Mavis Jarvis brooked no impudence, and all meekness disappeared as she reprimanded the young woman. 'Mind your manners, Ruth O'Leary, unless you wish for an appointment with the head.'

The girl stepped aside. 'Didn't mean no offence, miss. Just askin', that's all.'

'You'll be introduced in good time. That's all you need to know.'

Alice followed the secretary past the group, one girl whispering to another, 'I'll wager that arse is going to bring her a lot of unwanted attention.' Mavis seemed not to hear, Alice unsure whether she was meant to either.

Mavis stopped at the top of the last flight. 'Until told differently the girls will assume you're an addition to their ranks. And when they do find out who you are, you might find they resent you for your age.'

'I'll cope,' Alice assured her.

'Of course you will. I'll ask Mr Hughes to formally introduce you at breakfast in the morning. Now, before you eat let's sort out those clothes.'

Mavis escorted Alice back to her room, tummy full, requisitioned clothing folded over an arm. 'With the exception of Mr Hughes and the teaching staff, everyone sleeps on this floor,' the woman explained. 'There are some hundred and twenty girls residing here. They are split into dormitories, the girls distributed by age. Six dorms, twenty per room. We seem to have a glut of eighteen and nineteen-year-olds, so they have filled three. The under-eighteens occupy one and the twenty-plus, two.

'The landing door is locked at lights out. You'll be issued with a key tomorrow. Tonight I trust you can manage. It will be unlocked at six in the morning, so it won't be for long.'

'Who else with the exception of the pupils stays up here?' asked Alice, concerned she might be on her own.

'Pierce. You've met him. He upholds law and order in the twilight hours.'

'Is his room close to mine?'

'At the other end of the building. But you'll be fine.'

'What time's lights out?'

29

'Nine sharp.'

'My light included?'

'Of course not, Alice. Tuck yourself in whenever it suits. That said, I shall expect to see you ready, able and willing by seven.'

The day had worn late. Alice lay on the bed battle-scarred and exhausted, and yet still unable to yield to a merciful sleep. She detected Pierce's footfalls, leather striking polished wood. She clearly heard his firm and authoritative voice, the girl O'Leary warned for the second time that day.

Loneliness haunted, accentuated her misery. The last two days' events rolled back and forth, a soul-crushing tide whose waves dashed her spirit with increasing ferocity. Alice missed the impulsive Kate. She longed for the security the dizzy blonde's sisterly protection offered. She even yearned for involvement in one of her disastrous schemes. Chancing a return tempted almost irresistibly.

Much had happened in the last thirty-six hours, the young woman's world turned upside down. Her life it seemed had been built on lies and deceit, upon fables and ill-founded aspirations. Not one of her so-called loved ones had the courage to tell her the truth, of her parentage. Not one had the decency to explain the circumstances of her arrival in that world. All had gone, died. There was no one left to ask. No one to answer her many questions. No one except, *Richard*.

A realisation she hadn't washed since leaving for Barker's appalled her. Time against her, she had simply changed clothes on her return to Howell House. She idly scratched, feeling distinctly dirty. Another reason clung portentously to the peripheral of her recognition, that sword of Damocles temporarily dulled.

'You can't wash that sort of unholy dirt from your body, Hussey. Perversion doesn't cleanse. It's payment in kind.'

Alice had forgotten to ask about ablutions. Nosing into the hallway, eyes searching for a clue, a sign on a door, she wandered slowly, anxious not to disturb anyone. In one hand hung a wash bag, containing soap, flannel and a safety razor. Thrown over the free arm was a hand towel and pyjamas.

Barefoot, the blonde Ruth O'Leary approached silently from behind. ''Ello, lamb,' startled Alice, who spun on her heels, hand on heart.

'God, you made me jump!' She smiled nervously. 'Ruth, isn't it?'

'Yeah, that's it. Wa'cha after? The karzy?'

'I need a bath and I forgot to ask Miss Jarvis where it is.'

'I'll show yer. Better still, why don't yer get ready and let me run it for yer. Yer can leave yer togs in yer room. We're all gels together 'ere.'

'Except for Pierce,' Alice reminded.

'Oh, yer won't see that git again 'til morning. He'll 'ave curled up wiv a bottle for comfort, and I don't mean the hot water type, neither.'

'I'll slip my pyjamas on just to be safe.' Alice glanced up and down the hallway. 'Where is it, anyway?'

Ruth indicated a point halfway along. 'There. It's marked the Ritz Suite. Someone once had a sense of humour.'

'You sure you don't mind?' Alice checked.

'Course not. Always willin' to help a new girl.'

'Ah,' Alice began.

'Later. Tell me later. Have to run your bath before it gets too late.' The teenager skipped backwards. 'What's yer name, anyway?'

'Alice Hussey.'

'Ten minutes, Alice.'

Stood before the bedroom window, Alice slipped the coarse shirt from her shoulders, buttons undone. She attempted to penetrate the dark outside, gaze focusing instead on her reflection. She studied it, seeing frailty, confidence and strength wilted, shoulders bowed beneath the load. Dark rings hollowed her eyes, the once fresh young face appearing haunted. Her hair hung lank, the lustre and bounce devastated. Sighing, she reached behind, a flick of adept fingers releasing the bra. Pressure eased, the garment hung loose, cups precariously balanced. Alice considered again that ghostly image, seeing the temptress, the urge to play the part quickly dismissed. Disenchanted, believing herself used, she snatched the bra and threw it to a corner.

'Tits and arse do not the woman make,' she muttered, yanking down the skirt.

'But they invoke temptation, Hussey. Breasts attract hands, groping, mauling hands. You should know that. Buttocks, especially deeply divided, well-rounded buttocks, spawn the brute. You should know that too, Hussey.'

Naked, Alice drew on the pyjama trousers, fitting snug to thighs and buttocks. Wondering if her bath was ready and dismissing the spectre of Harris, she wriggled into the top. She had worn such nightclothes to raid the butler's pockets with disastrous results.

The rap on her door came at the right moment. Ruth waited outside, friendly smile and chirpy attitude welcoming. 'Bath's ready,' she announced.

The pair walked the hundred feet side by side. 'Where was yer before yer came 'ere then?' O'Leary enquired.

'Here and there,' Alice replied, avoiding a precise answer.

'And yer looks like butter wouldn't melt!'

First impressions, Alice thought. A chance to set the scales. 'I can look after myself.'

''Ard case, eh? A wolf in sheep's clothing. Better keep an eye on you then, 'adn't I?'

Ruth pushed the bathroom door open for Alice. She curtsied and urged her forward with a wave of the hand. 'Yer barf awaits, me lady.'

A zinc bath lay on a square of worn linoleum, the room inhospitable. Cream paint covered skirting boards, window frames and the run of large linen cupboards down either side. Beneath the window lay the source of water, a single standpipe.

Suspicious, Alice closed the distance, bent and tested the water. 'It's cold,' she reported. 'Bloody freezing.'

O'Leary folded her arms. 'Welcome to the fucking Ritz, Hussey. Baaa. Baaa. Baaa.'

Alice straightened. 'There's no hot water, is there?'

Ruth shook her head, expression contemptuously amused.

'No copper or boiler either?'

O'Leary sneered.

'Is it always like this?'

'Come winter, come snow, come ice on the inside of the windows. Adolescent gels need to be curbed; stop our 'ormones from runnin' riot. Who knows what we might get up to if our passions ain't chilled a bit. After all, most of us is whores, ain't we? Besides, we're young an' sturdy, we don't need no such luxuries. I'll tell yer one thing, no one stays very long in there first thing in the mornin'.'

'I'll speak to Mr Hughes; see if something can't be done,' Alice promised, with the best intentions.

O'Leary laughed. 'Oh yer will, will yer? Gawd, gel, you got a lot to learn you 'ave.'

'Perhaps I have.'

'An' the first thing you should learn is respect. We might be common, but we ain't fuckin' stupid. Time for your initiation, Miss head-in-the-clouds Hussey.'

Stunned, Alice reeled stupefied as the closet doors burst open, a horde of young women rushing silently around her. Before she could cry out they were upon her. Arms pinned to her sides she struggled in vain, someone behind thrusting a wet flannel into her mouth, then securing it with a strip of cloth. Gagged she could offer no protest, explanation or cry for help.

The mob parted to allow O'Leary to face her. The girl grabbed her by the hair and pushing her face close, taunted, 'We'll give yer lots to tell Geoffrey whip-arse Hughes in the morning, gel. First the cold bath, just to make sure yer bum is nice and frozen.' Ruth tore the wash bag from Alice's hand, rummaged inside and produced the razor. 'Then a shave, so's we can all get properly acquainted, like. And then yer can do the rounds; meet everyone on an intimate footing – real intimate, that is.'

O'Leary stepped back. 'Chuck 'er in, gels. Strip 'er and give 'er a real 'ard scrubbin'.'

Alice hit the water facedown, the shock snatching her breath. Immediately hands gripped her pyjama trousers, peeled them from her hips, naked bottom rapidly unveiled. Alice hung tenaciously to the bath sides, face above water, the soaked garment tossed to the floor.

Twisting, turning, kicking, Alice battled against the loss of her top. The bathwater churned, slopped and splashed, Alice's attackers becoming almost as wet as she. The jacket edged up, fists clutching, holding down her thighs. Breasts peeked naked, lurching, tossed corpulence glistening wet. She let the rim go, freeing her arms to defend herself.

Defiant, Alice yanked the top down, the wet fabric moulding to her torso, adhering to her breasts. She sat, crossed arms covering her chest, pride overriding desire. She seethed, cold green eyes warning retaliation.

O'Leary leant close. 'Who whipped yer then, Alice? Who caned yer arse? Was that at borstal, or have you been here longer than just today? Nice to see yer ain't no stranger to the bum slash, cos yer's certainly gonna get more than yer fair share 'ere. And especially tonight.' She straightened. 'Tie the new lamb's 'ands, an' scrub 'er down.'

Arms forcibly wrenched behind her, a dressing gown cord was used to tie the girl's wrists together. Two assailants pinioned her arms to the outside of the bath, holding Alice in a sitting position, and the redhead recoiled at the production of a half dozen scrubbing brushes. She twisted, kicked and tried desperately to evade their chaffing contact, then bucked and jerked as the Hope inmates began their sadistic initiation.

The top yanked up, tough bristles rubbed simultaneously at thighs, groin, belly and breasts. A tide of fire, burning and stinging, swept like a carpet of lava over her naked body. The girls gleefully worked with gusto, elbow grease used in generous proportions. The bristles scoured, her skin ripening bright red, flesh rapidly growing unbearably sore.

'Enough!' shouted O'Leary. 'Turn her over, and make sure her bum's given a good goin' over.'

Alice squealed, the shriek muffled, her body roughly turned, the bath rim cutting deep into her sore breasts. Again those devastating brushes swept her body; shoulders, back, buttocks and legs scuffed and abraded.

Two young women laboured feverishly on Alice's behind, brushes worked in circles, cheeks quivering, flesh surrendering to a deep hue of scarlet. O'Leary knelt, leaning on the bath, eyes riveted. 'I just love the motion of a full, firm butt. I finds it quite fascinatin'. 'Specially when it's set jumpin' by the cut of a cane. Gawd, that really does do something for me cunny.'

She laid a hand to Alice's bottom. 'My, he did hit you hard, didn't he. Bet they stung for fucking ever…

'Okay, enough, she looks like a bleedin' lobster now, don't she, gels? Still, look on the bright side, Alice; it's good for your complexion. When it stops burning you'll thank us. All that dead skin rubbed away.' She laughed. 'And a fair bit of live skin too, I shouldn't wonder.

'Now, who's gonna shave this poor little darlin'?' Ruth pushed a finger between Alice's thighs, the cold digit urged between her vulva. 'Mr Whip Arse don't like body hair. Mr Whip Arse gives us extras if we don't stay smooth and shorn, so we're just saving you a bit of aggro, that's all.'

They hauled Alice out and lay her on her back. Four girls prised her legs apart, Ruth pushing between, kneeling, razor held high. 'I won't nick yer if yer don't struggle. So be clever and lay still cos it's just *gotta* be done.'

Alice stared up at a circle of smirking faces. The mob held her so she couldn't move. Lecherous hands felt, squeezed and groped her breasts, Alice trying to determine who did exactly what. She sensed the touch and glide of razor, cold steel slicing through her pubic mane. She thanked providence for the new blade, for without it the ordeal would have been a lot worse.

O'Leary bent to her offensive task, sharp steel removing every trace of hair abroad the pubic mound. Alice jerked in utter humiliation as Ruth held her vaginal lips, the instrument slicing away the strands and wisps adjacent. 'There,' she finally said. 'Just like a plucked chicken.' Then hand held out she demanded, 'Alcohol.'

Ruth rubbed the spirit onto her fingers and palms. 'Just in case, Alice. Can't have no infections down here, can we? That would spoil a fuckin' good time, wouldn't it? And I bet with this body, you've had a fair few fucking good times. Hughes is gonna just love you, baby.'

Fire ignited Alice's mound, her sex lips set alight she writhed, but worse, a disturbing sexual glow expanded, permeated, drove relentlessly into her belly.

'Is there no depravation you won't stoop to? Your body is Satan's chalice where any debauched monster may drink. The more deformed the vile act, the greater your warped response.'

The group withdrew to the cupboards leaving Alice naked on the floor; hands still tied behind her, gag effectively keeping her silent. She rolled onto a side; her mottled and blotched body lustrous with water. The silence baffled her. She looked about, trying to discern what they were up to. All stood perfectly still, observing her.

Alice manoeuvred onto her knees, face kissing the floor. She waited. Nothing. Slowly she straightened, showing no emotion, expression impassive. Her body stung. Her fanny prickled. That sexual warmth lingered, hovered, expectation loosing random bursts of energy. Alice struggled to her feet. She stared at her tormentors, daring them to commit another atrocity. O'Leary had intimated a whipping, and the prospect of such wrung the nerves of arousal.

At Ruth's signal each girl opened a door and took out a towel. Alice noted the tight end knot and wetness of material. She waited, pride stopping her from running, stubbornness keeping her from cowering.

Pain blasted a buttock, the slap of knot on bare flesh explicit. She looked over a shoulder catching the blur of another towel in full flight. Alice tensed for the impact, the large wet knot cracking loudly on the other flank, the sting intense.

Tied hands longed to comfort the lingering smart, but Alice refused to tender the satisfaction. For the first time she could count heads. There were twenty packing that room, the compliment of one dormitory, she assumed. Another pair made their move, towels swung high. The room echoed to their footfalls and then the double clap of a torturous meeting.

Alice winced, backside ablaze. Then defiant she stared directly at Ruth, the smile masked by her gag. But O'Leary read the message and raised a hand, clicking the fingers. Every girl advanced on Alice, those towels held ready, threatening.

Alice backed to the door before the storm struck. Heavy knots hit with alarming force and rapidity. The fact she faced them meant nothing. Her upper arms, hips and thighs screamed under the barrage. Alice doubled, offering them another target. Lashes rained mercilessly on her back, shoulders, forearms and loins. The girl twisted, marked bottom placed in range. Primitive lust controlling, the women took full advantage, a flurry of blows announcing a refreshed onslaught.

Alice chewed the rag, eyelids screwed tight. Her knees gave, weakened legs buckling. Slowly she sank to the floor, buttocks shuddering, flesh heaving, the extensive flogging uninterrupted. Her head rested against the door, her back bowed, her ravaged bottom still receiving, and there she held her ground, backside torched.

O'Leary pushed to the front and held up a hand, and immediately the punishment ceased. The blonde crouched. Intrigued, she stroked Alice's body while studying the plethora of marks. Her dreamy, sensuous pale-blue eyes met Alice's. A communication took place, an understanding. Ruth shook her head; full lips parted seductively, the glimmer of a smile suggested affection.

Unabashed, O'Leary scrutinised Alice's body, gaze lingering on her bosom. 'I know this gel,' she began. 'She has this thing about whips and canes and the like. They don't scare her. No, far from it; she only has to see a flexed stick and she goes all goose bumpy.'

Ruth glanced at another girl loitering close by. 'You know her, don't yer, Cas? You know who I'm talking about. You can vouch for what she's like.'

'If it's who I think it is, yeah, I can.'

'Always in trouble, she is. Always up there waiting outside the principal's office. Some say she won't ever get out of this dump. Some reckon she don't want to. But I think she knows different. I think she knows the game she plays. I reckon she'll be out before anyone else.

'That initiation ain't the most pleasant of introductions, but you, Alice, barely turned a hair. I seen those that cowered like gutless vermin and them that sobbed their bleedin' hearts out. But you, Alice, you got grit. Or you got some'at else.'

She reached about the redhead, loosening the cord. 'She 'as a thing about restriction as well. Ropes or straps, she don't mind.'

O'Leary released the gag, Alice spitting the flannel out. 'She ain't fussy whether it's done or do, if yer knows what I mean. She reckons it's as much fun either way.

'Now you, Alice, if I let yer know there was six of the best waiting for yer in every dorm, what would yer say?'

Alice settled on her bare bottom, wincing, back resting against the door. 'I guess I'd say that I'm a member of staff, not a new inmate. I guess that's what I'd say.'

While the others showed fear or astonishment, O'Leary simply laughed. 'Nice one, Al. Nice one. And I suppose that's how you're going to chat with Hughes like an equal. Nah, you ain't no staff. Too young by 'alf. Staff are all old grizzlies 'ere. And you got your uniform, ain't yer? Staff don't wear uniforms. But I admire yer strategy.'

'And in the morning when you find out I'm telling the truth, everyone of you will be waiting on Mr Hughes.'

'We will anyway if yer's telling the honest.'

'I could turn a blind eye to what's happened. High jinks. A case of mistaken position. Not that I condone the barbarism of the initiation.'

'Yer'd do that for us, would yer?'

'I don't want to be the cause of trouble on my first day.'

'Who caned you, miss staff member? Was it a leavin' pressie from the last job, eh?'

'That is my business.'

'Course it is. It's like you seeing your initiation through to the bitter end. That's my business.'

'Believe me, Ruth, I have accepted the position of girl Friday.'

'Nah, don't think I will. First stop "B" dorm.'

Alice was hoisted bodily from the floor and ushered along the hallway by zealous hands. O'Leary opened the door, Alice pushed roughly through. A carpet slipper waited on a formica tabletop, a large woman perched beside it.

''Ere y'are, Drake. All scrubbed up and pruned. Best tell 'er the rules, though.'

Alice couldn't help feeling Drake looked more like a man than a woman. Ugly wouldn't describe, and she was to discover that aspect wasn't reserved just for the outside. With arms like hams struggling to remain folded, Drake opened her slit of a mouth, and with a voice deep, masculine, she detailed with unrestrained delight, 'You lay over the table of your own accord and you get six. Refuse and you get nine. Struggle when you're helped and you get a dozen. Understood?'

Alice refused any acknowledgement.

'You got ten seconds to either nod or shake your head.'

At the count of six Alice nodded.

'Good. You understand English. Well, what's it to be?'

The word 'penance' probed the fog of despondency. Divine punishment for her sins. The obscure chance dangled enticingly, to atone for the terrible transgressions she had participated in; an opportunity to partially cleanse her soul. Did it matter who wielded the flagellant? If she offered herself to God's hostile hand, then wouldn't Drake be his disciple?

Alice stepped forward, then hesitated. If she sought penance, then that should be insufferable, surely. The path to absolution

39

could never be easy. The level of suffering was not her choice. She had to leave that to fate.

'Well?' grunted Drake.

'Get fucked,' Alice hissed in proud defiance.

Ruth settled beside her. 'And there I was just beginning to respect yer. I thought you had bottle.'

'You'll regret this come morning, O'Leary,' Alice vowed. 'And tell me this; why should I satisfy your sick lust? Why should I submit to you?'

'You're beginning to piss me off, Al. We all look forward to new gels arriving; it gives us one night of excitement amidst a God-awful existence. It gives the new gel a chance to show some spunk. And then she's one of us. And when the next inmate arrives she joins in. But you? You're taking the shine off it.'

'And tomorrow I'm going to take the shine off you.'

'I'll tell you what, gel; you're either a real 'ard case or yer's tellin' the truth.'

Alice laughed.

'What's funny?' snapped O'Leary.

'Divine intervention, Ruth. Divine intervention. And don't it baffle yer? Eh, gel?'

Drake struggled from her perch with the grace of a walrus, the slipper held menacingly. 'Well, Hussey, are you going to do as you're told or not?'

'You want me over that table, then you put me over that table,' Alice contested uncompromisingly.

Drake possessed the strength of an ox and hoisted Alice clear of the floor with one arm, a fist clutching a handful of pyjama top. Carried the few feet, Drake then slammed the redhead facedown on the table, groin butted to the edge.

It was only a standard size eight carpet slipper, but when it slammed into a sore buttock Alice could barely contain the shock. A second reaped havoc on the sister cheek, her bum alight.

'Not hard enough,' chilled O'Leary, grinning sadistically. 'She ain't screamed, Drake, so you ain't hitting her hard enough.'

Drake smirked, raised biceps bulging, slipper readied for a swingeing blow. Alice braced herself for the worst, her bum already burning madly.

'What the hell's going on?' stopped Drake in her tracks. Pierce strode in, bloodshot eyes glaring. Tall with a barrel chest he personified the perfect sergeant major. The man glowered. 'Nobody move. Now I asked a question. I would appreciate a bloody answer.'

An arm swept with surprising speed, large hand seizing Ruth, fingers sinking painfully into her neck. 'Well, O'Leary? When there's mischief you're generally at the forefront.'

'Just a late night get together,' she offered lamely.

'Lights out was fifteen minutes ago. You know that, O'Leary. You should all be tucked up in your beds by now.'

He urged Ruth forward, his other hand seizing Alice similarly, lifting her, the girl hauling her top down as far as it would go. 'And don't think I haven't noticed that heated butt, young lady. I take it you have an acceptable explanation?'

Both hung immobilised in his tenacious embrace, the man exerting an excruciating pressure. 'There is a choice as I see it. You can either explain this rum business to me, or you can confide in Mr Hughes tomorrow. What will it be?'

O'Leary squeaked first. 'We were initiating Alice.'

'Ah!' he exclaimed. 'That would explain the lack of lower cover.' Pierce forced Alice over, scrutinising her vulnerable backside. 'And the marks.'

Still holding both, O'Leary squirming, Alice doubled, he admonished, 'Initiation is frowned upon, as you all well know. It is a punishable infringement. Absence from your dormitories after lights out is a punishable infringement.' He squeezed Alice's neck harder. 'And gallivanting with your bum hanging out is also a punishable infringement.'

Embarrassment summoned an inexplicable exhilaration; Alice's buttocks prickling, itching for attention. Her flesh heated by the assault of brush and towel begged further abuse. The girl knew she should speak out, explain her situation, if not demand fair deference, but the irresistible hand of passion obscured logic, foggy tentacles clouding reason. All Alice could think of was where her peculiar situation would lead.

The man jerked her upright and forced her head round to face him. 'So, what to do?'

'I'm sure you have a remedy,' Ruth whispered.

Grinning tight-lipped he forced O'Leary over until her nose nearly met her knees. 'Oh yes, O'Leary, I have a remedy. Not one any of you will appreciate, but being the considerate soul I am, I have a compromise.'

Alice joined Ruth, lips close to patellae.

'Two lambs. I require two volunteers, and to them I shall dispense a short but very sharp reminder of the rules and regulations applying to this institution.' He surveyed the forty or so inmates scattered about the dormitory. 'What, no takers? Does no one want to play the martyr? It is within my remit to take each and every one of you to task. I am duty bound to file a report first thing in the morning.'

Pierce shook the two girls he held. 'Perhaps these two might play the sacrificial lambs. After all, one is in a state of readiness and the other deserving. Does no one want to put their best foot forward to save their sisters?'

All hung their heads. Not one wished to replace Alice or Ruth.

'So be it.' Pierce yanked Ruth upright. 'My room, O'Leary. Make yourself available. You know what's expected.'

Ruth sidled from the dormitory.

'Now one more chance for one of you to do the right thing. Do you really want to see a new inmate sent to Pierce's room? Eh? Do you? Don't any of you feel the slightest bit of sympathy?'

His gibes were met with a tense silence.

'Alice,' he tightened his grip, 'looks like you are elected. Pierce's room, at the end of the hallway. Follow O'Leary's example. I'll be with you very shortly.'

Alice left, padding to where she assumed the custodian's

room was. She smiled sardonically. Divine intervention. No sway over her reparation. God's punishment. This was as it should be. And when Pierce discovered she wasn't an inmate, well, he'd be in an awkward position, wouldn't he? A bird in the hand, so to speak.

'You think you're off the hook, don't you?' Pierce strutted among the girls. 'Well, I can assure you, you are not. Not one of you craven miscreants will miss out on Pierce's education. Not one. I want six of you outside my room tomorrow night. I don't care which six. Draw lots. Then another six the night after, and so on. You misbegotten trollops will rue this night.'

The door sported the sign *Pierce*. Ajar, Alice pushed it fully open. The room, dimly lit, proved larger than expected. On the far side, against the wall, lay the man's cot. To the right stood a small circular dining table. To the left a bookcase, radio, gas ring and wardrobe. And in the centre the four chairs from the table.

Ruth had arranged them in pairs, two side by side facing the window, the other two placed in the opposite direction. The girl knelt, naked, legs parted, knees on the polished wooden seats. She bent over, backrest delving her lower belly, hands flat to the floor. She said nothing, face concealed by the fall of blonde tresses.

Alice, stomach churning, took up a similar position on the other seats. The fact occurred that she didn't have to undergo Pierce's punishment. The man would not dare to force the issue. All she had to do was tell the truth.

'I deserve this,' kept her there, comely bottom raised, legs parted, her sex on display. Fate had conjured a specific trial. God had contrived this. If she failed, then surely she would be cast down. Why else would she be there? Why should Pierce walk in? Why would he select her? Was it a sign of divine judgement?

'Ha! Do you really expect me to believe that? God's reparation does not involve flagrant exposure, such an explicit offering. Look at you, Hussey. Your loins shout "have me!".

They invite. They are poised to unsettle. There is only one message tendered, and that is unmitigated profligacy, boundless conceit.

'*Shaven genitalia displayed so outrageously, poised to entrap. Is that what you hope for, Alice? Want Pierce's cock, do you? Your intent is obvious, to persuade with your cunt. Alice, you entice. You incite. You possess the devil's tools. You are his disciple, and it would seem Satan has prepared his instrument well.*'

Knees uncomfortable, the wood hard, she wriggled, hanging breasts pressuring wet cloth, Alice so very aware of every inch of her vulnerable bottom. She glanced at Ruth, the girl keeping the stance.

Ears listened intently for the telltale thud of boots on wooden floorboards. Hearts thumped with apprehension, pulsed with suppressed sexual excitement. Goose bumps set the skin to shiver, the cool night air and abundant nervous energy culpable. Nipples reached for erection, the buzz of anticipation tingling, their hides electrified. Tenterhooks probed guts and bowel, stretched buttocks acutely sensitive, clitorises translating uncertainty into sexual curiosity. Fidgety thighs wavered, minds longing to close the gap, psyches drawing a charge from their plight. The bizarre charge derived from subservience, the quirky kick delivered by masculine domination, the crazy predicament of abject submission – to not only permit another to inflict horrors without protest, but to actually prepare and proffer the target.

Faces burned scarlet, the mask of humiliation gaining ground. 'Sorry,' tendered, if barely audible, surprised Alice. 'Didn't mean to land yer here.'

'There's things you don't know. Things you'll never know. I'm here not because of you, but for a reason you could never understand. I want no questions asked tomorrow. No tittle tattle. No unsuitable comments. That's the price of my silence, Ruth.'

'You are going to work here, aren't you?'

Alice didn't answer.

'If you don't have to be here, then don't be. Take my word for it, this won't be no picnic.'

'I have to be here. My sanity depends on it.'

'I don't understand, that's for sure. Why take a whipping, a Pierce whipping at that, when yer don't 'ave to?'

'We agreed, no questions.'

'Yer said tomorrow. It ain't tomorrow.'

'How long have you been here, and how long does Pierce usually leave a person dangling?'

'I got a two year minimum, and I've been 'ere six months. The longer Pierce leaves us the better. Yer really don't wanna hurry his idea of discipline.'

'How do you feel at the moment?'

'What, apart from 'anging on the edge of a precipice?'

'Yes, apart from that.'

'You mean the starkers and degrading position bit, don't yer? Supposed to be part of the punishment. Pierce will tell yer that losing yer togs inclines yer more to obedience. He reckons stripped to the skin bashes the shit out of yer ego. I reckon he's probably right.

'Mind you, sometimes it does some'at else. Now and again it can get quite interesting. Every so often the weird and wonderful 'appens.'

'Now?' Alice asked, particularly interested.

'Yeah, now.'

'Skin feel alright, does it?'

'Tingling.'

'A glow in the tummy?'

'Lower than that.'

'That girl you were talking about; is she…?'

'Right, ladies,' Pierce's voice boomed, 'sorry to keep you waiting.' He picked up a thick, broad, lengthy strap. 'O'Leary… question for you: caught off limits after light's out, how many? How many to punish you and deter you from further escapades?'

'One from you will do that, Mr Pierce.'

45

'Oh, I don't think so, girl.' Heavy leather struck soft backside with alarming expeditiousness, the meeting brutally effective.

Ruth sucked air. 'Christ!' discharged with the exhalation.

That almighty slap pitched Alice into a frenetic contradictory dilemma. Head spinning, she cursed her irrepressible enthusiasm, that disorderly fondness for the sound of smitten flesh. She wanted to suffer, not succumb to the throes of sexual euphoria.

'Have another go, O'Leary. Try and recall what I promised you the last time.'

'Would that be the time yer punishment *didn't* involve pulverisin' me arse?'

Swingeing implement collided with fired cheek, Ruth yelping. 'Strewth!'

'Now that wasn't the answer I wanted to hear, was it O'Leary?'

'No sir.'

'Miss Hussey, I wonder if you would be so kind as to join me?'

Puzzled, Alice climbed from the chair. Self-conscious, she pulled the hem of her top down, trying to cover her groin. The attempt effected a flattening of chest, breasts squeezed, emphasising their existence. Pierce tossed her a shirt. 'Put that on.'

The girl hesitated, dumbfounded, the blue cotton caught in a hand.

'Don't stand there looking gormless!' the man barked. 'Take off that wet rag and put the damned shirt on.'

'But...'

'What's up?' Pierce questioned slyly. 'Suddenly bashful?' He pointed at her lower body. 'But you're not wearing any knickers, girl.'

Alice hastily considered her predicament. Refuse? And then what? Deep, troublesome waters loomed, forbidding. Alice faltered; then tight-lipped she reached for the hem, accepting she would have to expose something. What though? Her bosom or striped rump?

She half turned, uncertainty biting deep. She stooped, whipped off the top, Pierce treated to the jerk and twitch of a liberated breast as well as the intoxicating quiver of her delectable buttocks, and smirked guilefully. Alice slipped the flannel garment on. 'I don't understand,' she imparted, fastening the buttons.

'What is there to understand?' he retorted. 'You'll catch a chill wearing wet clothes.'

'Not that.' Alice faced Pierce, unable to look him directly in the eye. 'I thought you were going to cane me.' She could see the rod in the periphery of her vision, the rattan and prospect of feeling it's bite intensifying that unfathomable desire.

He offered her the rod, ten millimetres of inert flexile violence. Alice shrugged. 'What do I want that for?'

'Live your entire life in a state of confusion do you, Hussey?'

She lifted her face, large intelligent green eyes defiant. 'Of late, I guess I do.'

'Well, allow me to elucidate.' Pierce pointed at O'Leary. 'This has misbehaved. And this will be thrashed. I want you to thrash it. Is that clear?' he asked, as if she was a child.

'That's not my responsibility,' she countered.

Pierce riposted, nodding. 'I think you'll find it is.'

'Are you ordering me to?'

'No, Miss Hussey, I'm asking you to.'

'And if I decline?'

'Quite simple; O'Leary will never forgive you. Do I make myself clear?'

'Do what he says,' whispered Ruth, suffering second thoughts.

Alice's arm fell, the cane vertical. 'How many?' she conceded, emotions jumbled.

'Nine of your best. With all your strength. You understand me this time?'

Alice nodded, tummy cartwheeling. The unexpected reared its contrary head, undermining purpose and determination. The swarm of butterflies stirring her stomach argued against any angelic aspirations or spiritual contrition.

'Why do you beat her, Alice? Is it your duty? Is it revenge? Or is it because the devil beckons and you cannot resist? That is the way of perversion. You can no more deny your abandoned urges than you can the fact you received him willingly; that you readily responded. You cannot change. You bear the brand of devil-child, of damnation. You can't resist the temptation. No more pretence. Do your master's bidding. No more nonsense about penance and sins. What are you waiting for? Be what you are. What I have always said you are. You are destined for perdition. Satan drives, Satan rewards and Satan awaits.'

Betwixt and between, goaded by a guilty conscience, persuaded by Ruth's imploring face, encouraged by Pierce's blackmail; Alice's enthusiasm was curbed by the thrill she experienced.

The rattan levelled, rested upon pale, tensed buttocks.

'Hard, Alice,' reminded Pierce. 'Leave the minx in no doubt.'

'Go on, Alice, please,' whispered O'Leary.

'Go on, Alice, for you are lost anyway. Appease those badgering demons. Indulge in the marking of her innocent young bottom. Wallow in the wretch's anguished cry. Accept your malign euphoria. Ogle the stripe flush with hell's colour. Orgasm to the puffy welts thrusting from tortured crimson flesh. Like a drug, isn't it? Addictive. You long to feel that sexual euphoria, don't you? Hit her, Alice. Go on, surrender completely to your master.'

A flash, too quick for the human eye. Hearts accelerated, pulses driven by sadistic, masochistic obsession. Thick rod hit, cut into yielding buttocks. The cane's girth briefly engulfed, supple flesh lay crushed before an irresistible force. The slap seemed to stand in time, bottom launched, stung flesh rippling, cheeks shuddering. Slowed, surreal, the tip warped, quivered, the dance predictive, announcing her agony before the confirming shriek.

O'Leary's shoulders dipped, naked back twisting this way

and that, hips pressed hard to the chair-back, flanks dimpled, buttocks twitching. Bewitching, the stripe flourished, scarlet edged into the pallid line, strength gathering quickly.

With hell's red-hot tongs still squeezing Ruth's tortured flesh, Alice launched the second terror. *'Be what they call me. Why even try to don the sackcloth and ashes? I'm not temptation. It's so easy to point the finger of accusation. And what of Richard? He doesn't wilt from dispensing corporal punishment. So what makes him the divine catalyst and me the devil's disciple?'*

O'Leary seized the chair legs, fists tightened, knuckles white. Teeth ground as fire penetrated, unendurable agony squeezing the contents of her stomach. She groaned, that and the subsequent curses muted.

Pierce stood, hands clasped behind his back, bearing proud. O'Leary's obvious suffering pleased. The strength in Alice's arm surprised, the cane connecting with a ferocious if delicious splat. Rattan struck lower corpulence, burrowed, lifted that scorched meat. Motivated by the searing hurt the girl's hips rose, knees leaving the rigour of hard wood, backside ascending before the whole came down with a jolt. The resultant tremor of posterior cheeks provoked, aroused the inflamed further, Pierce reacting sexually. Fingers gripped his stiff cock through the pocket lining, his hand stuffed there to cosset the disturbed.

'You shy from the consecrated, for fear of being discovered. Tell me the girl's naked backside recoiling beneath the violence of your rod doesn't proffer sexual stimulation. Tell me you aren't giddy with euphoria. Tell me that and I will call you a liar.'

'Being a religious zealot doesn't make a saint. Spouting fine rhetoric doesn't make one right.'

The rattan slashed, O'Leary yelping.

'You use your privileged position to bully and confuse me.'

A malicious downward stroke drove the rod briefly into upper heights, the tip adopting the curve, whipping a sensitive hip.

'All I ever wanted was a little love. A bit of affection. A

49

cuddle. Just an arm about the shoulder would have done; the touch of a comforting hand. Not him. Not heart of stone Richard.'

Hurtling rod bit furiously into pained flesh.

'I lost what I thought were my parents!'

O'Leary climbed the back of the seat, her buttocks torched, legs straightened, body angled.

'Then he announces he's not my uncle. After he...! The evil bastard!'

The cane swished vertically, slashing raised buttocks.

'I have no one left!'

A leg ascended, kicking desperately, the cane narrowly missing the foot, careering insufferably into upper thighs.

'The devious bastard pretended!'

Ruth attempted evasion, her torso sliding towards the floor, her ravaged bottom withdrawn, legs frantically shuffling, but Alice followed, arm raised high, rattan slicing plumped buttocks.

'He enjoyed the lie, the calculating shithouse!'

O'Leary's groin met the edge of the seat, her back arched, her breasts flat to the floor. Cruelly, Alice placed a foot on the girl's shoulder, pinning her, and the cane whipped Ruth's flank.

'All the while he knew!'

Again the rod bent to that vandalised hide.

'Bastard!' Alice hissed, lashing the girl. 'Bastard!' she spat, that mauled butt suffering a fourteenth.

'For Christ's sake Mr Pierce!' Ruth shrieked. 'For Christ's sake stop 'er!'

Mesmerised, Pierce followed the swift descent of the fifteenth, the welted flesh further crippled.

'Anythin' Mr Pierce. I'll do anythin' yer asks. Just stop this mad cow!' Ruth wriggled, feverishly attempting an escape. Her right knee found the floor, her left leg still caught on the chair. Alice eyed that division, the vulnerable vagina, and lifted the cane above her shoulder... but Pierce seized her wrist, preventing the downward sweep.

'Bastard!' Alice growled.

'Maybe,' agreed Pierce. 'But I think that's enough.'

Ruth wriggled from beneath Alice's foot, and knelt, hands tending her raw bottom. 'I guess I might 'ave deserved that,' she offered, wincing.

Edward took the cane from Alice and lay it to one side. 'Best get back to your dorm, O'Leary.'

Ruth turned, showed her back to pick up her nightdress, and Alice stared in horror. Fifteen purpled welts marred the girl's rump. Each stripe thick and bloated from scarlet flesh, the ends mauve.

'Did I...?'

'Yes, Alice, you whipped her like a demon possessed.'

'No, I...'

'Now, young lady.'

Alice glanced about the room, O'Leary having gone, her and Pierce were left alone.

51

Chapter Three

'I suppose it's only fair I take the same as Ruth,' Alice suggested, guilt weighing heavy.

'I don't believe that would be a wise move on my behalf.'

'No?' Alice asked, dumbfounded.

'I think I would have a difficult time explaining it to Mr Hughes.'

Resolve faded, the girl folded her arms, shirt hem rising accordingly. 'I don't understand.'

Pierce smiled, his head cocked to one side he studied the pleasant display of thigh. 'No Alice, it's me who doesn't understand. I know you were taken on today. Geoff told me. He asked me to keep an eye on you. Which I did. And that's why you're standing before me now and not doing the circuit of the dormitories. Those animals would have thrashed you without mercy, you know. So why?'

She shrugged. 'I told Ruth. She didn't believe me. I was issued with a pinafore, you see, because I don't have anything suitable at present. So the girls thought I was a new inmate.'

'That I can see, and those miserable wretches will pay the price. That is already in hand.'

'No, please, I don't bear them any grudge. Better if you let it die.'

'I'll not mention the matter to Mr, Hughes; that is my only concession. They knew what to expect if they were caught. In that they will not be disappointed.'

Pierce studied Alice, looking her over from head to toe. 'You're damned attractive.'

'Thank you.'

'Now, explain to me why you didn't tell me who you are?'

'I didn't think you would believe me.'

'So, you would have let me cane you?' He scratched his head. 'None of this is making any sense at all. What sort of girl doesn't bat an eye when…? You were near naked, Alice, barely a bloody stitch, and yet you offered no protest. You didn't seem to give a damn. I'd like to know why.'

She shrugged. 'It's been a long day. I'm very tired.'

'It's almost as if you wanted me to see you in the buff. And then coming here for a caning…'

'Twenty girls soaked me and then stripped me, Mr Pierce. I fought, but there is only so much a person can do against those odds. What was I supposed to do? And as for coming here, it got me away from them. I would have told you. It is all very unfortunate.'

'Bollocks!' Pierce pushed her, his palm slapping her shoulder. 'You're lying.'

Alice moved back a couple of steps. 'No…'

Pierce swooped, grapping her shirt, but Alice slapped his hand away and continued a steady retreat.

Edward pointed a finger accusingly. 'You bent over the chairs. You wanted me to cane you. You wanted me to see you like that.' He tugged at his tie knot and flicked the top button clear. 'But for some reason you've changed your mind. I'll tell you, Alice, seeing these girls can be a trial. Whipping their behinds, although part of the job, does have an effect. But when it comes to a real sexy looker, and a member of staff at that, flaunting everything she's got, well I don't mind admitting that really turns the screw, that does.'

'You're mistaken.' She slapped away the man's other hand, snatching at her shirt.

'If you like, Alice, I could forget who you are. I could treat you like O'Leary, if that's what you want. We could go a step further. I've got some rope somewhere. I mean, if you have a problem, a hang up with doing it freely, that could be taken care of.'

The image flashed and her tummy somersaulted. She gasped, Pierce believing her to be insulted. 'Capricious or just a bloody tease?' he asked angrily.

'Neither.' Alice hugged her body, spun, turning her back on the man. 'I guess you deserve an explanation, but not now.'

He eyed the fall of her shirt, the manner it clung to the small of her back, the provocative way it draped over protruding buttocks, the shape and division clearly discernible. 'Yeah, an explanation would be nice, but perhaps you should give that to Mr Hughes in the morning, eh?'

Alice looked over her shoulder, suddenly afraid. 'No, I can't. I couldn't possibly. Look, give me a few days. Too much has happened recently. I need to sort my feelings.'

Pierce shrugged. 'Okay, you've got until Wednesday. I'll not say anything in the meantime. You come here after lights out, and if you explain your feelings so that this dense oaf can understand, and fully explain your strange behaviour tonight, then we'll drop the whole weird matter, okay?'

Face burning, Alice nodded.

'Good. Best get yourself to bed then.'

Alice walked awkwardly to the door, knowing he watched her intensely. She reached for the handle. 'I'll wash your shirt before I return it,' she said, embarrassed.

'Whatever.'

She opened the door.

'Oh, Alice.'

'Yes?'

'I shall look forward to Wednesday night. I have to admit, you have what I would call, the perfect bum.'

Head down, exasperated, she went back to her room.

Sleep resisted, Alice tossing and turning. Having kept the shirt on she kicked restlessly, blankets and sheet pushed clear. Madness seemed to edge closer, lucidity waxing and waning. She felt no fear, no dread. Her psyche, her body ached for severity. She rolled onto her front, shirt hoisted, rounded bottom prominent, the flesh so alive, skin tingling. Eyes closed she imagined, longed to hear, the acute swish, the all-consuming bite, and then jerk to the scald of slashing cane. Punishment for sins ceased to play any part. Alice longed to be beaten purely for the sexual bliss it offered.

That strange hunger ate at her libido, vexing rationality. The same mental motion picture kept running though her overwrought mind. The seed sown by Pierce plagued her. She saw herself tied, the ropes cutting, biting deep into tender flesh. The chair supported her contorted body, bent over the back, wrists bound to the front legs. Pierce had secured her torso and arms. Thick rough jute encircled her waist twice before tethering her to the top of the chair-back. Several feet hung unused, the girl highly aroused by its intended use.

Another three coils gripped her bared breasts, one below, one above and one biting into her ample bosom. The released bra dangled, cups lost beneath the shirt, which was pulled up, the tail lying over her head. Another free length fell from her compressed cleavage, to trail over the seat and disappear between the vertical rails of the back.

Alice turned abruptly, moaning. Her hands ran to her crotch, legs parted wide. *'Oh, those hands. Hot and sweaty they cup me so gently, the touch light, promising. Fingers stroke, the feeling distant through the cotton.'* Her hands explored, pushing up beneath the shirt, fingers toying with her firm breasts.

'Fingertips touch bare skin, my exposed breasts.' She twisted, hips mobile. *'They're inside my bra. The cups are yanked clear, fingers probe, the grasp rough.'* One hand remained attentive to her aroused breasts, the other moved back to her crotch, fingers spread, pressed to her moist sex lips.

'Kneaded, squeezed, mauled, and I can't do a thing about it. Yes, I'm tied, and oh so tight. I want to scream but I'm gagged, the stocking cutting into the corners of my mouth.'

A finger parted delicate lips and sunk its tip, exploring.

'My bra falls away, hanging tits full and firm, suspended, quivering with the tiniest movement. A rope. Tied.'

Her hips rolled, buttocks alternately pressured, flesh constantly fluid in motion.

'Placed about my ribs. Oh yes, tits tied! Oh, what a sensation! So coarse, wrenched so tight, so very tight.'

Her free hand joined its twin, eight sisters playing freely.

'Another coil pulled tight above my tits, the friction burns.'

Three sisters probed her wet tunnel, the fourth pushing towards the puckered entrance to her anus. Three fondled, circled delicately about the clitoris, the nub rapidly swelling.

'Now the ultimate, resting against my nipples. It tightens, sinks into the supple flesh. I can barely breathe. My breasts are divided, nipples squashed.'

Stimulating needles delved her groin, bristles brushed her crotch. *'It would have to be Pierce. Lake was too detached, too authoritative. Richard too zealous, obnoxious. The toady of toad hall. Harris, ugh! Jay? No, too close, too much the lover. Pierce is perfect. Strict, masculine, he would whip with no regrets, without fear or favour.'*

Alice rolled onto her front, pushing that perfect behind up. *'I could do with it now. Twenty strokes with a whippy rattan. Oh, I can hear it, that sharp swish, the solid whop as it beats my bare bum. Then the unbearable smart followed by that indescribable burn.'*

Her fingers pushed deep, thrusting into that wet burrow. *'"I'll tie you down, Alice. I'll bind you so you can't move, girl".'* Her fingers worked faster. *'Sweet heaven. Tied down by him, my bare arse whipped by him. My cheeks like a sheet of corrugated iron, smothered in welts, a tortured, ploughed field. Flogged while I writhe and squeal and beg.'*

Her free hand settled on those raised flanks, fingers stroking. *'And now Pierce feels my scalded cheeks. His hand wanders. No, Pierce, not there. Not between my legs. You shouldn't feel my cunny. You shouldn't!'*

Her body tensed, every muscle rigid. Alice seized the pillow, fingers clawing, and she bit it. 'Oh, sweet fuck.'

Orgasm in retreat, mind and body soothed, her purged

thoughts quickly returned to Edward Pierce. She could have happily trotted down the corridor, knocked on his door and said 'let's do it'. She could be lying there with a sizzling rump. What the hell was this insanity? What drove her to such flagrant extremes? She didn't know, but the urge was so strong.

Alice shivered, pulling the bedding over her. It didn't help knowing he would. All she had to do was ask. But if she were to explain, where would she begin? If she could, and he understood, how would she know she wasn't fooling myself? How could she be sure she wasn't asking for sexual reasons? How could she be sure she'd be paying the fee for that sin?

It would hurt. It *should* hurt. Had she the courage? What would Pierce ultimately think of her? Did she care? She guessed she did.

A knock on the door roused Alice. Rubbing tired eyes she checked the time, three in the morning. 'Who is it?' she called out.

'It's Mavis, Alice.'

Shaking the sleep from her mind she opened the door. 'I thought you went home at night, Mavis.'

'And I normally stay there until eight. You have a visitor, Alice. A very determined gentleman, I must say. He's waiting in the common room on the ground floor.'

'Did he say who he is?'

'Why, your father of course.'

'Father? I'd best slip a dress on.'

'He said don't fuss, he knows what you are.'

Alice ran to the hall door, Mavis leaning past as she tried the handle. 'It's locked. We can't have you running amok, can we? I saw what you did to O'Leary. Poor thing.' A large brass key turned in the lock, the door opening. 'There you are, Alice. Don't be long now.'

She ran down the flights, bare feet slapping lightly on stone. Panting she reached the common room door, and paused, checking her hair in a glass pane. Anxious, she opened the door.

A tall grey-haired man waited with his back to her. 'Daddy? Is that really you?'

Reginald Hussey slowly turned and smiled. 'Been a while, hasn't it, Alice?'

'Where have you been? And where's mother?'

'More to the point, Alice, where have you been? What the devil have you been up to?'

'I don't follow you, daddy.'

'Daddy? Come now, you know I'm not your father. Richard told you that. Like he told me a lot of things about you.'

'Such as?'

'Don't be impertinent. Why aren't you at school?'

'I'm trying to find my mother.'

'Your mother's dead. You know that.'

Alice's heart fell to her stomach like a stone. 'No, I mean Rose.'

'Rose? What do you want to find that mad slut for?'

'Is she mad?'

'As a hatter.'

'Where is she, father?'

'Here, of course.'

'Where?'

'Use your eyes, girl. There. Look.'

Alice followed the pointing finger and in a corner, tied in a straitjacket, squatted herself.

'She likes being tied up,' her father divulged, ashamed. 'She likes other perverted acts as well. She's very much like you, isn't she, Alice?'

The girl nodded, belittled and shamefaced.

'There's no point you being here. And there's no merit in being in Chapel En Frith, snug in bed with a husband and father old enough to be your own. Go home, Alice. Go to school. Be what you set out to be. Don't end up a tart like your mother.'

'Home?' Anger displaced guilt. 'I have no home.'

'Of course you do. Richard has extended the hand of bonhomie. Accept it.'

'But…'

'But what? He's not your uncle? I know that. But he might be. We never did find out with whom your mother slept. Richard was a lot different then. Some say he could be the father of the little bastard girl.'

'Little bastard girl.'

'Little bastard girl.'

'Little bastard girl. Little bastard girl.'

'That's you, and now you know.'

'Richard!'

'Daddy, please.'

'No, never!'

'We can choose our friends, eh, but we can't pick our…'

'You can't be.'

'Why not? I've lived in Southport all my life, as did Rose.'

'That's sick!'

'Of course it isn't. Why do you think I am so concerned about your future? You should be at college, Alice. I've had Heptonstall ring me, asking where you are. They're not pleased. A damn good thrashing awaits when you do get there, I shouldn't wonder.'

'And that's your answer to everything, isn't it?'

'You know that's untrue. There are other ways to punish a loose girl. You know that. Discipline by example?' Richard smirked. 'You have a penchant for being tied up, I seem to recall. So I tied you up. Or rather, I had you bound. Remember that, Alice? That irksome fat boy with the pug face? Rather apt, I thought.'

'You beat him into submission. He was terrified of you…'

'I punished him for an act of depravity, the same as you. What would you have me do? Smile politely and say sorry to disturb you? Would that be the act of a responsible guardian? Would you expect your father to take such a frivolous course?'

'I…'

'Of course you wouldn't. He would be guilty of a dereliction of duty, wouldn't he? You'd grow evermore promiscuous. You'd believe licentiousness to be a way of life. You wouldn't see it for the evil trap it is. You'd be into prostitution and all sorts before you spotted the rot. That is the way of Satan. Those are his scurrilous, insidious tricks.'

Richard wagged his finger in her face, chilled eyes behind those round glasses menacing. 'He lays the table with precision, every tasty morsel inviting. He provides such splendid flavours, spice and zest, the tang of mischief. That's how it seems at first, Alice – naughty. And naughtiness in the child is expected. The child delights in the odd wayward turn. It thrives on the nectar of mischief. But for the reins of the astute guardian the child would be sucked into that eternal abyss of turpitude.'

Alice made to answer, vocal chords failing.

'What has Satan laid your table with, Alice? What delights does he entice you with?' His hands settled on her shoulders, his eyes boring into hers. 'What tune do you dance to?'

Thumbs tucked beneath the shirt opening, Richard grinning. 'With some the bait is money, luxury, good living. For others it's power, like Hitler.' He leant close to her ear, breath surprisingly fresh, and whispered. 'Your lure is the flesh. He draws you with glimpses of a promised land. He lulls you into believing yourself different. He taints the fruit so you perceive it in a different light.'

Richard straightened. 'And his payment, Alice?' Arms tensed, fists snapping aside, buttons giving to the force, the girl's chest bared. 'The consummate body.'

Alice made no attempt to cover herself. She stood, arms by her sides, entranced by the man's declamation. 'He doesn't lose, does he, Alice? You sing his song for a handful of fleshly diversions, and Satan remodels your body. You become a more useful tool for serving him; such is the cunning and guile of this monster.

'But I am no easy victim, for I see his guise.' He cupped his hands to her breasts, stroking the cool spheres. 'But I can see the temptation. I feel it. You present such an awesome bait. Many will fall at your feet. Many will be pitched into the fires of hell because of you, Alice.'

Richard filled his hands, Alice's breasts probed and squeezed. 'So what does he entice you with? A spontaneous fire in your belly whenever you come close to a man's cock? The heady scent of euphoria at his simple intimate touch? Does he nag you with constant dreams, leaving you wet between the legs? Does he drag your fingers down between your legs to comfort his itch?' Alice sensed Richard's own fingers there, stroking, pawing, intimidating her. She breathed in deeply.

'Does Satan reward you with inexplicable gratification, when bonds are drawn tightly about your sweet, curvaceous body? Does he make those cutting ropes seem erotically exhilarating? Do you long to feel them biting into intimate places?' His forefinger parted her sex lips, moving back and forth. 'Do you long to feel the sink of rope *here*, Alice? Cutting deep into your vagina, your pussy, *your cunt*?'

Richard withdrew the finger, purposefully placing it in his mouth and sucking. 'Hmmm… woman, Alice. Woman. These are all simple tricks to such an adept. You become addicted, always lusting for those few moments of absolute pleasure. And he provides them gladly. Satan is happy to toy with your cunt, Alice. And all the while he does you slide closer and closer to the point of no return.'

He laid a hand to her shoulder and turned her. He bent her over, lifting the shirttail clear of her naked bottom. He stroked, his palm slipping over those sleek dunes. 'You long to feel the slap of a whipping implement, don't you, Alice? At times the urgency is debilitating.' Richard lifted an arm and delivered a hefty smack to a flank. 'Is it simmering? Has the smart been turned? Has it become an aphrodisiac, filling your belly with fire, the glow of insatiable lust? Not yet? Of course not. It takes a while, doesn't it, Alice?'

He began a steady rhythm, slapping each buttock in turn. 'It takes time to reel the fish in. But that interval provides both parties with opportunity. The chance to exaggerate the lust, for the lechery in them to expand; whereby it consumes all objections, leading them to the path of utter profanation, to complete ignominy.'

Her behind burned intensely, the heat penetrating, burrowing to her sexual nucleus. Orgasm strengthened, flowed, ebbed and then struck its peak. Alice sat upright, eyes blinking. Curiously she delved beneath the covers, fingers feeling between her legs, and frowned at the warm fluids meeting that foray.

She leapt from the bed, and lifting the shirt checked her backside against a mirror. Only the faint lines of his caning marred that fetching rump. Alice straightened, tossing long auburn hair from her face. Dumbstruck she gazed stupidly about the room. 'He could have been here,' she said to herself. 'Those were his words. My head doesn't think that way. What the hell is going on?'

Most dreams, nightmares remove their traces shortly after waking, so that after an hour one can barely recall them. But Richard's visitation stayed, remained precisely clear.

'Nothing makes any sense any more,' she mumbled. 'How can he get to me here? He doesn't even know where I am. But what he said; it all rings so true. Except, Richard my father?' She shook her head vigorously. 'No way, but, he might know a bit more than he's letting on.'

She stole along the hallway with soap, flannel and towel, determined to wash, albeit in cold water. Relieved to find the washroom empty she quietly closed the door and stripped, and naked she stood before the basin trying to work up a lather.

'There's hot water in the bathroom next to mine,' the unmistakable voice of Pierce informed her.

Alice spun, grabbing the towel en route. She faced the big man, towel barely concealing her. 'Do you mind, Mr Pierce?' she snapped.

He shrugged affably. 'No, not at all. Just thought you'd like to know.' Closing the door behind him he called back. 'I've seen it all already, Alice. There's no surprises left.'

Smiling at the man's cheek she resumed, tensing as she heard the door open again. 'Oh, and it's extremely nice too,' Pierce added. 'Very tasty.'

Alice turned to throw the towel at him, the door slamming shut. For the first time in forty-eight hours she laughed, the partial submission relieving her tensions. She warmed to Edward Pierce, the man not as insensitive as she first thought.

Dressed in the shirt and pinafore supplied, Alice nosed downstairs, Pierce having unlocked all doors. She met Mavis on the ground floor, the woman just arrived.

'Good night?' Miss Jarvis enquired.

'Interesting,' Alice replied.

'No problems, I take it?'

'No, Mavis, no problems.'

'See, I was right, wasn't I? Now, I haven't caught up with Mr Hughes yet. But I will speak to him this morning and sort out those matters I promised. I dare say he will wish to speak with you himself at some juncture. But in the meantime, I'll show you the galley and what to do when the girls come down. Which won't be long now.'

Mavis introduced Alice to cook, a burly lump of a woman with crimson cheeks. 'Right,' harrumphed the servant, 'it's oat porridge for them that wants it, and oat porridge for them that don't.' She heaved a large pot towards Alice. 'One and a half ladles per crim, whether they want it or not. Then, my dear, our duty is done. We offered it, didn't we?' Alice struggled, cook slapping her hard on the back, her act of camaraderie.

Pierce opened the double doors that led from the corridor, winking at Alice as he took up position alongside. Silently, with only the squeak of shoe leather on polished wood, the girls filed in. Each collected a plain white ceramic bowl from a stack and then held it out before Alice, head bowed. Each received the requisite ladle and a half of heavy, grey, salt-flavoured porridge.

Face after face appeared to carry their unappealing stodge to long bench tables. Alice slopped porridge automatically, the scrape of ladle, flop of oatmeal the only sounds. No one would eat until they were all seated and Mr Hughes provided the nod.

She recognised some, those that abused her the night before. Still, no one was sure of Alice's position, the inmates often taking turns at dishing up meals. Then Ruth stood before her, eyeing her with scepticism. She cast a surreptitious glance towards Pierce. 'I'll catch *you* later,' she whispered.

Hughes entered, every girl standing, the scrape of chairs raucous, jarring Alice's nerves. She checked the time on a large clock mounted high on the wall. Eight precisely. Accompanied by what she presumed were a half dozen tutors, all grimfaced, Hughes signalled for them to begin. The females consumed that tasteless sludge in an orderly and mannerly fashion, all bar one.

Pierce strolled the lines, peering and checking every bowl. He lifted the full one, carrying it to Hughes. The principal fixed his gaze on the culprit. 'Wareholme, we waste nothing in this establishment. Do you have a medical reason for refusing good and wholesome food?'

The young woman rose and placed her hands behind her back. Ramrod straight she answered. 'I'd sooner finish my time in borstal than eat that shite every morning, sir!'

'By that I assume you have no sound reason for not eating it?' The man's voice, persona, wielded a cold hostility. His timbre threatened without the use of direct intimidation. Confidence and authority oozed from every pore.

'It's shite, sir. Cold, lumpy, stick-in-the-throat shite.'

'Let me make a couple of points clear, Wareholme, as you are relatively new. I decide whether you return to whence you came, not you. You are expected to adhere rigidly to what we term as Hope protocol. Failure to do so will invoke the tenth commandment.' Hughes lifted an eyebrow. 'Will you recite the tenth commandment please, Wareholme.'

The girl shuffled her feet anxiously. 'I must expect to be penalised for any infringement, indiscretion, or disobedience, sir.'

'The porridge, will you finish it?'

Sandra Wareholme searched the faces of those about her. Alice detected a conspiracy. It seemed to her the girl had made a boast, and those companions were not about to let her renege on that.

'Well, Wareholme?' Hughes persisted.

'I'll no eat that shite, sir,' she spat, her Scottish brogue coming to the fore. 'Not today, not tomorrow, not again. And I say that with the utmost respect to you, sir.'

Alice noted the way she trembled, knees close to knocking. But Sarah held her chin high. She refused to show fear or back down.

Unimpressed, Geoffrey Hughes relaxed, legs crossed, one arm slung casually over the back of his chair. 'Sandra,' he said quietly, voice carrying in that tense silence. 'You know I will not back down. You know what you can expect. I will give you one more chance. Either finish your breakfast, or give me good reason why you cannot. There is no, will not.'

The tall, ginger-haired girl took a deep breath. 'No, sir.'

Studying his fingers, expression concerned, he disclosed matter-of-factly, 'We seem to be tackling direct disobedience, use of unacceptable language and an attempt to incite insurgency. Do you agree, Wareholme?'

'I apologise for the use of the word shite, sir. It seemed the only appropriate description. If, in refusing to eat that shite I am guilty of disobedience, then so be it, sir. And I refute your accusation with regard to the last part, sir.' The girl's lips twitched, eyes sparkling.

Alice watched with bated breath, as did everyone else. Hughes stood in mortal danger of producing a heroine. Sandra Wareholme stood her ground, facing him with determination and backbone. She understood perfectly the likely result, as well as her future standing within that penal community.

'Very well,' conceded Hughes. 'You are forthwith excused breakfast.'

Sandra fought back the grin, expression unable to conceal her surprise.

'And lunch and tea,' added the man. 'When you finally come to your senses do let me know. Your porridge will be awaiting you.'

The principal stood, and stepping casually, approached the girl and her cohorts. 'Morton, stand up. And you, Wisbeck. And I think we'll have Smith, Catterall and Jenkins on their feet as well.

'Now, ladies, Hope does not tolerate cliques. Conspiratorial groups are strictly forbidden, and for good reason. Order must be maintained for the benefit of all. Mutinous conduct will ultimately wreck the opportunities Hope offers. Rules bring about stability. Discipline retains that stability.

'Now tell me, you six wise rogues, that you have not contemplated disruption. That you have not sought to undermine the stability of the Hope-Ashby Preparatory College.'

Hughes received nothing in return but silence and petulant faces.

'You see!' The man half turned, announcing his deduction. 'You expected a martyr, a heroine of the piece, a poor downtrodden waif, rising like some Joan of Arc. A saint willing to suffer the inquisition to demonstrate her virtues. And what have you instead? A scheming brat, ladies. A brat that has readily, and without prior complaint, eaten her porridge every morning for the last forty-six days. A proven incorrigible that opines that what is good enough for everyone else is shite.

'So what to do with this irksome rabble? I'll not force anyone to eat what they find unpalatable; that goes for every one of you. Any that wish to miss the wholesome nourishment of Avena sativa can sit with an empty bowl instead.'

Hughes stood legs apart, fists resting on hips. 'Well, Sandra Wareholme? Where's the bravado? Where's the rousing defiance? Lost your tongue?'

The limelight skilfully plucked from her wretched stance, Sandra had to try to salvage what she could, so with her voice lacking that earlier decisiveness she suggested, 'Perhaps if the shi… porridge, was served with a spoonful of sugar, sir, then the lumpy mess might travel the gullet a little easier.'

Hughes ambled behind the nerve-racked girl, hands gripping jacket lapels. He nodded. 'Morton, Wisbeck, Smith, Catterall and Jenkins wait outside my office.'

He waited for the five to leave. 'Did you draw the shortest straw, Sandra? Is that it?'

'No, sir.'

'Oh come now, we will get to the *bottom* of this eventually. And the longer this goes on the more disruption you cause. So, what do I have to do to get to the truth?'

'The truth is…'

Hughes continued drowning her excuse. 'Is, Sandra, that you thought you could undermine my authority. You had the ridiculous fancy that the whole school would rise to your defence. But I can assure you it will take more than one cocky brat from the heathen lowlands to do that.'

Lips twisting, face a snarl, eyes mad as hell, Sandra turned on the principal. 'You dare to insult Scotland!' She spat in his face. 'Pig! Fucking English pig!'

All breathing ceased. Furious, simmering, only her pride kept Sandra from begging. She waited, nervousness concealed, for Hughes' reaction.

'Put your P.E. kit on, and run the quadrangle until I call you.' He wiped the spittle from his face, expression satisfied. 'Clear the hall.'

As the girls filed out Geoffrey Hughes strolled towards Alice. He looked her up and down, seemingly bemused. 'A little drama for your first day, eh, Alice?'

'Yes sir,' she replied respectfully.

'It's a continual war. They provoke and we defend.'

'I thought you handled it very well, sir,' Alice praised.

A smile flickered. 'I didn't introduce you for one good reason, Alice. But this is no place to discuss that. Perhaps you would be good enough to accompany me to my office.'

'Before we go I have a question, Mr Hughes.'

67

'Certainly.'

'I've not eaten yet; do I take the same meals as the inmates?'

'Not inmates, Alice. Never inmates, crims, convicts or prisoners. They are students. They are here to learn, not to serve time.' The man scrutinised the pot, and the dreadful grey mess caked to the sides. 'And no, you're not expected to eat that shite.'

Hughes deliberately took Alice via the quadrangle, an open rectangle bordered by the buildings. There, anybody would be subjected to the scrutiny or scorn of several classes. Sandra, in plimsolls, white shorts and vest, already jogged. She followed the perimeter made from asphalt, her path directly alongside the classroom windows.

Hughes opened a door onto the quad, Alice following the man outside. Rain fell, dropping vertically, Sandra already wet. She trotted past the pair, Hughes studying her healthy stride, the sturdy build and athletic gait.

'She's a fit lass, Alice; that will stand her in good stead. The rule when running the quad is not to stop. Gauge the duration, your stamina and strength, and run within your limits. She'll receive one stroke for every time she falters.'

'How long does she have to run for?' Alice enquired.

'Until I say stop.' He checked his watch. 'It's now half eight, or near enough. We'll see how she's doing at half past twelve.'

Four hours? Alice didn't believe she could manage four minutes.

Tall Sandra was, strong of build too, but Alice noticed as the vest and shorts stuck to her body, semi-transparent with rain, that she possessed a good figure, and the odd fact struck her that a high percentage of the 'students' *were* acutely attractive.

The Scot wore nothing beneath the kit, that slowly becoming more obvious. Generous breasts gleamed pink, nipples poking tantalisingly. Tight shorts gripped tenaciously, the soaking merely adding a sheer quality. She ran by, the pair treated to her back, buttocks plainly visible, lurching with every stride.

'I shall cane her with those on,' Hughes announced

unexpectedly. 'While they are still wet.'

He opened a door on the opposite side of the quad, ushering Alice through. 'And what if she doesn't falter, sir?'

'Oh, she will… eventually.'

Chapter Four

They climbed to the second floor, the principal's stride energetic. In the long hallway waited the five miscreants, each conspicuously nervous. Hughes unlocked the study door. 'Morton, you can demonstrate your mettle first. The rest of you wait outside the p. r.'

Alice watched the group mooch to that other room, their body language crying apprehension.

'Now, Alice,' Hughes beckoned her into the study, 'shut the door please.

'Your dress is unacceptable. I cannot have you on active duty, so to speak, indiscernible from the ranks. Have you nothing else?'

'No, I'm sorry, sir. I left most of my wardrobe in Chapel. Miss Jarvis was kind enough to issue me with this.'

'Have you any money?'

'Some.'

Hughes opened a drawer, took out a small notepad and with a fountain pen quickly drafted a note. He offered it to Alice. 'Sharpes in the High Street. I have an account. You will need a complete wardrobe. Your 'uniform' must consist of white blouse, black skirt and stockings.' He pointed at her. 'I don't want to be able to see your bra underneath, either.'

Alice felt her face warm.

'Get what you need, but don't go mad. Allow for soiling, so at least two of everything. If that's the only colour of bra you have, then you'd best purchase a couple of white ones.'

He took a five-pound note out of his wallet. 'I don't have an account with Skinners the shoe shop, so use this. A sensible pair of black shoes, low heels. Two hours. Come back looking like a member of staff and not a...'

'*Student*, sir?'

'Precisely.'

Alice opened the door. 'And, Alice,' Hughes called after her. She half turned. 'Yes?'

'The underwear. The only criteria is that it cannot be discerned through your clothing.' He smiled; Alice offered the attractive side of the man. 'Lace. Half cups. Whatever you like.'

Outside she hovered, curiosity biting deep. With Morton inside the room, probably overwrought with anxiety by then, the remaining four hung on tenterhooks directly opposite the executioner's door.

Smith caught Alice's interest. Hostile, remote powder-blue eyes challenged her impudently. Shoulder length mousy hair bunched thickly, framed a heavily freckled elfin face. Thin lips beneath a small turned-up nose sneered contemptuously. At five feet two, Rachel Smith presented an effeminate, rather than feminine frame.

Geoffrey Hughes emerged from the next door down, rolling his sleeves up as he walked. He stopped, listening. He glanced over a shoulder. 'Alice? Is there a problem?'

'No, sir.'

'Then please go about your business.'

Unhurried, Alice dawdled, ears pricked. She heard Hughes' voice, indistinct, contained by the partition walls. As she passed his study the first solid connection between rump and cane reached her ears. Alice gasped. Her bottom clenched. Did she really want that? Did she really yearn for the humbling subservience, the crushed pride? Could that ever be a source of sexual gratification?

Twenty paces away and the second stroke echoed more faintly. Alice sighed, bum flesh tingling.

Another ten paces and the third bit stressed buttocks. Alice pushed the hair from her brow, a flush rising, cheeks heated.

She reached the top of the stairs as Morton's backside reeled to the sixth. There it might have ended, Alice would never know as the stairwell obstructed any further eavesdropping.

Pierce unlocked the main doors to let Alice back in. 'So what did you buy?' he asked amicably.

'What Mr Hughes said I should buy.' She opened one of the bags, Pierce peering inside.

'Black and white.' He chuckled. 'If only life were, eh? Black and white instead of all those little grey areas. Geoff has a thing about black and white.' He nudged Alice. 'A fetish about nuns, I reckon.'

'I wouldn't think so.'

'Why not?'

'He seems so proper and dedicated.'

'Ha!' Pierce slipped an arm around her waist and squeezed. 'You've a lot to learn.' He peered deeper into the bag. 'What, no undies? No black laced lingerie? Oh, Alice. Such delectable bits should be cosseted by the finest, most expensive silk.' His hand wandered to her buttock, Alice gently prising it free.

He closed on her ear, whispering, 'Black silk and white rope, now that would be an interesting contrast.'

'And red stripes, Alice. Very distinctive. Hard to keep saying no, isn't it?' She shivered.

'I can do more than make you shiver, Alice,' Pierce offered, misinterpreting the reaction. 'Tomorrow night, after lights out.'

The door banged shut as she climbed the stairs to the top floor. On the second she paused to check on Sandra, and looking down from the hallway window she spotted the tall Scot bent, hands against the wall. Wareholme threw her head back, tossing wet ginger curls, then hands on hips she shook first one leg then the other.

The rain had ceased, her kit dried by the heat of her body. Alice checked her watch: twelve-thirty.

'Wareholme!' Hughes' voice boomed. 'Did I say you could take a rest?'

Hands on her waist she bent, trying to catch her breath. 'Had it,' she wheezed. 'Can't run any more.'

'I suppose you would have me believe that this is your first rest?'

'Aye sir, it is. You dinnae think I would readily give you the excuse?'

'No, Wareholme, I dinnae think that at all. But there again I dinnae need excuses, do I? Not when I have an oaf of a girl providing me with plenty of reason.'

Hughes raised the arm hidden from Alice's view. A thick rattan glinted, which he flexed and twisted, gaze not lifting from Sandra, a satisfied smirk informative. He swished the brute, the sound having the desired effect on Wareholme. He continued to mimic her accent. 'Will you no eat your porridge tomorrow, brave Scot?'

Sandra eyed that cane warily. 'I'm done protesting, sir. I've said my piece.'

'The democratic way is by polite complaint, not rebellion. Now, how will it taste?'

Sandra chewed her bottom lip, intractability etched in that attractive but seasoned face. 'Like shite, I shouldn'a wonder.'

Hughes acknowledged her defiance, a trace of amusement discernible. 'You'd best adopt the position, hadn't you?'

Gait uneasy, she sauntered to the middle of the quad, granite chips crunching beneath her feet. Her arms fell loosely by her side and head laid back, eyelids blinking against a clearing sky she readied herself; the sprinter before a race. Then she flopped over, fingers engaging toes.

Hughes studied her for a few moments. White shorts fitted like a glove. Well-rounded, amply padded buttocks stretched cotton cloth. Long, strong, well-formed sun-kissed legs squeezed together, thighs smooth, skin faultless.

Smiling, the principal strolled to a nearby standpipe, a zinc-plated bucket left beneath. He filled that then carried the pail to the unsuspecting girl. Held above her he tipped, cold water pouring, soaking her shorts and body. He tossed it back across the yard. 'Pre-emptive cooling, Wareholme,' he explained, the taunt aimed only at her.

He rested a hand on that bowed back, cane tucked beneath the arm. The other hand flashed the short distance, slapping a buttock with force. It lingered, fingers gently rubbing stung flesh.

Alice leant on the sill, intrigued, aroused by anticipation. She assumed Hughes had to make an example of Sandra, to deter others from following her lead, and that example had to be public, or be pointless.

The arm flicked up, descended, slapping the same cheek, the same spot. Flesh quivered, the flank stung. The principal said nothing, his attention taken by the rows of faces lined up behind the windows.

'Well, Sandra,' he said quietly, 'you have your moment of glory. Your audience watches and waits. The question is, how will Sandra the Bruce bear up?'

His palm connected heavily with that burning cheek, discomfort edging higher. 'Those animals will leech off your misery. They want to see you hurting. And the more you hurt the happier those animals will be.' He slapped her again, the patch sore.

'Do you think they give a damn about your pain? They see you as the fool, the simpleton, the lamebrain stupid enough to bitch about porridge. The mad Scot crazy enough to call me a fucking English pig.'

Her buttock wobbled to another connection, the pain approaching sickening. 'I know you drew the short straw, Sandra. I know they cajoled you into provoking me. Now they're laughing, joking about the red-haired jackass who won't be able to sit for a week.'

Only Wareholme heard the man. Only Wareholme was meant to, and she sucked air as yet another scorcher edged her closer to purgatory.

'I can make you wish you were never born, tough Glaswegian bitch. That Gorbals reputation won't serve you here. That's just my hand. Imagine if I whip your sweet backside repeatedly, on the same spot, with the cane. Imagine that, Sandra.'

Hughes leant back, examining that reddened cheek. He raised his arm and struck, once, twice, three times in quick succession. Sandra Wareholme squealed. She tried to straighten, hips swaying evasively.

'There, that fed their lust for blood.' He mimicked her brogue 'The mad Scot isna as hard as she would have them believe. The tough Gorbals lass cannae take her medicine.'

Another volatile swipe had the girl reaching, hands trying to defend that blistering hurt.

'All is not lost. Not quite yet. There is an alternative.'

'And what might that be?' she asked, voice strained.

'Oh, so you're interested? You don't want me to carve your arse up in front of these morons, just to prove a point?'

'I'm listening, sir.'

'You are? Good. We'll have a chat tomorrow; after you've eaten your porridge. Yes? But unfortunately I am obliged to execute a prior judgement. Just look upon it as a small taste of what to expect should you disappoint me.'

The principal stepped back, levelled the rod, lifted it high and struck. Tensed wet buttocks gave before an explosive stroke. A tidal wave of excruciating fire swept through those hindquarters, Sandra gagging, but before she could muster her resolve that brute of a cane swept in again and cannoned into raging buttocks, doubling the agony. The girl bit hard, trying not to scream.

Alice pressed a hand between her legs, comforting her own inferno, massaging, an intense spasm raking her crotch. She turned from the window as the third echoed about the quad, the Scot's bum shuddering, the scald pitching her into the pit of hell.

Alice stared at the ceiling, lungs heaving, the sweat of lust dampening her forehead. 'Oh, God, I need that,' she whispered. 'I need that so badly.'

She failed to see Hughes stride away, cane tapping his calf, the expectant mob disappointed, and Sandra Wareholme sorrowfully rubbing a butchered backside.

That afternoon, dressed in the newly acquired clothes, Alice was called to Geoffrey Hughes' office. There she was assigned a number of clerical jobs, the man working and watching. He kept an interested eye on that awesome figure, the swirl of pleated black skirt entrancing. When she reached high, his calculating gaze fell upon her revealed lower thighs. Alice's bending produced a marked enthusiasm, whether she offered that engaging bottom or the pressure of youthful breasts in tight white cotton.

'May I ask why you were caned by Miss Lake?' he asked, unexpectedly.

'Oh.' She scratched her scalp, wondering how he knew. 'Nothing terribly serious. I absconded. I was a boarder.'

'I spoke with the good lady earlier. She said that was the only blemish on an otherwise perfect record. It was a painful experience, I presume.'

Unsettled by the question she replied, 'Doesn't the cane always hurt?'

Hughes returned his attention to the paperwork. 'I suppose it does at that.'

She observed the man for a few moments, mind ticking over, that insane desire blinding commonsense. 'Yes, Mr Hughes, it was extremely painful. But I deserved it.'

She hung on his reply, heart pounding, mentally begging him to propose a repeat. Instead the man skirted, delved the possibilities, hanging them on the line to wear another time. 'I imagine that happened some time ago?'

'Oh no, only a few months since.'

'You seem so mature.'

'I said I was eighteen; I am nearly, but not quite.'

'Still young enough to require guidance and the odd prompt, then.'

'Yes, I suppose I am, sir.'

76

'Still, work hard and apply yourself and you shouldn't need such.'

Alice smiled. 'I will do my best.'

She returned to her filing, pondering the short exchange. What was it all about? Was it a veiled warning? Was he trying to find out how she felt about chastisement? The conversation dogged her, feeling she might have been expected to take the lead, let her superior know in a roundabout way her inclinations. But how could she?

That evening she lay staring at the ceiling trying to analyse her feelings. Perhaps what she needed was a simple, damn good poking. She threw her legs apart. 'There you go, Pierce. Have this on me.'

Restless, the evening hot and sultry, Alice pushed open a window. Undoing her blouse she pulled it apart and leaned on the sill, trying to catch the slight breeze. She wondered where Jay was. Was Katy at Heptonstall? Had she been flogged yet? She laughed at the thought. She should get herself arrested and convicted; the Hope would suit her. Caned whenever she wanted, *and* at the drop of a hat.

'God, I'm bored,' she mumbled. 'Bored, and so horny. Why am I so horny? Just the thought of a cane on my bare bum makes me want to scream with frustration.'

She opened her door, peering outside to check the hall was clear. 'Wonder why Hughes let that girl off so lightly? Three strokes. Nothing really.' His cane ripping into wet, short-covered buttocks flashed before her eyes and she threw her arms about her body, shivering. She needed a diversion before she went completely mad. The way she felt poor old Pierce wouldn't be safe in his bed.

Coast clear Alice crept to the main landing doors. Still relatively early she padded barefoot to the second floor. The girls would be in the common rooms on the ground floor, so the first should be devoid of all human existence. Alice checked down the hallway, a light showing that Hughes still worked. She wanted to look at that room. Why did he cane the girls there? Why not his study? What was so special about that particular office?

Slowly she advanced, drawing level with Hughes' study, and caught the sound of voices. He was busy, that was good. She crept onward, reaching the room without incident. She tried the handle, the door swinging open. She peered into the gloom, eyes slowly adjusting. Beside a cupboard the room was devoid of furniture, except for one item squatting indistinct in the gloom. Curious, unable to resist further investigation, Alice moved nearer, quietly shutting the door behind her.

Closer inspection confirmed her suspicions. The piece cried corporal punishment. Thirty inches high it would support the average person's tummy, legs nigh on straight. The top was slatted, slightly dished and reinforced by a rectangular cradle. Four stout legs, supported by cross members fore, aft and at the sides, met with two heavy feet, set front to back, providing the apparatus with stability.

Alice knelt, examining it with enthusiasm. She had never seen the like, not even in Jay's basement. Six inches from the top, riveted to the front legs, were two heavy leather cuffs. Another pair hung unfastened halfway down the rear struts. Alice felt them. Her fingers stroked the old polished leather; the suede inner glossed by use and the sweat of God knows how many suffering girls.

A buckle riveted to the rectangular top glinted in the moonlight, a long strap dangling on the far side. So this was the secret weapon. This was why the girls were always brought here. Strapped down, legs parted, bottom thrust and stretched… and then caned.

Alice rose, leant forward, placing her palms on the slatted surface. But would that be with knickers on or off? Off, and Hughes would be able to see everything a girl had.

She settled, wood hard against her stomach, her shapely legs bent slightly to accommodate the position. What a piece of equipment! She parted her legs until her knees met with the feel of leather, completely restricted, unable to move, bum a sitting

78

target.

Hands felt for the forward rear straps. She gasped, belly alight, rear end and sex feeling exquisitely vulnerable.

Eyes adjusting to the dark, Alice noticed a key in the cupboard door. She rose and opened it, and gasped. She delved, pulling implements free, inspecting and then returning them.

Why did he want all these? There had to be a dozen canes. Then there were the straps, paddles and whips. What did he want whips for?

She lifted one, a three-foot, single-tailed, plaited lash. 'How do you fancy that across your bare arse, Alice?' she whispered, perplexed, then swung it, tail emitting a dull whoosh. She visualised herself on that bench, the whip used on her. She shivered, then shrugged. 'Perhaps not,' she mused, replacing it.

Cupboard door shut, the girl wandered back to the bench. She circled it, fingertips running over worn slats, imagination let loose, passion rising. Thoroughly immersed she failed to hear the slight click of shoe leather on the tiled floor in the office next door. She remained blissfully unaware of the eyes that snooped, concerned, of the voyeur that watched her every move through a two-way mirror set in the wall.

Alice pulled the shirt from the skirt's waistband. Already unfastened, she flicked it clear of her breasts. Little by little she gave to that perplexing compulsion. Warm, toned tummy touched, settled on cool inflexible wood. Her legs stretched at an angle, toes curled to the floor. She looked over her shoulder, checking the door, then hands drifted behind her back. Her bra undone she lifted the cups, freeing her breasts. Exposure, peril, the risk of discovery egged her on.

Her respiration shallow and rapid, sensual tension was stretched to sexual urgency. Intoxicated she plunged headlong towards hormonal madness, the frenzy that eradicated commonsense. Those realms of fantasy and reality merged, besieged a mind seeking solace, gripped a libido demanding gratification. She edged into a surreal world, subconscious masking the absurdities, tendering the plot and overseeing fulfilment of an all-consuming lust.

Alice wrenched the blouse from her arms, dropping it to the floor, bra following. Naked to the waist she settled her wrists against the cuffs, gauging how a tormentor might see her.

The mirror, eight feet away caught her eye, Alice abruptly turning her head, staring directly at the reflection. The figure behind jerked back, thinking for a moment the girl knew.

Illuminated by moonlight feeding directly in through the windows, Alice could make out her image. 'Oh God,' she whispered. 'What a position.'

Back, skirt-covered bottom and upper arms glowed beneath that soft luminosity. The shadows hung black and heavy, exaggerating the visible curves of breasts and highlighting the girl's prominent facial features. Her witness studied Alice with keen interest.

All objections devoured, inhibitions lost to the crushing sexual turmoil, Alice loosened her skirt. Hips wriggling, fingers urged the garment down, silken dunes basking in that ghostly radiance. Ebony laced panties hugged those contours, probed the sumptuous flesh, moulded between those lustrous cheeks. Provocatively her legs parted, knees locating the straps, Alice acquainting herself with the feel of complete submission.

She reached behind, grabbed a strap and fed it through the buckle. Tightened it pressured a thigh, held the limb fast, crowning the salaciousness. Twisting in the opposite direction she secured the other limb.

Alice lay, thighs spread, wallowing in that raw vulnerability. Untroubled by the possibility of detection, concern blunted, she tossed the wide strap over the small of her back. Fed through the clasp she pulled, tugged until her belly pressed against the slats and her rump thrust up. The retaining pin she flicked up with a forefinger, driving it into a hole as she released the strap.

Again she viewed her shadowy reflection. The slope of back, pinioned at the base, then rising abruptly, buttocks captured. Alice wriggled, tested the straps. Her lower body was held, the grip of leather an aphrodisiac.

Windows shut and barred, the atmosphere hung sultry, clammy air and exertion encouraging a sweat. Breathing laboured, her mind probed ever deeper into the abyss of possibility. Alice composed a scenario, visualising herself awaiting the lash. That exquisite body writhed, movement slow and exaggerated. Hips rolled, thighs pulling against the straps, leather delving lower back.

'Waiting to be whipped,' she mumbled, expression fraught. 'Waiting to be whipped.' She hissed. Sexual delirium stifled caution, the fantasy dancing so close to reality. Mundane ideals and objections purged, she focused all her energies on consummation of that dream.

Burning with passion, body slick with sweat, her torso heaved and pitched. Moist hands gripped the legs, pushing her shoulders up, face screwed with concentration. The vaults of mental perception ground open, her torturer taking centre stage. Face elusive he closed on her, coiled whip in hand.

Each exhalation carried a whimper, the short exclamation of a brewing storm. The incarnation proved so perfect her creation could have stood beside her. Fingers delved the loop of cuff, the urge for complete restriction irresistible. Her forearm thrust, knuckles grinding against leather. Oiled with sweat the appendage passed, wrist shackled.

Eyelids still tightly clenched Alice forced the other hand, the cuff eventually surrendering, and there the near-naked girl rested, her mind in another world.

So many images hailed that delusion, adding their excitation. The feel of biting straps aided and abetted. Faces filled the void; Jay, Harris, Pierce and Hughes, but the ogre Richard reigned supreme.

Alice tried to reject the monstrous concept, others temporarily fitting the bill, but the notion pursued her relentlessly. The vision firmed, eradicating all else. He wore that smug, conceited mask, that *I have you banged to rights* expression. The whip he caressed, emphasising its presence.

Her buttock muscles clenched, twitched apprehensively. She tugged on those restraining cuffs as if wishing to escape. The glow in her belly expanded, teasing with the possibility of orgasm.

'Whore,' the man spat. *'It is just that you should be spread in such a fashion. The Jezebel with her legs parted wide. Would that be an invitation? Perhaps when I have punished you I might proffer another warning on the sins of the flesh.'*

Her body jerked to the imaginary lash. She gasped, back arching, the reflex accentuating her ardour.

Her spectator watched intrigued, the young woman's gyrations raising numerous questions. Alice's energetic squirming, contortions and jerks paraded her inclination beyond the shadow of any doubt. A knowledgeable smile played, the observer comprehending.

Alice pushed right up, leather strap wet with sweat, gripping, biting into her back. Gleaming breasts swayed and trembled. Her supportive arms shook with effort and the aftermath of a body-racking climax.

She lay awhile twitching with the rumbles of extreme excitation. She shivered, her energy depleted, feeling the descending chill.

With satisfaction came the gradual infiltration of guilt, remorse for that vice. The possibility of being found near naked and strapped to the bench penetrated the euphoria. Ravished by the tempestuous upheaval her muscles inclined to torpidity. Her arm limp she tugged, the leather gripping with tenacity. Fear gripped, she yanked, the cuff refusing her passage.

'Oh God,' she whispered. 'Please, no.' Again she tried, her wrist firmly held. She wrenched on the other, which similarly clutched. Fear turned to panic, Alice feverishly jerking on her bonds. The sweat that had enabled the forward pass had dried, and that same perspiration lined the strap, enhancing its grip. She settled, belly beginning to feel the effects of the hard, probing slats. Closing on hysteria, her mind refused logical consideration.

She whispered in the dark, 'How am I going to explain this?

What am I going to say to Mr Hughes when he eventually finds me? Oh, why did I do it?'

She remained there, a haunting half hour passing slowly. Her body ached, muscles cramped. Periodically she attempted escape, those hide fetters offering no opportunity.

Tears of shame ran down her cheeks. Gone was that thirst for punishment. In its place stood the promise she would never succumb again. What would be the gain in remaining there all night? A miracle was not about to happen. Hughes would find her in the morning.

Tomorrow seemed distant, a long and uncomfortable night stretched ahead of her. The edge of that slatted top dug painfully into her ribs, the portentous brush of wood against shivering breasts no longer fodder for incitement. Those same narrow pieces stuck to her abdomen, leaving their colourful impression.

What would Hughes do? Cane her? She laughed sardonically. No, he would berate her, ask a multitude of questions guaranteed to extend her embarrassment. The man would stroll in unawares of the perverted slut bound to the bench. He would stand there aghast, the near naked trollop offering in detail every part of her anatomy. Then she would hear his outraged voice, and she would surely die of humiliation.

Her ears detected the snap of high heels out in the hallway. Mavis, perhaps? Alice opened her mouth to call, but resolve failed her. The steps approached, ceasing outside the door. Her heart stopped. She didn't dare breathe. She distinctly heard the handle turn, and then the room was flooded with artificial light.

The ensuing silence remained uninterrupted. Alice stared at the floor, the courage to see who, absent. The click of heels, slow, methodical. Alice squeezed her eyes shut, face burning. The person strode, circling her. Click. Click. Click. Click.

'If you're waiting on Mr Hughes, then I'm sure you'll be pleased to know he's forgotten you. He's gone home.'

Alice didn't recognise the voice. It held that element of surprised, but not shocked, and thankfully not outraged. 'No,' she whispered.

'No, what?'

'I'm not waiting on Mr Hughes.'

'I see. You seem to be in a bit of a predicament. Someone's idea of a joke, perhaps?'

'I'm just glad a woman has found me, and not a man.'

The woman laughed. 'Oh, that I *can* understand. So who are you? I don't recognise the bum.'

The remark pressed home her dire situation all the more. 'I'm Alice. Alice Hussey.'

'Ah, yes, the new girl Friday. They said you were a beautiful girl. I can see no reason to contest that. So Alice, how did you wind up strapped to Mr Hughes' whipping bench?'

'I've been here a while. I'm cold and terribly, terribly embarrassed. Do you think you could release me first?'

'Release you? But if I'm not happy with your explanation I might have to strap you down again.'

Alice found the courage. She lifted and turned her head to see with whom she spoke. Intelligent hazel eyes met her interest, the woman reading her mind. 'Doctor Sheila Doodney. Hi.'

'Do doctors cane people?'

'This one does. Frequently.' She laid a cool hand to Alice's bottom, who swallowed hard as the doctor pressed her fingers into that deliciously compacted flesh. 'For what reason, flicks through your mind. The answers are complex and many faceted. Therapy, in some cases, to dissuade malingerers in others. A bit like a boarding school matron, I suppose. I also teach, so I am expected to uphold discipline. And, Alice... so what do you think the *and* is?' She brushed stray blonde strands of hair from her brow, the rest tied back in a ponytail.

'Girls found in the dark strapped to a whipping bench?' Alice guessed tentatively.

'No, strangely not until now. Do you think I should whip you? Make the most of this unprecedented opportunity?' Sheila rested fists on narrow hips, suit jacket open.

'I probably deserve it.'

Sheila ran a fingernail from the girl's bottom the length of her

84

back, then went on. 'The other reason I flog backside is purely because I enjoy it. Now the question is do you, Alice, have a similar preoccupation?' Alice caught the scent of expensive perfume, the smell reminding her of Jenny.

'I strapped myself down. Does that answer your question?'

'Partly. Confession is good for the soul, it's said. Do you agree?'

'Sometimes.'

'Catholic?'

'Yes. A bad one.'

'Others will be quick to judge you, leave it to them. So you're prepared, served up, one might say. I assume you've had the aperitif? Do you desire the main course?'

'Not really.'

'The bugler sounded the charge. The gallant six hundred stormed the cannons. And when the balls started ripping them apart their courage faltered. Sweet, ecstatic fantasy. Glorious sexual ideals. We exorcise them, but they come back. Is that not so, Alice?

'Are you sexually active? Are you in a relationship? Have you experienced a climax in the last couple of hours?'

'Yes, no and yes.'

'Oh dear, then your hormones will be in recess. A caned bottom will hurt most cruelly, I suspect. A sinful Catholic endures a penance, I believe. Is that so, Alice?'

'Yes.'

'Should you suffer a penance?'

The doctor inadvertently hit the nail directly on the head. Alice surrendered to tears. 'Yes,' she blubbed. 'Yes, I should.'

'Have you been a bad girl?'

Alice nodded, tears running freely.

'And will a thorough caning absolve you?'

'It might.'

'Will it ease your conscience?'

She shook her head. 'I doubt it.'

Sheila leant and unfastened the cuffs. 'No caning tonight.

85

Maybe tomorrow, we'll see. Release yourself and get dressed.'

The woman waited until Alice had donned her clothes. 'I am a psychologist, Alice. There is much I understand, much I can commiserate with. And there again, there is much I would like to know. I believe you need to unburden yourself. You can talk to me. I have taken the Hippocratic oath. Anything you care to tell me will be in the strictest confidence.'

Relieved at the outcome, Alice still felt dreadfully humbled. 'Do you really cane the girls?' she asked, believing that to be a ruse.

Sheila smiled. 'Oh yes, Alice. And my immediate instinct was to cane you. Had you been a student here, then I would have. Still, perhaps I've helped you sort your thoughts out a little?'

'What time do you want to see me?' Alice enquired.

'Not I you. Surely you wish to chat with me?' Sheila smiled.

'When I finish work?'

'Quite acceptable. Goodnight, my dear.'

On the landing between flights she ran directly into Ruth O'Leary.

'Said I'd see you later, didn't I?' the young woman reminded. Alice tried to pass, but Ruth grabbed her blouse. 'What's yer hurry? I thought we could chat about the weather. You know, whether yer is staff or inmate, or just plain bloody snoop.'

Alice seized her wrist, pulling it from the blouse. 'At this moment I am just plain bloody pissed off.'

Ruth pondered, her scrutiny of the redhead prolonged. Tired, Alice headed up the stairs. 'Hughes always introduces new starters, but he ain't you.' Ruth ascended in pursuit. 'Bit of an enigma, ain't yer?' The blonde caught up. 'And that business last night; now that really do puzzle me.'

They reached the top floor, Alice pausing. 'There's no mystery there. I told you who I was, and you chose not to believe me. Just think yourself lucky it didn't go any further.'

'Lucky? Jeezuz! I slept on my belly last night cos of you. You had your revenge. You took that out on my arse. Fuck, the girls could have hung hockey sticks on the welts.'

Alice closed her eyes. 'What did you just say?'

'The stripes; they were that raised the girls could have—'

'Hung hockey sticks on them,' Alice joined her, grinning.

'What's the matter wiv you?' O'Leary demanded. 'What's so amusing…?'

Alice giggled, then laughed outright.

'Come on, what's so funny?'

Alice began to lose control. She hugged her body, hysterics taking her.

'You're fucking mad!'

The redhead gasped. 'I know. Oh Christ, how I know.' She leaned against the wall, tensions, the horrors of the last few days coming to the fore, and still giggling insanely she slid to the floor.

With Ruth standing over her completely dumbfounded by her utter loss of control, Alice calmed, sucked air, chest heaving, tears staining her cheeks.

O'Leary knelt. 'Madness passed, 'as it?'

Alice shook her head. 'No Ruth, I don't think it ever will. I suspect it'll worsen by the day.'

'While there's still a thread of sanity left then, answer me this. Why didn't you tell Pierce you were a member of staff? Why did yer 'appily take up that position? I mean, Jeezuz, it were nowhere near decent, were it? Yer don't 'ave to do that unless yer's a… Unless yer 'ave to.'

Alice pulled a face of resignation. 'I thought I had to. It seemed appropriate.'

'I don't follow you. Why would you have to?'

'Things you don't know. Matters you will never understand. But be assured Ruth, I am no snoop. And if Pierce keeps his word, then Mr Hughes will never know what happened last night.'

O'Leary squatted, arms about her shins, jaw resting on her knees. 'Thanks for that. Pierce is bad enough, but Hughes?' She shivered.

'Did I hurt you badly?' Alice enquired, regretting the incident.

'I'm sittin' ain't I? I guess it weren't that bad. I've had worse. A hell of a lot worse. Ever been birched?'

Alice nodded.

'Some'at in common, eh? Ever had yer tits caned?'

Alice pursed her lips, face reflecting the assumed horror of such a punishment.

O'Leary glanced left and right, ensuring the hall remained empty, then back straight she unfastened her shirt. Peeling back the cloth she exposed her breasts. 'See?'

Alice scrutinised the girl. Surprisingly well endowed, breasts exquisitely firm and well rounded, those delightful orbs showed the marks of numerous tramlines.

'Who?' Alice mouthed rather than voiced.

Ruth shook her head. 'Can't say. I can't trust yer, not yet.'

'Pierce?' Alice persisted. 'Hughes?'

'Nah. Like I said, I can't say. But it was a novel experience, that I will admit.'

'Now we're both puzzled,' Alice remarked.

'You trust me and I'll trust you, eh?' Ruth offered.

'You show me yours and I'll show you mine,' Alice riposted.

'Eh? Well I've shown you mine. So let's 'ave a decko at yours.'

'I don't think so,' Alice declined, thinking herself lucky to get off so lightly with the last madcap venture. 'I'm not, you know,' she added, least Ruth arrived at the wrong conclusion.

'What, queer?' Ruth laughed. 'Gawd gel, do you think I am?' She settled astride Alice's outstretched legs, then leaning forward, face close to Alice's, hands spread on the girl's thighs she disclosed, 'But when yer's doing time, yer needs to occupy yerself. I like a side of meat spreading me fanny just like any red-blooded gel do. But the pokey ain't got much to offer that way. So, we make do.'

'But I'm not an inmate, am I?' Alice reminded.

'No, you're not, so how about nippin' down the shops and buying us a couple of pound of cock. Nice stiff 'ard ones.'

Alice chuckled. 'If I could I would.'

'Yer know, I think yer might at that. Shall we call a truce? We done you and you done me, so we're quits.' She offered her hand, Alice accepting.

'Now tell me why yer fell about laughing?'

'I have a friend. A very close friend. Kate. She's completely mad. She once said exactly the same thing, so it just struck me as hilarious. She's a blonde too.'

'Yep, mad as hatters, us blondes. You just watch and wait, and yer'll see.'

Chapter Five

Alice stretched out, feeling less troubled. She still had Pierce to fend off, but hoped he would listen to reason. All the while perversion remained in her head those fantasies could cause no trouble. It seemed to her that the second she tried to realise the dream, all horrors descended. Her mind was a Pandora's box, and should be left well alone.

Using Pierce's shirt as a nightgown she turned on her side, arms hugging her pillow. She drifted, sleep engulfing her.

Inconsequential dreams flittered; the only common thread her past. Carters and her parents' home offered a feeling of security, and her subconscious snatched at that whilst fending off the horrors of being orphaned, and the ensuing loneliness.

Skipping from euphoric comfort to encroaching homesickness, Pierce abruptly crashed those fragile mental barriers. Her concerns about the following day allowed his promise purchase. Hazy images and random propositions badgered. Ropes lay scattered about his room. Those chairs squatted, beckoning. Pierce's face loomed large, the pot-marked skin and ginger handlebar moustache startlingly clear. 'You promised me, Alice. You said I could tie you up.'

Alice refuted the suggestion. 'I did not!'

He held a soft white rope beneath her nose. 'It was agreed that if you couldn't explain, then you would participate. And you can't explain, can you Alice? What can you say? It's all a misunderstanding, won't wash. Why come to my room, Alice? Why come near-naked? Why bend over the chairs? Did you want me to see your cunny? Did you want a portion? Is that it? Been without too long, have you? Why not get it over with,

Alice? Let me tie you tight. Rope you so you can't move. I could let you off the cane this time. Just a little smacking instead. Just a bit of over the knee. Warm that lovely bum up. What do you say, Alice?'

The girl sat up, staring into the dark. She checked the time – ten-fifteen. 'What's the point leaving it until tomorrow?' she asked herself. 'If I sort it out now I might get a good night's kip, and God knows I need one.'

She pulled back the bedclothes, settling bare feet on the floor. Quickly she slipped on her panties and a skirt, and adjusting her hair she whispered, 'Just tell him straight. If he wants to see Hughes, then go ahead.' She reached the door, fingers around the handle. 'With any luck the girls will be sound asleep. With any luck Pierce will be too.'

Outside in the hallway she strode to his room. She didn't bother knocking, but waltzed straight in. Pierce lay on his cot, stark naked, a pornographic magazine in his hands. Startled, he slapped the journal down to cover his vitals. 'What the… not more trouble!'

'I'm not doing it,' she blurted.

'Not doing what?' he asked, puzzled and annoyed.

'I'm not coming here tomorrow night.'

'You could have waited until the morning to tell me that. Anyway, I didn't imagine you would.'

'No?' she questioned, surprised.

'No.'

'Why not?'

'Why should you? I assume you've all the answers for Mr Hughes.'

Taken aback, Pierce not reacting as expected, Alice found herself lost for words. 'I… I… of course I have.'

He shrugged. 'Then you don't have a problem, do you?'

'No.'

'Well it's been nice talking to you, but if you don't mind you have me at a disadvantage, if you hadn't noticed.'

'Oh yes, of course, I'm sorry.' She turned to face the door.

'Unless of course you fancy cuddling up to me?' Pierce added.

Her back to him, Alice admitted, 'Look, I haven't any answers.' She didn't see Pierce grin. 'Well, not any that will hold water. It would mean baring my soul, and I'd sooner leave here than do that.'

'You have somewhere to go, I take it?'

'Yes, as it happens. But I'd sooner stay. Can you give me a few weeks? I might be able to explain it to you then.'

'You've had a day, and you have until tomorrow night. Edward Pierce stands by his word. To be honest, I don't really give a damn about tales of hardship. You acted strangely to say the least, and I don't think anything you say will change my mind on that.'

'This is blackmail; you realise that?'

'This is no Enid Blyton story, Alice. This is the real world – real men, real women, and hard reality. You don't want to explain yourself, then you have to accept the consequences.'

What choice did she have? She needed to buy time. She had to keep Pierce quiet. It was her own stupid fault, anyway. It was Harris all over again. Perhaps she deserved this. Perhaps this was her punishment.

'Well Alice, either shut the door behind you or take your skirt off.'

'Maybe this is it; my punishment.'

She reached behind, fingers settling on the fastening.

'Or perhaps deep down I want this.'

She released the first button. Pierce leered, and sampled another gulp from the whiskey bottle.

'I have to let matters take their course. I wouldn't try to persuade a priest in his judgement.'

She released the other two buttons and let it fall. 'How do you want me?' she asked, uncertain.

'Come here,' Pierce said, tossing aside the magazine and sitting up.

Alice approached, trying to divert her gaze, the man in a state of arousal. She stood before him, Pierce reaching out, hands ascending her thighs, hips, then taking the elastic of her panties in his fingers. He savoured the moment.

'This will be it, won't it?' Alice sought reassurance. 'You'll forget about last night?'

He shook his head, Alice's tummy turning over. 'Can't do that. Couldn't ever forget last night. Same as I won't forget tonight. But you have my word I won't *say* anything.'

'And you won't try anything?'

'What do you take me for, some sort of pervert?' He grinned, tugging down her panties. He simmered awhile, contemplating on what lay behind that fragile cotton barrier, the shirt wavering with every deep breath Alice took. Pierce seized his bottle, swigging heavily on the alcohol, eyes gazing at Alice, taunting her.

'A good cognac should be savoured. One should scent the bouquet,' he briefed, leaning, sniffing close to her sex. 'Then one takes a sip.' A hand wandered up a thigh, over a hip to her waist. Sighing deeply he followed the indentation between hip and groin, fingers delicately descending. Alice shuddered.

His thumb ran over the nudity of her mound, then touched upon the foremost point of her vaginal lips. 'Did they shear you last night?' he asked, seeming sympathetic.

Alice nodded.

'That's a bit of a thing here. I've no idea why, but most of the girls are.'

Hands on her hips he turned her, and lifting the shirt he whistled softly. 'I don't think I've ever seen a better example of woman in my life. And I've seen a fair few. Christ, you'd give the devil himself the horn.'

He ran his hands over those protruding cheeks, fingers and thumbs pressing the flesh; Pierce drinking of her firm corpulence. 'What an arse, Alice. I say what a delightful, perfect piece of womanhood.'

She shuddered as his tongue slid the length of the division. She leapt from his hold. 'Don't do that. You can tie me, you can discipline me, but you don't maul me. And you certainly don't

93

lick me. Understand?'

Pierce pulled a face. 'You don't make the rules. Not in Pierce's room you don't.'

Alice angrily defended her position. 'Touching's one thing, but groping is another. I'm not a tart, and I'm not a piece of meat. I'm only doing this because I fucked up. And be warned; you renege on this agreement, then you'd better keep your door locked of a night.'

He held up his hands. 'You came here to sort things out. I didn't force you. Now, I've not misled you in any way. I've been straight right down the line. Either you do like I say, or piss off back to your room. Your decision, Alice.'

'You really are a worm,' she agreed, reluctantly. 'And I'd be happier if you put some pants on.'

Fingers curling around the thick stem, he asked, 'This old boy worry you, does he? Tell you what, hold it.'

She eyed the monster with animosity. 'No thank you.'

Pierce rose, the might of the man dwarfing her. He glared down on her, erection proud, the shaft long, stout and eager. 'That wasn't a request. Hold it.'

Reluctantly, tentatively she placed her hand on the column, the touch, the feel affecting her in a manner she deplored.

'See, it doesn't bite. Now look me in the eye and tell me you don't want it. When your arse is burning scarlet and the ropes are biting deep, tell me you don't want it then. Hard and thrusting in your tight little slit.'

'No, Mr Pierce, I don't want it. Not even if you were the last man on earth. I meant what I said earlier. What do you take me for? I'm here purely to keep your vindictive gob shut, and that's all.'

'A right good shafting might just improve your temperament. God, you're one cantankerous bitch.'

'Just get on with it,' she spat.

Pierce moved behind her and slapped a hand to her buttock, the girl's eyes widening. Fingers probed, squeezed the flesh, the man remarking, 'Nice and fleshy; just how I like it.' Jaw set he repeated the liberty on the other cheek. Her bum stung, tingled, proffered an unwanted thrill. 'You should have some respect. No more games.'

He threw an arm around her waist, lifting her. He slumped on the cot, Alice spread over his thighs, a brawny left arm pinning her down. Alice settled one hand on the floor, the other grabbing a fistful of eiderdown. Pierce slapped a buttock with aggression, the sting caustic. Alice bit her lip. The opposite cheek flattened, wobbled beneath his blow, burning insanely. The girl gasped.

'Ask Mr Pierce if you might have the honour of scratching his itching cock,' he demanded, slapping her rump again.

Alice failed to comprehend. 'What?'

He struck yet again, the sound of hand on flesh music to his ears. He emphasised the iteration with another hefty swipe. 'I said, ask Mr Pierce…'

Long auburn locks tumbled, obscuring her face. She grit her teeth, biting on the yelp. 'I heard you.' she growled.

'Well?' Arm rising high Pierce continued to pulverise that delicious backside.

'Get lost.'

Pierce doubled the pace, an inferno ignited. That tight corpulence coloured, the taut humps of her buttocks quickly warmed. 'I'll lay a pound to your penny you change your mind.'

'And… ouch! Pigs might… ouch! Fly. Ow!'

The minutes ticking by, she stuffed the bed sheet in her mouth to muffle her cries, biting on the cloth to stifle her agony. The man struck remorselessly, her backside raw, every slap sheer unadulterated torture. Alice twisted, wriggled, kicked and squealed. Her bottom the deepest carmine, and savagely hot, Pierce asked, 'Changed your mind yet?'

Pride intact she insisted, 'No.'

The man leant on her back. 'You know, Alice, my hand is getting sore. Time to rest it, I think.'

The girl relaxed, unwilling to admit it, but she was very close to tendering that request. Pierce reached, lifted a hairbrush from his bedside table and blasted her lustrous rump with it.

Alice reared. 'You said you were going to rest your hand!'

He laughed. 'You bet your sweet fanny I am.' Hard flat wood bit battered flesh. Alice tried desperately to escape, the man's arm too strong.

Her bum grew numb, the immediate soreness easing, but still that hiding proved no cakewalk. Every square inch of her crimson rump smarted. She felt his erect cock pressing against her groin. The spectre of indulgence raised its unwanted head, Alice rejecting it outright.

Unable to take any more, guessing he would beat her all night if necessary, Alice conceded. She hoped it was a case of Pierce asserting his authority rather than actually expecting her to carry it through. 'I'll do it!' she shrieked. 'I'll do it!'

Pierce kept on, hairbrush slapping the stricken. 'I hear you.'

'Please,' Alice managed, the word sticking in her throat. 'Please, it hurts.'

'Oh, I know it does,' Pierce taunted. 'Funnily enough, it's supposed to.'

'God,' she mumbled, kicking frantically. 'I said I'd do it.'

'What was that exactly?'

'You know.'

She fought against his arm, pushing up, back arching, heated crimson bottom heaving to his ardent slaps.

'No, Alice, you ask me nicely now.'

She endured another twenty vigorous smacks. 'Okay, okay, can I scratch the itch in your penis?'

Pierce persevered, Alice writhing, head tossed, hair flying. 'Not quite as I want. Try again.'

'Bastard,' drifted from her lips, face contorted with the insufferable fire. 'P-please c-can I scratch your cock, Mr P-Pierce?'

'That's better.' He laid the brush to one side. 'See, you can learn respect, even at your age. Mr Pierce could teach you a few other tricks, too. You just remember that when you're lying in your bed all alone. When you can't keep your fingers out of your fanny.'

'You're disgusting.'

'You mean you don't? Eighteen years old and you've never scratched that itch down here.' He thrust his hand between her legs, Alice's thighs trying to prevent the crude interference.

His grip relaxed, Alice managing to escape. She crawled on all fours, grabbing her panties. 'I shouldn't have come here. You men are all the same. You only want one thing. I thought you might be half decent, but you're just like all the rest.' She pushed up from the floor, rising to her feet. 'You go and tell Mr Hughes, and I'll tell him you didn't give me any alternative. My word against yours.'

Unimpressed, Pierce merely grinned. 'You know something, girl? You could be a top model with a body like that. You could earn a bloody fortune. Now I happen to know someone who could give you a start. You'd only have to pose, pretend you were doing it. Act like. This fellow knows someone who would publish the pics. Good money. Far more than you'd ever earn working for the Hope.'

He lay back on the bed, picking up the magazine. 'I don't expect you to make up your mind straight away.' And as she headed for the door, humiliated and angry, he added, 'You haven't obliged me yet.'

Alice stopped. 'What?'

'You begged. Under duress, I know, but you pleaded. Only right you go through with it. See, Alice, a disappointed dicky affects its control centre. You know how it is – once a month, when your hormones go barmy, all that venom and spite. Not getting close now, are you?'

Alice leant against the open door. 'What are you going on about?'

'I'm just saying, let dicky down and anything might happen.' Pierce nodded at the near vertical pole swaying between his legs.

Alice sashayed back, deliberately rolling her hips, expression steamy. She paused by his bed, her eyes flirtatious. She reached out slowly, fingers extended. Pierce watched, a burning desire anticipating succour.

She curled cool fingers around his stem, her demeanour raising the man's pulse. Her fist rose, riding the plum, extending the foreskin. Pierce's arrogant grin subsided, sexual tension replacing it.

The descent exposed his glistening plum, Pierce groaning, and Alice felt the enrapt jerk, the involuntary pump of excited cock. 'It seems a shame to use my nails on such a delicate area,' she whispered, her voice sex incarnate.

Pierce hung on tenterhooks as mouth open, tongue darting, her flushed face closed on his rampant shaft. The colour of his manhood darkened, Alice's fist tight, his plum turning mauve. 'Teeth?' she asked sensually.

'Vixen,' Pierce cursed. 'If you don't I'll go bloody mad.'

Her tongue wavered millimetres from that bloated dome, the man's penis as hard as it would ever get. Her shirt had risen with her bending, a crimson flank exposed. Her breasts, loose, swung and played with her shirt in the most delectable manner.

Pierce dangled on the edge of paradise. He'd been there hundreds of times before. Girls galore had sucked him off as a remission on the bum slash. But Alice drew something extra. Alice boiled his pot. Alice raised his pulse, his heartbeat and his temperature. Pierce suffered an overwhelming desire to stuff his impressive shaft hard between her legs. He wanted her pussy more than any other. No female had ever made him hunger so ravenously.

Alice plotted a cruelty. She sought revenge – to tempt, to raise his hopes, and then sink her fingernails deep into that sensitive monster.

Pierce's limited patience drew close to its end, the man becoming suspicious. Her fist relaxed, fingers positioning claw-like. Her lips drew tight over gleaming enamel, teeth poised to sink deep into that eager head.

Pierce's speed proved startling. His huge fist closed about hers, squeezing her hand, preventing the intended assault. At the same instant he seized her hair, holding her head painfully in position. 'Well, Alice?' he growled. 'What's keeping you? There's sexual anticipation, and then there's taking the fucking piss.'

'I… um…' The unexpected choked all excuse.

Pierce sneered. 'You fucking tease. You had no intentions, did you? What was it to be, fingernails cutting into my cock? A bite, perhaps?' He shook her head. 'Well?'

Alice stared at the one-eyed monster, the slit seeming to wink, glans the colour of a Victoria Plum. Her scalp screamed, Pierce's pull on her hair extreme.

'As I thought,' Eddie nigh on snarled. 'I'm close to coming, girl. Half naked girls with their tongues hanging out have that strange effect on me. But the point is, just how do you intend to appease me? Where do you want my wad of come?'

'Let me go,' Alice whined, close to tears. 'Please, just let me go.'

He forced her head down, her mouth meeting, lips giving to the press of earnest shaft. With ease he filled her mouth with salty meat. 'What?'

Alice fought the invasion, her back and neck no match for his strength.

'You can have it between your legs if you prefer,' Pierce taunted. 'Or up your arse. I've no real preference. But one thing is for sure, you're going to take my wad in one hole or the other.'

Spiritually crushed, Alice mentally crumbled. Defiance always seemed to spell defeat. Either she was stupid or she was stupid, she decided, guile and cunning forever evading her.

'Don't like it there, eh?' Pierce persisted. 'Okay…' Lifted and tossed like a rag doll Alice realised his full strength. She never stood a chance against him. With her face pushed into the blanket, Alice barely able to breathe, he hoisted her hips. Crudely parting her legs the enraged man forced a partial entry, the end of his shaft snug in Alice's dry burrow.

'More to your liking, tease? Shall I thrust? Do you want to feel my full meat, scratch it with your cunt?'

99

'Please…' escaped the trap of rough blanket.

'Was that, "yes please"?'

She shook her head, the subsequent pain in her scalp agonising.

'No? How about this little puckered hole then?'

The girl squirmed, red-hot razors slicing at her anus. She grit her teeth and begged, her smothered pleading pleasing Pierce.

The man opened her for the grief and pain it caused. He observed gleefully that immersion of glans before snatching it clear, and Alice sighed in relief.

Roughly turned, Alice stared up at him, the naked man over her, knees either side of her torso. He nursed that eager penis, the veins as proud as the shaft itself. He leaned forward, crotch descending close to her face, generous balls swinging, brushing her mouth and nose. His fist pumped the organ, a rapid back and forth motion, Pierce intent on masturbation.

Pinned to the bed, Alice could only watch. She had never seen a man wank himself; the act both disgusted and entranced. Pierce's hefty cock stirred something Alice preferred to ignore. The impression of it sunk deep in her fanny would not disperse, a mental picture prone to revisit for days after.

Pierce energetically massaged that column for some two minutes, the fleshy pole consuming her thoughts. Then he straightened and grunted.

Alice's gaze followed those impressive hair-flecked testicles. Puzzled, she noted the minor spasm, the drawing tight of scrotum, the satisfied jerk of climaxing balls. Pierce's gasp brought her focus to his tip, like some medieval knight's helmet. She frowned to the depression of his shaft, the apparent aiming of that red eye, then she recoiled in horror at the surge of viscous sperm, the seed raining audibly onto her face.

Wad after wad pumped from that *membrum virile*, Pierce deliberately spreading it, sperm fouling her eyes, nose, and mouth. She tossed her head, expression disgusted, stomach nauseated. As the final insult Pierce wiped his weakening erection across her lips, a trail of slimy seed left in its wake.

Laughing, he removed his weight, Alice rolling away, frantically wiping at her face. 'You filthy…' she raged, heaving. 'You disgusting pervert!'

She careened into the hallway wiping her face with her panties to see Ruth O'Leary leaning against her dormitory door. She said nothing, her smug expression and knowing look speaking volumes. Alice glanced down at the knickers in her hand, the utter shame too much to bear.

Downcast, miserable, blaming herself for her own stupidity, she stumbled back to her room. 'What now?' she said, punching her head, yanking on a clump of hair. 'I'm so stupid! Will I ever learn? The only friends you will ever have are your family, and you girl, haven't got one.'

Inside she crouched, back against the wall. She was on her own. No one was going to give her anything. All they wanted was to take, take, take and take. Let the scumbag go to Hughes. Let him say what he wanted. He probably would anyway. Would she ever trust Harris again? No, so she mustn't trust Pierce.'

Eyes closing she contemplated on how life had been so uncomplicated only a few months before, then rising, shoulders slumped, legs numbed, she flicked on the light.

'Good evening, Alice,' chilled her heart. 'And where have you been?'

Hardly daring she turned her head towards the one man in the world that terrified her beyond words. Richard smiled.

'This can't be,' she muttered. 'This isn't real.'

'Oh, I'm afraid it is, Alice. Mr Hughes rang Carters and that nice Miss Lake rang me. She was concerned, you see. She wondered why you'd cut short your education. But of course I knew nothing about your travels, did I? The last I heard, that playboy Howell was supposed to be looking after you. I'm not surprised. Still, he'll get his comeuppance in the next couple of days.'

'What have you done?' she demanded.

'Only what I promised, should you turn your back on me.'

He nodded at her hand. 'More to the point, what have *you*

done, and where have *you* been?'

Those panties hung incriminating, Alice suddenly very conscious about Pierce's emission still glistening on her face, and she dropped them as if they had stung her. 'Nothing,' she replied. 'Just went to the bathroom.'

Richard stood. 'Really?'

'Yes, unc… er, Richard.'

Smug, he informed Alice, tone level. 'Nigh on half an hour to visit the bathroom.' He stooped, picking up her panties. 'Couldn't you manage to pull them up?'

'I… um… I…'

He grabbed Alice by the hair, pulling her over. 'Who, Alice? Who have you been with?'

'I haven't been with anyone!' she cried.

'Listen to me, girl. I promised your father I would look after you. I vowed I would be there for you until you're twenty-one. I have no intention of reneging on that promise. No matter where you go, where you run to, or where you hide, I will find you.' He pulled her head back. 'Now, where have you been?'

'Father?' she gasped, the tendons in her throat strained. 'You don't even know who my father is.'

He moved closer, face looming, hostile eyes lancing her guilt. Round spectacles framed the contempt. 'Oh, I know who your father is.'

He twisted her hair, roots pulled, her scalp on fire. Tearful green eyes begged. 'Who?' she whispered, terrified of the answer.

'What's on your birth certificate Alice?'

'Nothing. There's no name.'

'You're thinking me, aren't you?'

'No, I don't know.'

'Would I father a bastard? Would I? Could *you* possibly be my daughter? A tart. A whore. A perverted Jezebel.' He eased the pressure. 'That would be interesting, wouldn't it? Don't you think so, Alice? You, the devil's spawn, the offspring of me, God's unerring disciple. Perhaps you should look to the incubus, for your father is most likely Satan.'

Richard threw her onto the bed. Alice lay, not daring to move. 'You fear me, don't you, Alice?'

She rammed a thumb in her mouth, nodding.

'So you should. I hold the key to your future. Only I can unlock the secrets you wish to know. Only I can ensure your sanity.' He reached down, flicking up her shirt. He stroked those trounced buttocks.

'I can lead you on the path to salvation. I have the strength to minister your exorcism. I will rid you of these demons, Alice. I will take you to still waters. No more the devil urges. The thirst for corruption will be quenched. Do you hear me, child? I alone can save you.'

Tears wetted her cheeks, her nerves in tatters. 'I do need *someone*.'

'Of course you do, Alice. I think you know now that Jonathan Howell only wanted one thing.'

Alice nodded.

'And that is the way of most men. I am the nearest you have to family, Alice. We don't always see eye to eye, but I do have your interests at heart. Do you really want to remain in this infernal place?'

She shook her head.

'Don't you need a shoulder to cry on? Don't you want a loving cuddle?'

'Yes,' she admitted, weeping openly.

'Then let me hold you. Let me make up for those bad times.'

She threw herself into his arms, Richard embracing, pulling her to him. He stroked her hair. 'So tell me, Alice. You can you know. I won't be mad, I promise. Where were you? Who spanked your bottom, and why?'

'Edward Pierce, uncle,' she sobbed. 'I made a mistake.'

'A habit of yours, it would seem. What was this mistake?'

Alice buried her face in his shoulder, choked she couldn't reply.

'Okay, who is Pierce?'

'He's the custodian. A corrupt slime-ball.'

'And he had cause to discipline you?'

'No, uncle, that's just it. He tricked me.'

'But you said you made a mistake.'

'Yes, but it was innocent.'

'So, why let him beat you? This sounds very much like Harris to me.'

She pushed away from him, accusing. 'You're only being nice so I'll admit to something, aren't you?'

'So you do have an admission, then? What did Pierce catch you doing, Alice? Was it like with Malcolm? Has that vile licentiousness resurfaced, or did it never go away? Or were you at it with some young buck. Oh, I forget, he wouldn't have to be young to please you, would he? No, someone *my* age would do, wouldn't he?'

'You're twisting everything.'

'Me? Twisting things? No, I think you will find it's you that's twisted.'

'Yes, of course I'm twisted. Why else would I… I…'

'What Alice? Why else would you what?'

'Sleep with you,' she nearly screamed.

'Sleep? You didn't sleep. You took me, remember? You tempted me. You drew me to your bed. Don't tell me you've managed to dismiss that cursed seduction from your mind. The way you used your body. The manner you swayed your naked hips. Is that what you did with this Pierce? Is it? Did you entice him? Did you? Come on, Alice, face the truth. Stop running away. See yourself for what you are.'

She covered her face, fingers raking her forehead. 'Yes, yes, yes, I did bait you, I know. But it was only because Kate suggested it…'

'Kate? Katy Howell? I might have guessed she would figure in all this somewhere. If she told you to jump off a cliff I suppose you would.'

'No, of course…'

'Don't blame Kate for your own ill-conceived behaviour. You

are of your own making. You are what you are. You wanted to bed me. God knows what you hoped to procure from it.'

'I thought you wanted to teach me a lesson?'

'In that I failed miserably; here you are, Pierce's bed still warm.'

'No, I didn't sleep with him.' Alice felt weary and confused.

'You didn't sleep with me either, but I seem to recall a particular union. I also remember a certain satisfaction; much as you *hated* every second of it.'

'I don't know why that happened.'

'Eighteen and you don't know the facts of life? Next you'll be telling me you didn't know what a penis is for.'

She lay back, sobbing. 'Leave me alone, Richard. For God's sake just get out and leave me alone.'

He stood, fastened his jacket. 'Very well, Alice, but as I said, I am ultimately responsible for you. I will come back, and you will come home with me eventually.'

She watched the door close, and arms about her body, shivering, mind close to shattering, she whispered, 'Oh God, what have I done? What did I ever do to deserve this? All I ever wanted was to graduate, find a soul mate, marry and have a couple of children. But I don't think that's ever going to happen. I'm damned. I'm damned.'

Alice woke with a start, daylight flooding the room. She gazed stupidly at the carpet, rough against her cheek, disturbed as she fought for clarity, the fog of sleep slowly lifting. She stretched, her body stiff, aching.

Richard!

The recollection knifed her gut. She sprang up, checking, quite expecting to see the vile man seated somewhere. Relief flooded her body, the room quite empty. It was another nightmare. The cold light of day restored her logical perception. But he could have been there. She'd not broken the trail completely. What he said, about Lake, that could happen. It would be just like her to do that, ring him, give her whereabouts away.

She rubbed the sleep from her eyes. There was nothing she could do about that now. Hughes had already spoken to Stagnant, and if she was going to ring Richard she would have done so by now.

She ran fingers through her hair, idly checking the time on her wristwatch. Staring in disbelief she cursed. No, it couldn't be!

Desperate, Alice began searching for her skirt. She crouched on all fours, bottom in the air, checking under the bed. 'This is insane,' she mumbled. 'The damn thing's got to be here somewhere.'

She rose, stood, scratching her head. Glancing about she caught sight of her rear in the mirror fixed to the wardrobe. 'Ah,' she exclaimed, 'I must have hung it up.' She opened the door, pulling the few garments back and forth. 'Shit!'

Panic rising, and already an hour late, she yanked a short skirt from its hanger. 'This'll have to do.' Curious she aimed her bottom at the mirror, warily lifting the shirt, her. She frowned, her head in a spin. 'What the...?' Discoloured, her bottom displayed the marks of a harsh spanking. She could discern hand and fingerprints, the contusions a dull red.

'How?' she muttered, exasperated, her lateness making her flustered. 'Who?' She stood awhile gawping. 'Richard? No, even if he was here he didn't do that.'

An image flashed, too fast for Alice to grasp. 'Something...' she whispered. 'There's something else. Something else happened last night...'

Quickly she washed, brushed her long hair, and quickly finished dressing. The short skirt riding several inches above the knee left her feeling uneasy. Should she bend the tops of her stockings would be revealed, and it hugged her bottom a touch too tightly, emphasising the swell of her buttocks and the line of her panties.

Alice ran the several flights downstairs and along to the main hall. She burst in, flustered, flushed, and over one hundred faces lifted, turned in her direction, expressions questioning.

Hughes stood. Adjusting his jacket, he leant on the table.

'Nice of you to join us, Miss Hussey. Enjoy your lay in?'

'I'm so sorry,' Alice pleaded. 'I…'

'Did we wear you out yesterday? Is that it? Too tired to rise for the *second* day. What time shall we see you tomorrow? Lunchtime, perhaps?'

She held her hands out. 'I… I've no excuse, sir. My profound apologies.'

'Well I suppose that's something. No lies. No deceit. No lame excuses. Take a leaf from Miss Hussey's book, girls. Alice doesn't insult my intelligence with a load of cock and bull.'

Alice smiled weakly; the fear eased, nerves settling.

'No, Alice is late, and Alice admits she's late. She also admits that she was incapable of rising from her slumbers. That on her *second* day she has proved herself unreliable.'

Chastened, her face burned. She wrung her hands, grimacing with embarrassment. Too short a time in which to make her mark on an adult world, she readily succumbed to Hughes' sarcasm, as if she had never left school.

'Which hedgerow was it, Miss Hussey?'

She looked up. 'Sorry sir?'

'Why? What else have you done?'

'I'm not with you, Mr Hughes.'

'That is blatantly obvious. Perhaps a cold shower might wake you up, hm?'

Dumbfounded she shrugged.

'If you tell me which hedgerow blocked your path here, I'll have Mr Pierce cut it down.'

'Damn, you'd give the devil himself the horn!'

Alice jerked, the mental jolt electric. Nauseous, almost too frightened to pressure her memory, she settled her attention on Edward Pierce. The man smirked. He eased back his tunic, the glimpse of a neatly folded black skirt promoting her fears.

'Well, Miss Hussey, I'm waiting.'

Alice felt very much the solitary figure, so alone, the fool for Hughes' verbal assault. Six months before she would have fought her ground, rebuffed the tirade with intelligence and grit. But confidence crushed, seeing herself as a useless misfit, she folded before the principal's onslaught.

She waved a hand, indicating her auburn hair. 'Didn't have time to brush it properly. Sorry.'

'Didn't have time?' Hughes repeated, derisory. 'In my world there are twenty-four hours to the day. I find time to work, eat, sleep, play and wash. In my world personal pride is foremost. Those daily ablutions are necessary. Is sleep more important to you, Alice?'

She knew there was no point in reply; she had no excuse, no defence. As usual she deserved what she got.

'Obviously it is,' Hughes finished.

Sheila Doodney took hold of Hughes' sleeve and gently tugged. The man looked at her, bent, and the doctor whispered in his ear. The man nodded, shrugged and straightened.

'Very well, Hussey, take that cold shower, and after I would like a chat in my office.'

Ruth caught Alice's attention, pursing her lips, inferring an unpleasant time awaited.

Alice paused by Edward Pierce. 'Can I have my skirt, please?'

'Tonight, Alice,' he said quietly. '*Come* again.'

She didn't feel like arguing, especially after Hughes' condescending words. But she needed an answer to a vital question, so chanced the remark, 'You spanked me hard last night, you know.'

'No more than you deserved.'

The principal's odd wit aimed at another interrupted any further comment. 'Well Sandra, how do you like your porridge this morning?'

Alice hung back, intrigued to see the outcome.

'I think I will be sick, sir,' the young woman replied.

'Oh, sick is it? Doesn't the mix meet with your approval then?'

A mouthful remained, Wareholme heaving. She shook her head.

'But Sandra, you are privileged; no one else is treated to sugar.'

The girl laid her head on her arms, retching.

Hughes smiled without mirth. 'I suppose it clashes with the salt, eh? Not to mention the pepper and mustard.'

'Where's the showers?' Alice asked Pierce.

'The principal most likely referred to the one next-door to his study. Seeing as he wants a little *chat* like.' The man twiddled with his moustache. 'Might be wise to pad your knickers, too.'

Alice caught Sheila's smile as she left, the woman winking good-humouredly. She ignored Pierce's comment, deciding the doctor had offered some valid point in an advisory capacity. The wink meant something, and the manner in which it was dealt offered Alice hope.

A door on the left of the principal's study marked *Private* led to his personal washroom. A subliminal link triggered that frustrating and impregnable abyss of her subconscious, choosing the moment to launch a clue to the previous night. Alice hesitated. 'Pierce, naked?' she questioned, perturbed, but the mental doors slammed shut, Alice's struggles to recall more hopeless.

She stripped, peeled the skirt from her hips, and tossed the shirt to one side. She unfastened the bra and let it fall, panties following. She shivered, body erupting in sensual goose bumps. Naked in an alien and precarious environment encouraged a teasing awareness, no lock on the door accentuating it. Evocative possibilities filtered through to that disturbed conscience. Gratuitous pictures fired from the core of her being lacerated propriety. The depths of her sex prickled sensually. Alice smiled, the possibility of Hughes walking in on her posing a peculiar attraction.

She stepped naked into the trough, drawing the flimsy, semitransparent curtain behind her. She estimated him to be about forty-five, easily more than twice her age, but with a certain rugged appeal. Shaking her head she dismissed the thought. She wasn't there to become embroiled in yet another precarious dalliance; she had more than enough to occupy her.

Alice fumbled with the taps, producing a warm spray. Who

would know? As long as she didn't end up lobster-red and give the game away. She luxuriated in that deluge, the shower a novelty, fine needles of water proving oddly arousing. Thoroughly immersed she failed to hear the door open, or notice a shadow move across the closet.

Hughes scowled, finger and thumb rubbing a chisel jaw. He could discern the outline, the pink of a naked female body. The female form seen through the haze of steam and curtain communicated a certain *je ne sais quoi*. The mystery about what lay beyond intrigued, flirted with intimacy.

Alice presented a tantalising presence, the profile and contours of evocative bottom veiled in obscurity, her physique a mere ghost. Even so, the fullness of that well-rounded behind, the protrusion of fleshy buttocks and that sublime division proved intoxicatingly perceptible.

She dropped the soap and bent, bottom adhering to that diaphanous shroud, the curtain moulding to her curves. Geoffrey Hughes lay his head to one side, studying the revelation, unsure who took the liberty.

Alice tried to make sense of the previous night, scratching at the few indistinct impressions submitted by a grudging subconscious. *'If I was with Pierce, why can't I remember a thing? And if I wasn't, how did he get hold of my skirt? What did I do? How far did I go? Split personality, I must be a schizophrenic. Was that mother's insanity? Is it hereditary? Am I going mad?'*

Alice seemed not to notice the reddening of breasts and belly, awareness consumed by that quandary. She probed the depths, mind refusing, the block frustrating. *'If I can't remember Pierce, but can recall every detail about Richard, what does that tell me?'* She felt the burn and squealed, jumping back.

Eyebrows knitting Hughes pursed his lips, acutely annoyed, and as Alice braved the scalding water to struggle with the hot faucet, the principal unbuckled his belt.

'Damn! Shit! Damn!' sounded from behind the curtain, Hughes doubling the two inch belt as Alice cursed. 'Oh you

110

bastard thing, you! Why won't you turn off?'

Twisting, wriggling beneath that skin-searing deluge, hands taking turns, continuously recoiling with the burn, Alice inadvertently advertised her youthful agility. She treated Hughes to a display of nubile flesh, wet body repeatedly pressed to the clinging curtain. She paraded the cock-inspiring tremble of intimate parts, the lurch and sway of seductive breasts, and shudder of jostled buttocks. The misty veil between only served to enhance that delightful apparition.

Concerned she begged, voice a suppressed whisper. 'Please… oh come on, *please*. Don't do this to me.' Her skin approaching that undesirable lobster colour, Alice submitted to the tide of rage. A flannel wrapped about the valve she applied every ounce of her strength. 'Come on… come *on*! What are you trying to do, get me into trouble? I'm not even supposed to be using you, you bastard, bastard, *bastard*!'

She twisted beneath the tap, full pink moons thrust into the curtain. Not knowing which miscreant took the liberty, or why, Hughes struck, and the almighty crack of leather biting wet gossamer-enveloped buttocks slammed off the walls. Alice reared, hands flying to the stricken, her backside ignited, the shock stupefying.

Thunderstruck she flinched as Hughes' cloth-protected hand intervened to turn off the tap. She cringed with the slap of a towel against her chest, and holding it against her breasts she shrank before searching fingers, Hughes determined to bring the impudent urchin to book. She spun as the principal drew the curtain, offering her back and exposed bum in preference to bosom and crotch.

The man's eyes settled on that fleshy rump, the mark of his belt conspicuous against the mottled bruising induced by Pierce. He reached, seized an ear and led the girl, dignity slaughtered, from behind the curtain. He didn't even attempt to look at her face. Geoffrey Hughes had no interest in who or why, only in providing a painful lesson and deterrent. The reasons and excuses he would dismiss later.

He hoisted the mortified girl by her ear, Alice rising to tiptoe. She clung to the towel, folded arms pinning the cloth, soft pillows of flesh playing peek-a-boo. Her hair wet and darkened looked more black than auburn; had it not been Hughes might have recognised her. But as it stood he firmly believed he held a mischievous inmate, keen on extending her personal standing.

Hughes was well used to their tricks and what they were prepared to endure, just to prove their courage and to achieve a rise in status. Under such circumstances he brooked no impertinence and accepted no excuses. His response was generally rapid, ruthless and relentless. The girl's called it the three R's.

Hughes couldn't immediately identify the intruder, the voluptuous backside he was about to redden alien to him. But there again, he hadn't had the pleasure of every girl in the building, many having the sense to steer clear of his rod.

Alice dangling by the ear, unsure what to do, what to say, reeled to the prolific slap of leather. His belt stunned a flank, cheek leaping before the stroke, a sickening fire left in its wake.

'You damned hussy!' stifled any immediate protest, Alice thrown into a state of flux. The apparent use of her name only served to confirm the man's intent, the use of the word 'damned' cutting to the quick.

'Your idea of a joke, is it?' he asked, whipping her butt with a brutal stinger. Alice's hips jerked forward, bottom cheeks clenching, the accusation leaving her nonplussed. 'Or did you think this would make you queen of the hornet's nest?' Hughes sneered, dealing three explosive discharges in a row. 'Well, let's see how the queen likes the acid burn of a few dozen stings herself.'

Disconcerted pitched headlong into utter confusion, Alice not understanding a word of his accusations. Her right buttock smarting aggressively, her ear feeling as if it was being torn off, she finally gave thought to the injustice of her predicament. Hughes whipped her backside as if she were a child, or worse, a slave. And what did she do in return? She meekly accepted

112

his rough handout. Did she subconsciously seek such abuse? Did she deliberately provoke those most likely to respond with physical indignity? She wasn't sure. But she *was* decided about her immediate susceptibility.

Humiliation and embarrassment tickled an elusive core, Hughes spanking her bare bottom, his complete dominance and her utter subservience adding their pennyworth. The concealment of her breasts, towel draped loosely over her shorn mound, focused her mind. Being virtually naked deluged her sexual hub with a multitude of staggering sensations, and each time Hughes' belt stung flesh close to her vagina the simmering pot bubbled a little more vigorously. She became acutely aware of the man's proximity, of what he saw, of what he glimpsed. Her head spun, mind dizzy with a bizarre euphoria. What she had longed for, what her mind and body craved, had at last befallen her.

Hughes struck, the slap tremendous, the right flank blasted, and her flesh still fired she took yet another, jerking to the exquisite fire.

The leather lifted, circled, bit and cut with a frenzied rhythm, Hughes announcing each detonation with one word. 'How… dare… you… use… my… personal… facilities…?'

It hadn't occurred to Alice that Hughes wasn't aware whose bum shook and heaved beneath the unremitting onslaught. She believed he punished her for being unpunctual, untidy, and ignoring his direct orders. The misuse of personal facilities proved a revelation.

He let go of her ear, clamping his hand to her neck instead. She offered no resistance, bending as the man urged, his fingers delving the sensitive muscles about the nape. Hughes tossed his belt to one side and took up the drubbing with his hand instead. Arm about her waist he rained hefty slaps to that sore right cheek and unpunished left alike. That bottom gave before the excessive force, flesh constantly mobile. 'You know the rules.' His hand deepened the scarlet. 'As an inmate you are not even permitted on this floor unless given specific permission.'

Her eyes flicked wide. Inmate?

'What was it,' he asked, hand pounding the raw, 'an inane dare again? Bravado? Or just plain stupidity?'

The penny dropped. He didn't know it was her!

'No one uses my private washroom. Absolutely no one.'

A dozen possibilities tumbled simultaneously. His abject apology, her vulnerable state. His embarrassed stammer, her commiserating attitude. His eyes riveted to her wet, towel-draped body. Maybe a... Pierce crashed the hallucination. A stark image filled her mind's eye, Pierce with fingers curled about a monstrous erection. Horror gripped her. What had she done?

She closed her eyes, the rhythmic slap and burn fuelling the sensual fire. That impressive shaft loomed ever larger, the thing pulsating, its head a grisly purple.

Her bum felt razor-cut, beaten flesh pulsating. A raw sensitivity groped, clawed at her hide and deeper. Every slap meeting with lower corpulence seemed to graze her sex, the sensation intoxicating, flesh ultra-sensitised with each connection, an internal glow forming, slowly overwhelming her.

The constant slap, slap, slap echoing distinctly about the closet, stressed the punitive act, impressed upon Alice her demeaning position, Hughes' controlling action and her meek compliance. She could never explain why, but she instinctively knew that was what she craved.

Hughes pulled Alice upright by her hair. He leant close, threatening. 'By rights you should be strapped over my bench and screaming to the bite of leather.'

She felt faint. The scene ran through her mind. That whip she had examined lashing her naked bottom, whipping her until the flesh heaved up in a plethora of welts, until her buttocks were crimson and despatching messages of acute ecstasy. And then to feel Hughes' cock between her legs, thrusting, stretching her tight vagina.

Hughes turned her face to him, saying, 'Now let's see who dares to use my washroom.' The man frowned. Alice opened her eyes and gazed into his, expecting. 'What?' Hughes mumbled. 'You?'

Her bottom as hot as Hades, crotch alight, she whispered, 'Yes sir, it's me.'

Obviously stunned he gathered his wits. 'Then please explain to me what you were doing in my shower. And will you account for the fact you didn't say who you were. I would appreciate you telling me why you let me strap and spank a member of staff without offering one word of protest.'

Alice noted the storm clouds looming, the man's eyes as black as thunder. 'I thought you were punishing me for being late,' she offered lamely.

'And you think a bare bottom spanking is just discipline?' he asked incredulously.

'Yes,' she replied. 'No,' she added, unsure. 'I don't know,' she concluded.

'This adds a whole new dimension to staff discipline. And if I just chastised you for lateness, justly in your mind, then what about that disgraceful outburst I witnessed? That eruption of vulgarity that expressed a severe lack of vocabulary. And then there is your admission to ignoring my explicit instructions. You now stand convicted of a catalogue of crimes, don't you? Perhaps I should now cane you for your those, hm?'

Alice chewed her lip. 'You mean…'

'Yes, Alice, I quote. "What are you trying to do, get me into trouble? I'm not even supposed to be using you, you bastard, bastard, bastard". Condemned by your own mouth, I believe.'

'I lost my temper. I'm sorry. And yes, I used the hot water against your implicit demand. I'm sorry.'

'I think you will be. Words are quite ineffective. Those scoundrels I am expected to mould into decent human beings use such all the time. You'd think they would learn, but they don't. Sorry is being doubled and suffering. And you had the temerity to use my washroom, not just the water. This is my private washroom. It was my soap and flannel you washed with. It is my towel you cover your embarrassment with. There are other facilities for members of staff.'

'I'm sorry, I didn't know,' Alice offered lamely.

'Didn't know is not a defence. It is common decency to honour another's privacy. When I said I wanted to see you in my office I meant just that. Damn it, girl, where do you hail from, the jungle? Respect! Where's your respect?'

Alice lowered her face, cheeks burning, mentally begging Hughes to inflict the worst. 'Well, what do you say Alice? Should I take the cane to your bottom?'

That decision proved one of the most arduous she had ever had to make, but slowly, heart beating, pulse racing, she nodded.

Eyebrows raised, Geoffrey Hughes sighed. 'Very well, I have a meeting in a few minutes. Dry yourself, get dressed, then come back at eleven. I will deal with you then.'

Chapter Six

The meeting was with Sandra Wareholme. The girl stood before Hughes' desk, legs apart, hands behind her back. 'You wanted to see me, sir?'

'How's the stomach?'

'Settling, sir. Your idea of a wee joke perhaps?'

'No joke, Wareholme. Yesterday we reached what I hope will prove an amicable agreement. Breakfast and those three stripes were just a taster of what you can expect should you let me down.'

'I expected far worse. What exactly have I agreed to, sir?'

'A job. What might be a watershed in your otherwise pointless existence. You're a nice looking, bonny and buxom young woman, and you have come to the attention of a colleague of mine. He would like to do a portfolio of you. There is the smell of hard cash here, Sandra. Money the Hope trust could well do with. You do the shoot, my associate fields the pictures, and with any luck we'll have ourselves a contract.'

'What sort of photographs would they be, sir?'

'Oh, don't get all innocent on me. You know damn well what sort. You're not that desirable.'

'Thank you for the compliment, sir. I take it you mean nude?'

'Sexy underwear, erotic, you know the sort.'

'Aye. So what's in it for me?'

'You will have a trade, Sandra. Hope will have provided you with an alternative to lying on your back with your legs parted. Be grateful.'

'Oh, I didnae just lay on my back, sir. I had a few more tricks than that.'

'I dare say you did. You follow this up and you are excused the workshop.'

'And the cane, sir?'

'Now would I want to mark the goods, Sandra? Do we have an understanding?'

'Aye sir, I believe we do.'

'Two o'clock. Pierce will take you. He will oversee the shoot; make sure you toe the line, and that the photographer doesn't get any fancy ideas. You do as you're told, Sandra, and I'll see your life at Hope becomes quite comfortable. You fuck with me, and I'll whip you to hell and back.'

'Yes, sir.' The girl didn't doubt a word he said.

Hughes had provided Alice with time to dwell on their appointment, the heat of the moment passed, a chill of anticipation taking hold. She had no doubt that if he had caned her there and then she would have writhed in ecstasy to every stroke, but she had two hours to contemplate, to grow nervous, to come to fear the meeting. That intense arousal waned, guilty hormones declining, leaving the impotent Alice to face the music cold.

What had urged her? That question nagged remorselessly. How did Hughes view her agreement? Did her think her weird? Did any respect for her as a person fly out of the window because of her submission? Would he treat her with contempt in the future? Doubts hounded Alice, the young woman certain she had made a grave mistake.

She spent those two fraught hours with Mavis, entering endless names in various registers: attendance, sickness, sundry lessons and workshops. Lastly and seemingly inauspicious, Mavis passed her the punishment record with a small pile of additions. Intrigued, apprehensive, Alice read.

Those five from the breakfast fiasco ranked as the latest. Hughes' handwriting listed Teresa Morton, twelve strokes for gross misconduct. Carol Wisbeck, fifteen strokes for the same.

Rachel Smith, ten cuts. Joan Catterall, twelve, and Linda Jenkins, twelve. Alice wriggled, her bottom already sore and bruised.

Some of the records were nearly a fortnight old. She entered one for Ruth O'Leary given some ten days before. She had difficulty translating Hughes' scrawl, but she was sure it read: Repeatedly and openly defiant, disobedient and insolent. Refused to apologise or mend her ways. Three-dozen strokes.

Alice fidgeted. What if Hughes decided she should be whipped so remorselessly? Fantasy made demands the body could not always meet. She laid her head in her hands. If only he had carried it out there and then.

Alice thumbed through the pages, astounded by the sheer volume of entries. A day didn't seem to pass without some girl falling foul of the principal's rod. O'Leary popped up at regular intervals. Six strokes here, nine there, but never less than six. In fact when Alice studied all those names, no one received less than the half dozen. A mandatory punishment perhaps, Alice wasn't sure, but she felt uneasy about the whole business.

Mavis leant over her, asking, 'Is that done yet?'

Alice shook her head. 'Not quite. Just this last few to do.'

'You're seeing Mr Hughes at eleven, aren't you?'

The girl's stomach rolled, that queasy feeling of emptiness settling. A lump formed in her chest. Her hands trembled, knees knocked, dread permeated every muscle, Alice wishing she had never consented.

'And you're going out this afternoon, so I understand.'

Alice looked up at Mavis, her face pale, mouth dry. 'Am I?'

'Oh, Mr Hughes hasn't told you yet. Best I say no more. And if you would be so kind not to say I mentioned it, I would be most grateful.'

'Yes, of course.' She resumed her work, nerves evident in the shaky handwriting. Going out? Where? What for? What had he in mind?

For the next hour Alice fretted. Concern nagged as to how many strokes, and how hard. She cogitated on the position she would have to assume, on Hughes' idea of presentation, the skirt, the panties or bare. Her mind kept returning to the shower and how she felt, how she craved a lengthy and painful thrashing. An ungovernable madness, Alice concluded. No rhyme or reason. The lust drove her mad when she couldn't appease the demons and absented itself when she could.

Her chin supported on her hands, fingers sunk in cheeks, Alice mused. Did she want to be dominated? Was that the key? Did she want to be used and controlled?

Perhaps that's what ailed her. Was she losing touch with the real world? Did she fuck Pierce last night? Imagine that, Alice Hussey going all the way. She couldn't even ask him because he wasn't trustworthy. So she had to live with it, hoping that somewhere along the line he put her out of her misery.

And dear old Uncle Richard came to see her. Or did he? It seemed like he did, but she couldn't be sure. It felt like her world was tipped upside down, and she thought sadly of her best friend. *'I'm losing my sanity, Kate. Mother was mad. Of course, you don't know, do you? Alice is a bastard, not an orphan at all. My mother and father could both be alive, so it would seem. Who my father is has yet to be revealed. But it could be Richard. Nice one that, eh? And mother? I know who my mother is. It's Rose. And she's incarcerated in a nuthouse somewhere.*

'Guess what, Kate, my second day here and I've been spanked twice already. And I'm due to be thrashed again in thirty-two minutes. I'm going to put it down to just desserts. It will be my penance for all those sins I haven't had absolved. It will be my punishment for trying to take your father away from your mother. It will be for all those sacrilegious thoughts and moments. I will suffer horribly for baiting Richard and for sleeping with him.

' See, I told you I was mad. Yes, I slept with Richard. Except I didn't sleep. No Kate, I fucked. I fucked my uncle, except he isn't my uncle; he's probably my father. Yes I fucked and I had an orgasm. What's the punishment for incest do you reckon? Burn in the fires of hell for evermore? But that's in the afterlife, isn't it? What's my choice in this life, eh? To seek absolution?

*To pay with agonised suffering? Will that eradicate the guilt?
I don't think so, Kate. This I will have to live with for the rest of
my mortal days. My sins are unforgivable. I am condemned by
my own actions, so I might as well be hung for the whole
sheep. That is my path, Kate. That is the way I have decided to
go. I am going to enjoy these relatively few mortal years, for I
have to face an eternity in hell. I am damned Kate. Damned.'*

'Have you finished that book, Alice?' brought the young
woman abruptly back to the moment.

'Yes, all done, Mavis.'

'Best get yourself off to Mr Hughes' office then. He despises
lateness.'

'And don't I know it,' Alice muttered, rising.

Mavis eyed the short tight skirt Alice wore. 'Where's the
black skirt you bought yesterday?'

'I spilt a drink down it,' Alice lied.

'The head won't like that skirt. What about the other one?'

'It got crumpled. It needs ironing.'

'A word from the wise, put on that summer dress. The pastel
pink cotton one, with the button front and pretty roses.'

'You think he'll like that better?'

'Mr Hughes hasn't told me why he wants to see you, Alice.
But I haven't worked for him for all these years not to know his
moods. I won't pry, but if it's what I think it is, then you'd be
better off appeasing the man's fetish for correct dress. Go on,
you have time. Go and change.'

Alice accepted Mavis at her word. She seemed one of the few
people in that building with a modicum of humanity. Pierce she
decided was corrupt. Every girl was a convicted criminal, and
Hughes she had yet to make her mind up about. Her sixth sense
insisted he was not trustworthy. Something about the man irked.

Alice stripped off her clothes, unable to resist examining her
bottom. The fury had faded, her buttocks showing the more
durable marks of chastisement, the fingerprints of the night
before and those freshly lain by Hughes. Could she take the
cane? That was the enduring question, but she faced the fact

that she had no choice.

She opened the drawer containing her few items of underwear. 'Why didn't I bring more?' she muttered. 'Why the devil did I leave it all at Howell House?'

She plucked a pair of white cotton panties from the few, drew them over her legs and hips and studied the result. They clung smoothly to her round bottom, the flesh beneath visible, the tone of her skin distinguishable. Would that matter? She very much doubted it. They hugged tightly, declaring the gorge between. Alice sighed, a prickle intensifying below.

She chose a white bra to match, the cups snugly cosseting her breasts. She stepped into a white suspender, pulling it to her trim waist. 'Now, Mr Hughes,' she whispered, 'let's see how you like black stockings. Let's see if Alice can take your breath away.'

The silk hosiery she caressed, stroked to her thighs, then sitting on the edge of the bed she smoothed them to within several inches of her cotton-covered crotch. There she clipped them before lifting first one limb and then the other, studying them in the mirror. 'There you are, Mr Hughes – long legs, slender, and oh so shapely. Feel these thighs, Mr Hughes.' Her hand stroked between her legs. 'Silky smooth… creamy… and see where they lead…' She fingered her vagina through the cotton gusset. 'Unused. Virgin. Tight, Mr Hughes. Oh, so very tight…'

She lay back, head resting on the pillow. Fingers ascended, teasing her body. They brushed against that supple mound devoid of curls, flitted over flat tummy. The tips flicked over the rise of ribs and delicately circled those tight, upright knolls of breast flesh. Alice moaned softly, her lips slightly parted. 'I've got the horn,' she whispered. Jesus, I'm so fucking randy again. Stay like this. Feel sexy. Keep yearning for that flogging and it'll be a cakewalk. It'll be what I've been begging for, for days.'

'Not penance, nor contrition then, Alice?'

She sat up, taking hold of the dress Mavis suggested she wore. 'No,' she replied to her conscience. 'It's devil-made lust.'

Checking her watch, deciding she still had time to linger, Alice pulled the dress over her head. She wriggled it down her torso, exaggerated bosom impeding its progress. Alice left the bottom three buttons fastened and the top three free, the gap exhibiting a swell of satin breast and provocatively deep cleavage to perfection.

The fabric lay snug to her back, hugging her body, announcing the slenderness of her waist. The dress gripped her bust, squeezing the fruits within, their prominence further elevated, emphatically announced. The cut clung to ribs and belly before surrendering to a flourish, the sweep of skirt. Alice admired the effect, the pastel fabric seemingly painted on her torso, before cascading over the thrust of divinely curved bottom.

Again she checked the time. She frowned and tapped the glass of her wristwatch, then threw her arms up and cried, 'Why? Why does nothing ever go to plan? What is the time, for Christ's sake?'

Her watch still indicating the same time it did at least five minutes earlier, she hurtled down the flight of stairs. She ran into the corridor, her leg catching on an old hook, her stocking rent and láddered. Breathless she knocked on Hughes' study door.

'Come,' he called.

Alice opened the door, eyes frantically looking for his wall clock, her hopes crumbling as she noted the time.

'Was it too much to hope for, Alice?' Hughes enquired sarcastically. 'For you to be on time?'

'I was diverted,' she mumbled. 'My watch stopped.'

'Ah, those *words* again. What about sorry? You seem to have forgotten that one.'

She shrugged and stared at the window, shoulders slumped.

'Miss Jenkins said you left her office some twenty minutes ago. Does it really take twenty-six minutes to walk thirty feet?'

'I went to my room to change,' she tried to explain.

'Into what, exactly? It certainly wasn't a punctual employee.'

'I caught my stocking on a nail running down here.'

'Calamity Jane. Or perhaps the perils of Pauline. You seem to fit both bills.'

'I couldn't agree more, sir. So why not give me a severe caning for my trouble.'

'Is that flippancy I detect?'

'No sir, it's total surrender.'

'Oh, I see. You are attempting to influence me by playing the hard-done-by. Suggest worse and perhaps I will show some leniency. I know every trick in the book, Alice. You are among professional tricksters and liars here. So maybe I will call your bluff.'

He lit his pipe and puffed, deep in thought. 'I mentioned in the shower this morning that there is a bench. It is located in the punishment room along the corridor. Those finding themselves strapped over it never wish to repeat the episode. Perhaps I should demonstrate its brutal purpose to you.'

A dream come true? Alice wasn't sure. But she had travelled that far, she had agreed to the caning, and she was severely tempted by the man's threat. But with her valour fading in the sights of the big guns, Alice hung her head and shrugged.

'Not today, though. Today I have a job for you. A chance to redeem yourself. I want you to play chaperone to that Scottish lout Sandra.'

'If I do well, don't mess up, you'll think twice about that punishment. Is that it?'

Hughes placed his pipe in the ashtray. 'Let's just say we'll see how you do. Take it from there.'

He folded his arms and leant back in the chair. 'Two o'clock. Don't be late.'

'Can I ask where I'll be going?'

'To Chester. It's a studio. Sandra will be doing a portfolio. Snap Davies is the photographer, an old acquaintance from my army days. If Wareholme turns out to be photogenic she could earn a damned good living. Snap pays well for successful girls, the sort that aren't too shy about what they do.'

'What time will we be back?'

'Why, do you want paying for overtime?'

'No, it's not that. I'm supposed to be seeing Dr Doodney after work.'

'Social, or business?'

'I have a few problems, she was going to try and help me.'

'She'll wait. Tell you what, when you get back come directly to my house. Sheila will be there. You can have your chat or psychoanalysis then.'

'It's just a chat,' Alice corrected, a little peeved.

'So all your marbles are in place; I'm glad to hear it.'

Alice left his office pondering on the opportunity. Happy to escape for a while, and a touch thrilled about the responsibility, she wasn't so sure about the marbles.

Alice served dinner, taking a particular interest in those few girls she knew, the ones that had recently met with Hughes' cane. How had they fared? Did they strut, stride or hobble? Did they appear content or dejected? She longed to ask personal questions, but of course could not. Then O'Leary stood before her, plate held out.

'Got an extra couple of spuds for an old mate then?' the girl asked, forthright.

Alice dumped the requisite number before suggesting. 'If you can meet me after lunch, then yes.'

Ruth winked. 'Not behind the bike sheds?'

'I want to ask you something, that's all.' Alice held the extras over her plate.

'Yeah, go on. Yer knows how to disappoint a gel, don't yer?'

Alice dropped the roast potatoes. 'One o'clock, in the quad. Make sure we're left alone.'

Ruth took her dinner, and glancing back she teased, 'If yer want sex, then the answer is yes.'

Alice found O'Leary easily enough, the girl shooing away her friends. 'Now what's all the secrecy about? We could have talked at dinner, the silence rule is only first thing.'

Alice stood close, a hand covering her mouth should anyone lip-read. 'I had to do the punishment book this morning.'

Ruth laughed. 'See someone's name keep cropping up, did yer?'

Alice nodded. 'You do seem to get yourself into a lot of hot water.'

'That's easy here. Just look at a geezer the wrong way and yer gets six of the best. I'm not really that troublesome, I just won't knuckle under. I've only got me pride left, and they ain't 'aving that. Anyway, I can take whatever they hand out.'

'That's really what I wanted to ask you. Does Hughes hit very hard?'

'You sound worried, gel. Due to get it for being late this morning, are yer?'

'I'm not sure. But if I am to be caned then I would like to prepare myself.'

'Try armour plating.'

'Do you mean...?'

'He's a fucking demon. Six means you'll have difficulty walking, let alone sittin'. Twelve, if yer survive, and yer'll sleep face down for a few nights. Any more and, no, yer don't wanna even think any more.'

'You received thirty-six ten days ago. That must have been bad.'

Ruth chuckled. 'He whipped me, Al. He strapped me to that fucking bench stark naked and whipped me. Whip as in leather plaited and fucking painful.'

'On the bottom, you mean?'

'It don't matter much where, Al. The outcome is the same. But no, not entirely on the butt. Hughes likes to play with your mind. You think he's going to hit yer and he don't. You think it will be hard and it's soft. And when yer expects soft, the bastard cripples yer. So he misdirects a few. Across the thighs for example, or to the lower back. Maybe one to crucify yer shoulders. And then there's the beaut between the legs.'

'He didn't whip your tits, did he?'

Ruth's eyes narrowed. 'I told yer, Al; you ain't close enough to know.'

'I'm going out with Wareholme this afternoon,' Alice blurted, the need to tell someone overpowering.

'I heard she'd been made an offer she couldn't refuse. So what's Hughes got her doin'?'

'A photo shoot.'

'What, that streak of carrot-topped Gorbals piss? Bet they're cock in the fanny shots. Or up the jacksy.'

'I think Sandra has a nice figure.'

Ruth looked Alice up and down. 'You've got the figure, Al. Wareholme's got the muscle, and a lot of that is in her head.'

'You sound jealous.'

Ruth shook her head. 'Nah. Ain't no room for that here. Good luck to her. But I'll bet you a long lingering kiss on the lips, in the dead of night, with no clothes on, that it ain't a straight up photo shoot. Knowing Hughes like I do, I'll wager my body that there's a twist somewhere.'

Alice spotted the man in question strolling amid the crowd. 'Look, best go; the head's on his rounds. I don't want either of us to get into any more trouble.'

Pierce drove, Alice and Sandra sitting in the back of a heavy Riley, a pair of steel handcuffs linking the pair together. Pierce held the key, and as far as he was concerned neither would escape.

Forty minutes later he turned the car onto a gravel drive. 'Here we are, ladies, how the other half do live.'

Both expected a half-mile of drive and a large mansion, but Snap Davies rented a large detached house, set thirty feet back from the main road behind a huge hedge.

Pierce waited for the girls to clamber out before announcing, 'I'll take the bracelets off inside.'

Self-conscious, the pair waited with him until a short, wiry man in his early thirties answered the door. Casually dressed with an open neck shirt, cuffs rolled up, he ran a hand through

127

thick blond curls. 'Pierce, nice to see you.' The pair shook hands.

Snap ran an eye over the two females. 'A brace. You brought me a brace. Excellent.'

'Not quite,' Pierce corrected, following the girls inside. 'Sandra's the dumb blonde. The redhead is Alice, our new... sorry Alice, what are you exactly?'

'Girl Friday,' she advised, shooting a glower at Pierce.

'Ah, that was it. A bit like a man Friday but without the nuts.'

Davies led them through to the back of the house, the doors off the hallway closed. White walls and ceiling and a polished wooden floor met Alice's curiosity. Wide French windows shed copious light into the ground floor studio, a large room equipped with the paraphernalia of the professional photographer.

Pierce loosed the handcuffs, both girls sub-consciously rubbing their wrists. Then ungraciously, not a chivalrous character, he gripped the back of Sandra's dress and jerked her forward. 'This one will do exactly as you please, if she knows what's good for her.' He nodded at Alice. 'And that one might if you can find the right buttons to press.'

Alice bit. 'I resent that, Mr Pierce.'

The man grinned maliciously. 'She's got very nice tits, Snap. Lovely shape, and nice sucklers they are.'

Alice's face burned, knowing her embarrassment showed. Her brows knitted, green eyes simmering with loathing.

'Gorgeous bum too, Snap. A backside that will take a fair lathering. I suspect there might be a few marks on it today, though.'

Sandra considered Alice, a smirk tucked away in her smug look.

'I think Mr Pierce likes to appear advantaged,' Alice defended. 'The man walked in on me when I was washing. Didn't you, Mr Pierce?'

'Oh, did I give the wrong impression? How remiss. It must have been someone else's arse I tanned last night.'

'There you go again, trying to sound like some Lothario.'

'Must be my age, girl; confused I guess. Yes, I suppose you

promising to *come* back tonight was a misunderstanding too.'

'Are you trying to make me out to be some sort of tart, Mr Pierce?'

The man shook his head. 'No Alice, not *some* sort of tart.'

Incensed, seeing she was losing the verbal battle, Alice took a swing at him, but Pierce caught her arm by the wrist, his grip painful. He held her hand aloft, his free arm taking her by surprise. For his age he moved swiftly, flicking up her skirt, his hand wedging between her legs and lifting. He pushed her back against a wall, fingers deliberately mauling her vagina. 'Don't try that again,' he warned, smiling coldly. 'Not unless you want me to turn you over my knee, right here in front of everyone.'

Humiliated, she stared daggers.

'I see your face scrubbed up well.' He let her go.

Taught a lesson. Put in her place. Made a complete fool of. All those terms went through Alice's head. Yet another nail had been hammered into her dignity, her pride choked, and puzzled about his last remark she decided on conceding for the time being.

Cocky, Pierce held out his arms. 'See? You just have to know the right buttons.'

Davies smiled to humour the man. 'You know where the projector is, Eddie. There's something ready to roll that I think you'll find interesting.'

Pierce indicated the girls. 'And these two?'

'They'll be fine. Go and put your feet up. Honestly, everything will be just fine.'

As soon as Pierce had left the room Davies approached Alice. 'Are you okay?'

She nodded, wiping her eyes with the back of a hand.

'Eddie's all mouth. I know that. I never take any notice of the man. Now, why don't you sit over there,' he pointed to a chair. 'While I chat with Sandy.'

Pierce had only intimated the truth, not spilled the beans on some sensational secret. Alice blamed herself for triggering her predicament. Had she acted rationally, like a normal levelheaded eighteen-year-old, then that humiliating scene would not have happened. Pierce would use his presumptive deductions to coerce and embarrass her. She presumed the man to be yet another vindictive, manipulating, sexually frustrated Harris. Alice was partly correct, but had no conception of the man's true designs.

She watched half interested, Snap attempting to extricate an expressive pose from Sandra, but patience wilting the man threw his hands in the air. 'For fuck's sake, Sandra, think woman, not wooden top. You're like a fucking mannequin. You're like a bloody erection, stiff, minus the excitement.'

'You said pout, so I fucking pouted,' Sandra disputed angrily.

'Yes pout, not sulk. You've a face like a smacked bum.'

'Look, why don't I just take my bloody clothes off. That's what you want, isn't it?'

'No, that's not what I want. Not what I want at all. Let me try to explain, Sandy. The punter buys the magazine. He turns the pages and stares at you. For him to want to stare at you, you first have to provoke him. Tits, fanny and arse don't necessarily provoke. In fact I've seen some that would put the average bloke off his Sunday roast.

'You smoulder. You present the package. You present it in a fashion that Mr Punter cannot resist. He sees Miss Wareholme and wants to, no, he yearns to screw her. He can't put the rag down. He's got the horn. All he can think of is shoving his cock in your fanny. Or perhaps somewhere else.'

Snap sighed. 'Now, can you see what I'm driving at?'

'I told you she was a dumb blonde.' Pierce stood in the doorway, leaning on the jam. 'All a whore knows is to lie flat on her back. By the time the sop gets his kit off, all he can think about is that slit between her legs. All she has to do is make sure the geezer can access it.'

Sandra bit. 'I did a hell of a lot more than that!'

'Well fucking do it now!' Pierce bellowed.

'It's different,' she countered. 'There's no passion here. It's all so fucking impersonal. How the hell can I feel sexy?'

Pierce scratched his head. 'Oh, I didn't realise you wanted a bit of realism. You should have said, Sandra.' The man unbuttoned his fly. 'Anything to keep the Glasgow bitch happy.'

Hand stuffed inside his trousers, Pierce advanced, Sandra unsure what to do. 'What do you reckon on some cocksucking, Snap? Do you reckon she could look provocative with eight inches shoved in her gob?'

'If Sandy's willing, then…'

'Oh Sandy will do whatever I ask, won't you Sandy?'

The girl eyed him warily.

Pierce rummaged inside his pants, grinning at the anxious girl. 'I think you get the picture, Sandra darling. Nice erotic poses for Mr Davies, or the alternative – a gobble, buggery and penetration, to put it mildly. So what's it to be?'

'Oh for goodness sake!' Alice intervened. 'Stop frightening the girl.'

'Frighten?' questioned Pierce. 'I'm not frightening Wareholme. Whores are only bothered about sex when they aren't getting it. Ain't that right, Sandra?'

Angered, Sandra criticised. 'You haven't the slightest idea have you, you great lummox?'

Alice pushed between the two men. 'I'm not pretending I know much about this game, but…'

'How did it go?' Geoffrey asked, having taken Edward to one side.

'How you reckoned it would. Alice seems to be a sucker for the lame duck. Sandra was hopeless. A bit like asking an all in wrestler to do Swan Lake. I expect she's good at seducing a bloke in a Glaswegian bed-sit, but raw sex and expressive imagery are two different animals.'

'So you're saying Wareholme failed?'

'The same as she'd fail her eleven plus, Geoff. She was never geared for it in the first place. But Alice? Now there's another story. That girl is sex on legs. She'd smoulder in sackcloth. I don't know what it is about her. Okay, she's a looker, especially with them eyes. Bewitching, yeah, that's it. She casts a spell on you, makes you want to beg for it.'

'Like all those whores we liberated in Paris you mean?'

'No, Geoff, not like them at all. Alice demands a respectful fucking. I think when you've sunk your dick in that one you would have plumbed the ultimate woman.'

'Did she pose for Snap?'

'Oh yeah, she did. She wouldn't take her kit off, though. But dressed in fatigues she could excite the impotent to action. She's a natural, Geoff. She's got more drawing power than Carol Lombard.'

'That's what I thought when I saw her walk through those gates on Monday.'

'What you done to your arm?' Pierce asked, noticing the bandage.

'Sprain,' Hughes replied. 'My caning arm as well. Bastard that, don't you think?'

'So do you want me to take over?'

'Kind of you to offer, Eddie, but I have someone else in mind.'

'There was one other matter.'

'Oh?' Hughes frowned, curious. 'What's that?'

'Wareholme got a bit fractious. Jealous, I guess. Or maybe she thought Alice overshadowed her; put her in jeopardy, so to speak.'

'How fractious? Physical?' Hughes' eyes narrowed.

'A push, but more verbal.'

'Did I mention Don Catchpole was interested?'

'What, in Wareholme?'

'Yes. A weekend. But I'm not happy with his security.'

'What's he offering?'

'Fifty for two separate weekends, a month apart.'

Pierce pursed his lips. 'Just think what Alice might be worth.'

Geoff waggled his finger. 'Not might be, Eddie. Not might be.'

'But she's a free agent. Unless you was thinking of seeing her nicked, sentenced and sent here.'

'No need. I believe I know how to pull her strings.'

Alice sat in another room with Sheila Doodney. 'Do you want to talk about last evening, Alice?'

'I think I owe you an explanation,' the girl replied, blushing.

'No need. We are what we are, and most of us can do very little about it. I said last night that I enjoy beating a backside. One might construe that as perverted. But is it? Aren't we as a race somewhat sadistic? One only has to look down the ages to see that. I don't beat the undeserving. I don't look for an excuse to. So, how I feel is immaterial.

'Masochism is untreatable. The desire to be dominated and punished is triggered by a tenuous agent and magnified by hormonal reaction. That chemistry alters the thinking process, exaggerates the urgency, and makes the person somewhat irrational. To that person the moment is crucial, what they yearn for holds an irresistible urgency. Once a masochist always a masochist, unless in later years it transmutes to sadism. But why try to treat the, shall we say, difference? The masochist will be the only one to suffer, and suffer is a misconception. The masochist doesn't suffer, not in the slightest. On the contrary; he stroke she submits to a sensation of euphoria.

'Am I making sense, Alice?'

'I think so. I can't help myself, that's what you're saying.'

'And why try to? Apart from the guilt when you've sobered from the effects of hormonal madness, did you not relish every second?'

Alice grudgingly nodded.

'So why fight it?

'Were you what one might term a good Catholic once?' Sheila added.

'I was brought up as such. And yes, I believe I was. I accepted the teachings. I find them credible. I believe in heaven and hell. I believe in God and Satan. I remain convinced that if I sin I should be punished – if not in this life, then in the hereafter. I think that is just.'

'And penance? What does that achieve?'

'There has to be a moral standard. The world would be a

horrendous place otherwise, literally a hell on earth. We can tolerate an element of evil but the majority have to be basically principled. As mortals we are permitted errors, a learning curve if you like. Temptation is all about, but we should be strong enough to resist. Of course not all do, or can. God, however, will forgive our sins if we seek absolution. But in return we should demonstrate regret. The penance must be a penalty. It should be something the sinner loathes or fears. Flagellation has long been the reserved penance for sinners in the Catholic Church, I understand. But how can one see that as a penalty if one, say, is sexually turned on by the prospect?'

'I suppose there is discipline and there is corporal punishment. The difference being that the latter is far more cold and brutal. There is evidence of erogenous zones being susceptible to flagellation. In other words, the beating of certain parts of the body has a sexual connection. That triggers a hormonal response. That connected with the release of endorphins can have quite a surprising effect.'

'I see.'

'Do you seek contrition?'

Alice nodded. 'I feel I should be… I feel I'm damned. I don't know if any penance would be severe enough to save my soul.'

'Do you want to tell me what troubles you?'

Alice shook her head. 'I can't. It's something I have to sort out myself. I either have to come to terms with it or go mad.'

'Coming to terms would be better.'

'Is madness hereditary?'

'There is some that would say so. Personally I remain sceptical. Why do you ask?'

'My mother was locked away just before she gave birth to me. I was raised by my uncle.'

'Was your mother married?'

Alice shook her head, the shame of illegitimacy weighing heavy.

'Then don't presume her mad. Eighteen years ago unmarried mothers were considered a disgrace to their family. So much so that extreme tactics were used to cleanse the family name.'

'But I am going mad, Sheila. Last night I did something. I went somewhere and can't remember it.'

'Then what makes you think you did if you can't recall the incident?'

'Evidence and flashes.'

'You may have walked in your sleep.'

'I did more than walk. Wouldn't pain wake me up?'

'Not necessarily. If it tuned in with your subconscious activity then pain would seem reasonable, and therefore not interfere with the trance.'

'That means anything could happen! How can I stop it occurring again?'

'Try tying an ankle to the bed. You might release yourself, but there again you might not. In which case the bond will disturb the dream.'

'Thank you, you've been a great help.'

'There is another possibility you might find worrying.'

'What?'

'Trauma. Whatever happened was so abhorrent you wiped it from your memory.'

Alice shivered.

Tired, Alice determined to leave the house unobtrusively, desirous of avoiding any criticism Hughes might make on her afternoon's exploits. She sighed wearily as the man's voice summoned. 'Alice! You're not creeping off, are you?'

'I thought I might catch an early night, sir,' she excused. 'I wouldn't want to be late in the morning.'

'Pierce, be a good fellow. Take yourself and Wareholme into the other room. I'd like a word with Alice in private.'

Alone with Hughes, apprehensive and unsure of his intent, Alice sought to defuse any censure. 'I'm sorry if I went too far this afternoon, sir. I didn't mean to show off. I suppose I might have got carried away a bit, but...'

'But you enjoyed yourself?'

Alice smiled. Those emerald pools twinkled. She nodded, face burning. 'Yes, I suppose I did.'

'And Snap made you an offer?'

'Yes, but I don't know if I could, or even if I would want to accept.'

'That's your right, of course…' Hughes seemed reluctant to continue.

'You think I should?'

'That really isn't for me to say.' He sucked on his pipe, thoughtful. 'What I will state though, and don't for one second construe this as priggish; I've known Snap for many a year. He's a brilliant photographer. He has connections. But.' He raised an eyebrow. 'His operation is risqué, and never anything else.'

Alice settled her bum on the arm of the settee. Crossing her legs she attempted a serious and adult appraisal. 'I would prefer artistic, Mr Hughes. I don't believe there is anything wrong with the human body. It's what prudes like Richard make of that.'

'Richard?'

She shook her head. 'A ghost from the past.'

Alice quickly changed the subject. 'You said Snap has connections. What sort?'

'The sort that could put you in ermine and champagne for the rest of your life.'

Alice's eyes widened. 'Really?'

'Don't go rushing into anything. You think on matters. You'll still be as desirable and stunning in six months' time. And if you are what the editors and public want, then waiting can do no harm.'

'I'm sure you're right.'

'Of course I am.'

'But you see no real harm in it? You would vouch for Mr Davies?'

'I am liberal minded, and as I have said, I have known Snap for years. He is in my opinion completely trustworthy.'

Hughes laid his pipe in an ashtray. 'But interesting as it is, this is not what I wanted to talk about, Alice.'

She straightened. 'Oh, I'm sorry. I didn't mean to witter on.'

Hughes held up his right hand, and indicating the bandage he said, 'I need a favour.'

'I'm no nurse.'

'But you can use a cane.'

'How do you mean?'

'You can whip a backside or two. That's all I'm asking.'

'I don't understand.'

'It's quite simple, Alice. I am incapacitated. I am unable to correct the wayward and incorrigible in the accepted manner. Those rogues and rascals would make much hay while this particular sun shines. I really do not fancy deferring punishments for the next fortnight or so. If these miscreants aren't kept on a tight leash they will take advantage. I want them to know that regardless of my plight, they will not be allowed to wander from the prescribed route.'

Puzzled expression relaxing, Alice asked, stunned, 'You want me to punish the girls?'

'Exactly that.'

'But…' The young woman stood, her manner agitated. 'There must be someone else.'

Hughes folded his arms. 'I'll pay you for the added responsibility.'

'It's not that.'

'Okay, I won't.' He grinned.

'I don't understand this,' she pleaded. 'I've done nothing but mess up since I started, so why me?'

'I have my reasons,' Hughes replied enigmatically.

'Care to share them with me?'

Hughes sighed. 'I trust you, Alice. Is that not enough?'

'Don't you think it a little ironic that I of all people should be chastising the girls?'

He shrugged. 'What irony?'

'Mr Hughes! It was my bottom you spanked in the shower

room. It was my naked bottom you whipped with your belt. And it is my bottom that quails at the threat of a caning.'

He pursed his lips, eyes twinkling. 'Then you are somewhat seasoned, I would say. All the more reason to offer the post to you.'

'Can I have time to think about it?'

He shook his head. 'Impress me. Provide me with an instant and reasoned reply.'

Alice felt he played with her. There was a teasing air about the man. She had no doubt regards her decision, but she remained sceptical about his motives. 'Yes,' she agreed confidently, 'I'll do it. Why? Because I'll not shy from responsibility.'

He slapped his thighs. 'Excellent.'

Alice subconsciously rubbed a buttock. 'Have you come to a decision about me yet?'

Hughes frowned. 'In what way?'

'Caning me.'

He held the injured arm aloft again. 'Can't, can I.'

'Not now, I realise that. But when your arm is better.'

'Worried, are you?' He gazed at her, mischievously inquisitive, his expression giving to audacity. 'Or is it a case of apprehensive excitation?'

Alice jerked, his perception so disturbingly accurate. 'I… I don't know what you mean, sir,' she blurted, startled.

'Don't you?' he approached her, confident of that notion and certain of his intentions. Holding her gaze, his eyes seemed to penetrate to her very core, tearing the dark secrets and truth from her heart. He placed his good hand to her chest, just above her right breast. 'We'll see,' he whispered, sliding fingers between the buttons and beneath the fabric.

Those cool fingers lay so close to the upper slopes of her breasts, their rise and fall suddenly exaggerated, her breathing ragged, uncertain. Alice wilted, surrendered unequivocally to an avalanche of primeval emotions. At that moment in time she would have permitted Hughes any sexual liberty.

'Your heart has a precise rhythm,' the man advised. 'Now Alice, listen to me.' He leaned to her neck, lips close to the skin, the girl sensing his warm breath. 'Once my wrist is healed I shall not only cane you, but I shall do so with vigour and on your defenceless bare bottom.'

Alice couldn't conceal the sharp intake of air. She could not control the increase in pulse, her heart thumping passionately.

'See,' Hughes whispered, 'your body speaks to me, Alice. It tells me much.'

'Fear,' she gasped, her mouth dry.

'Is it?' The man lifted his head and stared into her eyes. 'Are you sure, Alice? This is your chance. An opportunity for honesty. The time to admit to who you are, what you are. The moment to grasp that illusive fantasy you so often dream about.'

'I…' Her resolve fluctuated.

'You tremble, girl. But there is no smell of fear about you.' He bent again to her ear. 'You only have to admit the truth, Alice. You are a whisper from attaining what you yearn for.'

'I'm not sure what I am,' she managed. 'I just don't know.'

The man stepped away, his hand sliding from within her blouse. 'Then perhaps we can find out; determine your particular tastes.'

Alice took a deep breath. 'Perhaps I seek reparation and no more.'

Hughes smiled. 'A sinful girl, eh?'

An invisible hand pushed, her lust for castigation uncovering a flash of boldness. 'Yes sir, sinful indeed.'

'Perhaps confession is necessary,' Hughes suggested, delving.

Alice met his gaze. 'And a penance without fear or favour?'

Hughes nodded. 'Pierce will see you back to your room.'

'I don't need an escort, Pierce.'

'Governor's orders. See you back to your room, he said.'

'Perhaps you would like to give me my skirt back now.'

'As a token of good will, huh?'

139

'If that lets you dismount from your high perverted horse, then yes.'

'I'm up front. I never found the need for deceit. You can have your skirt back when you fulfil our agreement.'

'You know I never will.'

'Never say never.'

Alice halted. She turned and looked up at the custodian. 'I had a reason for behaving the way I did. Maybe it was in hindsight a confused motive. But whatever, I am under no obligation to explain matters to you, Pierce. Tell Mr Hughes what you think happened. Tell him it all. I don't care, Pierce. Frankly I don't give a damn. But I want that skirt back, and I *will* have it.'

Edward Pierce nodded. 'Shame. I suppose I shall have to play with someone else now. But whoever that might be, one fact is guaranteed.'

'And what would that be?'

'She won't be the corker you are.'

Certain no unwelcome eyes could stand witness, Hughes placed an arm about Sandra's shoulders. He guided her forward and into the front parlour. 'What did I promise you Sandra, should you fail me?'

Head bowed the girl wrung her shaking hands. 'It wasna my fault, sir.'

'No? Whose then? Mine?'

'No sir, of course not, sir.'

'Pierce, maybe. Or perhaps Alice stole your sensual finesse. It seems by Pierce's account she outshone you in every way. I send you, an experienced prostitute, and a naïve, eighteen-year-old chaperone shows you a trick or three.'

'I tried,' Sandra whimpered. 'I really did try sir.'

'You, Wareholme, have been trying ever since you arrived at Hope. Trying my patience. Now it has finally snapped.'

The young woman swallowed hard. 'Are you going to flog me?'

Hughes squeezed her shoulder, pulling her to him. 'Flog you, Sandra? As in whip your naked body? As in string you from that hook fixed in that old beam up there? Tempting, isn't it? Very, very tempting.'

Hughes pushed her forward, Sandra almost sent sprawling. 'But I have other fish to fry this night, and if you don't get your mission right very quickly it will be your backside sizzling.'

He pointed at a small furry bundle laid on the couch. 'For you, Sandra. I thought you'd be proud to wear a national emblem.'

She picked the item up. 'It's a sporran. Men wear the sporran in Scotland, sir.'

Hughes shrugged. 'The way you performed today it was hard to tell what sex you are. You certainly were no femme fatale. Anyway, it might tickle your fancy. Put it on.'

Sandra strung it about her waist.

'No. That is the only piece of clothing you wear.'

'Sir?'

'Just the sporran, Wareholme, and only the sporran.'

He watched her strip. Arms folded he smiled with satisfaction as the Scot peeled her blouse from her body and the skirt from her hips. 'Everything, Sandra. Every stitch.'

Embarrassed by the man's focussed attention she loosed her bra, firm, shapely and ample breasts exposed. She stooped, lowering her panties, Hughes revelling in the fall and swing of alluring tits. He smiled contentedly as she donned the sporran.

'Excellent. I now have no doubts about your sex. I think that pair qualifies you for womanhood. Now I would like to unearth an element of grace, if such a quality lurks in that artless body. Yonder lies a bookshelf. Help yourself to one of the tomes – heavy or light, small or large. It is of no consequence to me.'

He watched the girl move awkwardly away, the roll of her hips, the quiver of her buttocks enthralling. Sandra selected a small book, and faced him clutching it to cover her bosom.

'Place it on your head,' Hughes ordered.

Frowning, the girl obeyed, the lift and tremble of her breasts

141

delighting the principal.

'Now the test. You will note the two chairs placed back to back. I want you to climb over them without losing the book. Think you can do that?'

Sandra nodded, the book falling to the floor.

'Bad start, Sandy, but I have an incentive for you. The proverbial carrot.' Hughes produced a leather strap from behind his back. He held it up. 'One stroke for the first time you drop it. Two for the second time. Three for the third. Get the drift? Let's see if you can manage the trick before your arse glows in the dark.'

Chapter Seven

Alice flicked the light switch. 'What the?' she gasped as her eyes adjusted to the glare.

''Ello,' answered her, Ruth stretched out in Alice's bed, naked shoulders protruding from the covers.

'What are you doing here? If Pierce finds out he'll…'

'Why should he? You ain't gonna tell him are you?'

'Look, go back to your dorm before he misses you.'

'Can't, gel. I'm a bit tied up at the mo.'

'What?'

'Pull back the bedclothes and take a decko.'

Half expecting, hoping she was wrong, Alice yanked back the covers. 'God, you're mad, Ruth!'

'What, yer mean it don't do nothing for yer?'

'I can't think why you thought it would.'

'It does something for me, I can tell yer. That one yanked tight between me legs I reckon is sopping by now. Gawd, it don't 'alf cut into me fanny. It's right hard against me clit, rubbin' it somethin' cruel at times.'

'Who did this? You can't have tied yourself up.'

Ruth chuckled. 'If I could 'ave laid me hands to half a cucumber I'd have shoved it in me 'ole first. Christ, that would've been some feeling.'

'I'll untie you.'

'All the knots is at the back, Al. Yer'll 'ave to turn me over first.'

Alice pushed her hands beneath the girl, lifting and rolling her, and there the redhead paused, a scrawl in ink on Ruth's bottom taking her attention. Curious, she read the first sentence.

'My arse for your delectation.' The next read, 'Whip it as hard as you like and as often as you like.'

Another penned across her lower cheeks announced, 'Stick provided. A real good stinger.'

A rattan had been sunk between O'Leary's buttocks; one end nestled to her coccyx, the other between her calves, and Alice plucked it from the girl's behind.

'No one will hear, Al. They're all up the other end of the hallway behind closed doors. Yer can whip me arse as 'ard as yer wants.'

Alice flexed the rod, sensing the weight and suppleness of the brute.

'Yer can do whatever yer wants with me body. It's wrapped in rope just for you. My pressie to you.'

Alice glanced up, her reflection in the window catching her eye. A ghostly image, a transparent Alice Hussey. Martinet Hussey. Lesbian Hussey. Whore Hussey.

Confused by conflicting emotions, she surveyed the naked form laid out before her. She listened absently to Ruth's excited breathing, the hope, the lust in the girl's expectation. Her wrists and elbows were bound, bonds cutting deep into the joints. A rope led from her hands, navigating the waist, fibres sunk without a trace. The girl's hands bent at a crazy angle, knuckles pressed into the small of her back. A ligature led from between, disappearing into the valley of her arse. Another length encircled Ruth's thighs, three loops, all drawn to maximum pressure, the flesh beneath probed to the muscle. Other bindings encircled her knees and ankles, the burden there extreme.

Alice pushed a finger between those lustrous buttocks, the tip gauging the bite of rope within. She pursed her lips, dwelling on how that same ligature must cut into the girl's vagina.

Sandra ground her teeth, fingertips clawing at a monumental smart gripping her bottom. Three times she had attempted to conquer the chairs and three times she had failed at the first hurdle. Her backside blushed with the ferocity of Hughes assault. Six times that murderous leather wickedly slapped her vulnerable cheeks. Six times she quailed before its terrifying wrath.

Hughes stood idly watching, a hand in his trouser pocket flagrantly massaging his privates. 'Try again, Sandra. There's no rush. I have all night. You see, unlike some I don't have to rise first thing in the morning.'

Wincing, Sandra perched the book on her head. 'I'll never do it,' she wailed.

'Oh, you better had, for your own good. Or should I say for your backside's good. Four if you drop it this time.'

The blonde cautiously raised a knee, foot seeking the chair seat.

'By the time this night is over,' Hughes continued to nettle the girl, 'you should be able to dance the cancan with that book on your head.'

Sandra leant forward, hands seeking the chair-back.

'Discipline, Sandra. This is all about discipline. A characteristic you seem to lack.'

Hughes observed amused as her other foot left the floor, her torso slowly rising. He feasted on the broad scarlet stripes decorating her bare behind, and anticipated laying another four hefty swipes to that ravaged flesh.

'Self-discipline on the one hand, and a corrective lesson on the other.'

The girl tried to retain her balance, the chair feeling unstable, the rhythmic slap of leather on Hughes' palm unnerving her. Still she rose, arms lifted cruciform to steady her. And then she stood erect, both feet flat on the polished wooden seat. She permitted herself a presumptive smile.

'Talking of which, I have yet to deal with that assault on a member of staff.' Hughes strolled behind her, gaze centred on that reddened sphere. There he remained enjoying the view, the twitch of nervous buttocks, further disconcerting the female.

Fraught, expecting the violent crack of leather on sore flesh, Sandra made the mistake of trying to see where he was, and the book slid, hit her shoulder and fell with a thud to the floor.

'Oh shame, Sandra. You were doing *so* well too.'

Every muscled in her body bunched, knotted expectantly. She squeezed her eyelids tight, teeth clenched. Fingers curled, hands talon-like. An inch and a half of leather, a quarter thick struck her buttock with devastating force, the almighty crack spinning off the walls. Sandra swallowed the scream.

Her haunches straining, dimpled, flesh hot and fired, Hughes levelled a second, the blast of scalding fire sickening. A wail of agony escaped her, her hands clawing at her scalp.

The third consumed the other cheek, an awesome burn ripping through the flesh. Sandra jerked, hips thrown forward, a fruitless reaction to avoid the worst.

His last ignited another strip of scarlet meat, the hurt triggering tears, saline jewels cantering down her distorted face. Her hands fell to tend the inferno, skin reeling to the attempt.

Hughes banqueted on her pain, her distress. Her nudity was only partly responsible for the man's arousal. What he hoped would be a long and torturous road to total subjugation fed the rest of the man's libido. 'Care to try again?' he enquired sardonically.

Sandra stepped down from the chair, lambasted buttocks cradled in her hands. Focus fixed on the floor she asked calculatingly, as well as a hint of desperation, 'Is there anything I can do or say, sir, to change your mind?'

'What yer gonna do then, Al?' Ruth asked, hopeful.

'Untie you,' the girl replied without hesitation. 'I've no reason to hurt you.'

'But you wouldn't, would you? I enjoy it.' The young woman turned her face to Alice and whispered, 'I love it. The harder the better.'

Alice dropped the rod on the bed. 'I dare say sometime over the next few days I will have good reason, but for the time being I think it best you go back to your dorm.'

The blonde rolled onto her side and stared up at Alice. 'What d'yer mean, good reason?'

'You'll find out soon enough.' Alice tried to ignore what she saw, the allure of O'Leary's bound nakedness proving irresistible. Alice's eyes roamed, fed her frustration, a hunger for sins of the flesh. Thoughts, inappropriate notions petitioned propriety, that insatiable lust that lurked beneath the surface boiled and seethed. Bolts of euphoric energy haphazardly lanced sexually restless quarters. Desirous of Ruth's tethered state, temptation sneaked insidiously into the frame.

'Free me tit,' brought her back to the moment.

'What?'

'Me right tit's caught. Ease it out, Al.'

Alice could have rolled O'Leary onto her back, the voice of conscience whispering, *'There's no harm.'* She reached, slipped fingers about the fleshy knoll, and eased that seductive breast clear.

'That does something for me, Al. Does the feel of me do anything for you?'

'No,' Alice lied.

'What you worried about?' Ruth persisted. 'No one ain't gonna know. Keep turning yer back on what yer really want and before yer knows it yer'll be too bleedin' old.'

'And what do I really want, Ruth?' Alice glared down at the girl. 'I don't even know the answer to that one, so how would you?'

'I seen it in yer eyes, gel. An' I seen the way yer holds up under a beatin'. Yer's the same as me; it's just that I've faced up to it and you ain't. What is it? Do yer think yerself too good to be a masochistic lessie?'

'I guess a lot boils down to trust. Let's face it, Ruth, I'm not going to open up to someone unless I know them.'

'Yer won't get to know me the way you're carrying on.'

'No, you're probably right.'

'You sayin' yer don't trust me?'

'Why should I? You don't trust me. You said so yourself.'

Ruth frowned and chewed her lip. 'The marks on my tits,

right?'

Alice perched her bum on a chest of drawers. 'It was then, yes. But not knowing doesn't bother me. I'm not prying. But you said yourself, you didn't know me well enough.'

'Untie me wrists, Al. These ropes are killing me. Trust Drake to go over the top.'

Hughes closed the distance, Sandra wincing with apprehension. He stared at her breasts, leaving no question as to where his interest lay. 'Are you by any chance offering me the fruits of your body?'

Wareholme twitched nervously. She knew him not, her first dealings with him was when she opted to defy him. He radiated an aura. A malevolence. There was a cold hostility in his voice, his manner and his actions. Geoffrey Hughes scared her shitless.

Mouth dry, Sandra followed the raising of his hand, cold leather pressed to her breast. 'Answer me, Sandra. Are you suggesting a favour of the flesh?'

The twitch gave to trembles, nerves beyond her control. 'I... I'll do anything you want sir,' she replied, evasive.

'Anything? Now there's an offer worth consideration.' Hughes pursed his lips, masking his amusement. 'Put your hands on your head.' Sandra immediately complied, and he stepped back several paces, strap gripped by both fists, attention deliberately focussed on her chest. He snapped on the leather. 'I want you to suffer, Sandra. It's as simple as that.'

Her heart near seized as he lifted and propelled that devilish strap in an arc. She squealed in terror as the tip brushed her left breast, the realisation that he'd missed offering no succour.

She opened her eyes to Hughes' sadistic cackle, the man pouring a whiskey from a decanter. He lifted the glass and drained the contents in one gulp. 'That put the fear of God up you, didn't it, Wareholme?'

'What do you want from me?' she begged, at her wits' end.

'I want nothing from you, whore. It's what I'm going to give you. Hell, Sandra. Simple as that. Hell, consummate hell.'

'Why?' Tears fell.

'Why?' He laughed. 'Because you're a bag of shite. Because you're a heathen Scottish barbarian.' Hughes threw his hands apart. 'I don't need a reason, you stupid dumb cow! I am God. I make and break as I fucking please. And it pleases me to fucking break you.'

Sandra hugged herself. She had never felt so naked in all her life. Beyond susceptible, beyond helpless, Sandra experienced the grope of hopelessness.

Hughes downed a second large whiskey. 'And I'm not worried about you telling all to your mates. They won't be seeing you again.

'Tonight I play with you. Tonight I do whatever I feel like doing to you. Then tomorrow you go into service. You will become a useful member of society. You will earn a living.'

'Doing what?' she whined.

'You've no family to talk of, have you?'

'What's that got to do with anything?'

'If I've discharged you from this establishment, then there will be no one looking for you.'

'You're letting me go?' Her heart lifted.

Hughes laughed. 'You really are a stupid lummox, aren't you? When you were arrested and sent to borstal you lost your freedom, right? Then you opted to come here, where even more rights were stripped from you. Are you with me so far?'

The blonde nodded.

'I run this establishment. I decide when and if you are to be released. If I say you are released then no one will query that. So no one will check up. As far as the establishment is concerned you are out there somewhere in the big wide world.

'But you won't be. You will be one of Hope's lambs. You will be a little Oliver Twist. You will be earning for the Hope coffers. I have found you a job in hell, Sandra.'

Every inch of her naked flesh prickled. She had never before felt so alive, so dead. 'Why me? Is it because I'm a Scot?'

'No, it's because you fit the bill. But I will say if you hadn't drawn my attention to you, then we might not be having this conversation.'

'You're going to sell me, aren't you? I'll be no more than a slave.'

'That's about the size of it.'

'Have you no conscience?'

He shook his head. 'None whatsoever. Make no mistake; I am a ruthless bastard. I take great satisfaction from cruelty, especially toward young attractive women. I'm at my happiest when you are suffering, mentally or physically, and I am the worst enemy you could possibly imagine.'

Freed, the marks of ropes as stirring to Alice as the tethers themselves, Ruth rubbed at the numbed flesh. 'I went on a job. The geezer was a slimy, depraved little git. He 'ad me do him a few favours, yer know, of the sexual type.'

'No, I don't know. And what do you mean by "went on a job"?'

'If it gets out I told yer I'll really suffer for it. Let's just say tarts like me 'as a use in Hope. Us that don't have no inhibitions can do quite well. And the favours? Come on, Al, you're not that naïve.'

'No, I suppose not.'

'He were only a little git, but his pride and joy were a spectacle to behold. I ain't never seen a pair of bollocks so huge, and so fucking full, either. His squirts could 'ave put the fire of London out.

'Anyway, he had this fetish, one that drove him to distraction. So, for a fiver shoved in me tunnel an' nothing said about it, I let him whip me tits with a very flexible cane.'

Alice leant forward and ran a finger the length of a mark. 'Six strokes?'

'Nah, six on each tit.'

'Hurt much?'

'He made a meal of it. It weren't no whack, whack an' done with. The cane were thin, flexible like a whip, and cos it was so thin it didn't bruise. He had me stand with me hands behind me head. He reckoned if I squealed or tried to rub them he'd just start all over again.'

Ruth gently massaged a breast, fingertips depressing resilient skin. 'He built up to the first stroke. Got me on tenterhooks. I was shaking like a leaf, I can tell yer. Then he whipped me with the first one.' She ran a finger over her breast, indicating where. 'It stung like fuck, Al. It was all I could do to keep me gob shut. It stung and stung and fucking stung.'

Ruth leaned forward and laid a hand beside Alice's knee. 'He waits. He walks around me. He lashes me bare arse a half dozen times. Very rapid strokes, them was. So there I am stinging at both ends.'

Ruth stroked, caressed Alice's inner thigh. 'Oh, I liked the arse bit. Some'at about my arse, gel. It really responds to a thrashing. I just gets this swarm of hot fizzy bubbles inside, like swelling in me groin, filling me fanny with these delicious tingling sensations. I've come a few times that way. Well, more than a few times.'

The blonde's palm ascended, climbing ever closer to that inviting apex. Alice said nothing, nor gave any indication of approval or objection.

'Then the geezer comes full circle. He rests that cane on me other tit. He draws it back and forth. He taps a couple of times. Up goes the rod. Down it comes with one hell of a swish. Slap! It whips, bites right into me boob, bending round at the tip. Fuck me. I watched it, Al. Me tit leapt. It jerked with the impact. And that smart? Jesus H Christ! I thought he'd set me jug on fire.'

Ruth slipped from the bed to kneel before Alice. Her hand attained the redhead's cotton protected crotch, her fingers probing the soft sex lips beneath. 'Twelve of those, Al. And in between, dozens to me corrugated arse and thighs. Fuck me, gel, I was floating in paradise.'

Something snapped. All objections were effaced. Inhibitions melted. A tide of urgency swept over Alice. She fell to her knees, her mind crowded by irresistible pressures. Zealous demons splintered the shackles of conscience, crushing all constraints. They dominated immediate thought, action and response. Alice's body became a slave to her lust – a tool to finally assuage the devil's thirst.

Skirt pulled to her waist, thin cotton panties inviting invasion, Alice leant her forehead on Ruth's shoulder. Eyes closed, the redhead sighed. Ruth's body against hers launched a tidal wave of contentment, met the corrosive need for affection. It mattered not her intimate was another female, any moral objections lost to a sea of urgency. 'Tell me more,' she whispered.

Ruth accepted what she deemed an invitation, fingers sliding within those flimsy briefs. 'About what?'

Alice moaned to Ruth's digit overture, fingertips stroking her vagina. 'About your striping.'

'You tell me about yours instead,' O'Leary countered.

'That never happened. I'll tell you what could happen to a defenceless girl, though. That's if you want to hear it.'

'Go on then.'

Recollections abounded, sweet memories and horrors intermingled. Alice shivered to the unfastening of blouse buttons, anticipating *her* touch, *her* licentious feel of erotic tit flesh. A relative stranger, a female, groping her *there*. Goose bumps prickled her skin, her body sensually lit. A pang of self-reproach ricocheted, stinging insouciance, as her bra was eased aside. She gasped as curious fingers first courted then probed, feeling the warm, sleek knoll. 'An innocent girl could find herself with an older man she really fancies. A man more than twice her age, but so damned handsome and sexy she can't resist him.'

Alice stared up at the ceiling as Ruth descended her torso. Divinity battled devilry, there being no middle ground. An outright war between good and evil, she could see it no other way. Mortal flesh and blood embraced the sexual affection, her indoctrinated mind seeing it as an outrage. 'She could offer herself up on a plate. She could say she would do anything for him. Worse, she didn't say that, she just gave him what he wanted.'

Alice felt Ruth's lips caress a nipple, the subsequent bolt of ecstatic energy withering. 'Oh God,' she whispered unheard. 'She could find out he gets off on laying an implement to that young girl's bottom. Worse still, her bare bottom.'

Wet tongue darted, raided, aroused.

'Because she wants him so badly,' Alice sighed. 'To be honest, because the virgin wants his cock rammed hard into her cunt so badly…'

Ruth's seduction became more animated, her hands forcefully groping, tongue licking wildly. Her teeth first nibbled, then bit those succulent orbs.

Eyelids rested, covered green pools. Images danced, tempted and reminded. 'He had some cock, too. I sucked it, so I know. I had his thick shaft tight in my mouth. I licked the head, and drank his come.'

Ruth snatched at Alice's wrist, drawing it to her groin, guiding the girl's fingers to her shaven pussy. 'Finger-fuck me, for Christ's sake!'

'He caned me a few times. He could be so gentle and at other times so cruel.'

'What were his name?'

'Despair.'

'Oh shit, I knew him.'

'He's standing here right now, watching you two perverts play happy couples.'

Stunned, shocked to the core, the pair jerked apart. Alice leapt to her feet, turning her back on the intrusive Pierce, frantically trying to button her blouse. Ruth slumped back, knees drawn up, face an embarrassed scarlet.

Pierce strode by the blonde, his sights set on Alice. He shoved her hard against the wall, a hand raising her skirt, heavy mauler then grabbing a half covered buttock. 'Explains a lot, this little twosome, don't it? It's not a man you're after, is it? You're a queer girl, a lessie.'

Alice struggled, attempting to wriggle free, but Pierce used

153

his weight, held her firm, flat against the wall. 'How dare you?' she tried. 'How dare you burst into my room?'

'Burst in? I didn't burst in. I walked in. I knocked, but you didn't seem to hear. Must have been completely absorbed, eh?'

'What I do, in the privacy of my room, has got nothing to do with you.'

'Never said it had. I am confused, though. How can such a pair of good-looking birds be so butch? Eh, how come?'

'Will you get your hand out of my pants and let me go?'

Pierce pressed his body against her back. 'Feel that, Alice? Can you feel that manhood? It likes you. It wants to introduce itself to your,' he leant to her ear, 'tight cunt hole.'

'You can dream!' she hissed.

'No?' The big man spun her round and thrust her shoulders against the wall. Keeping her there with one hand and an elbow he flicked her blouse apart. The man whistled. 'Forgotten how sweet they were. Mind if I partake?'

Before Alice could object his hands smothered those shapely orbs, Pierce's leer telling her how much he enjoyed the grope. 'Wait outside, O'Leary. Me and Alice have a little bit of business to attend to.'

Ruth didn't need telling twice, she scurried from the floor and headed for the door. 'Don't worry, blondie,' he called after her, 'I'm good for a fair few fucks before I'm, er, fucked. You'll get your share.'

The door shut, Pierce looked Alice in the eyes. 'Where do we go from here, Hussey?'

'You're asking me? The piece of shit with his hands glued to my tits is asking me?'

'I understand you were heading up the ladder, but I think that sort of promotion would be more for the straight, dependable, professional employee, not a fucking deviant.'

'Blackmail?' Alice smiled. 'You think you can have me by promising to keep this quiet? Well fuck you, Eddie Pierce. Tell Mr Hughes. I couldn't give a damn.'

'Couldn't you now? Perhaps you might give a damn about

me thrashing that lovely arse of yours.'

'We've been there, Pierce. You have no power to do so.'

He stepped away. 'O'Leary!' he bawled, and the young woman stepped back into the room looking exceedingly sheepish.

'You are off limits.'

She nodded, face pale.

'You're breaking the curfew.'

Stooped, hugging herself, fingers digging into upper arms, she nodded again.

'You were discovered in a compromising position with a member of staff; a disgusting clinch with another female. You know what to expect, don't you?'

'Yeah,' she mumbled.

'Trouble is, it will be doubled.'

Startled, her mouth fell open.

'Yes, doubled. Lover girl here won't accept any responsibility, so you will have to suffer her lot as well.'

Ruth stared at the floor, fingers squeezing with fingers. 'That's okay.'

Alice gripped Pierce's wrists, her nails sinking into the man's skin, but jaw set, ignoring the pain, he forced a smile.

'It's not okay,' Alice objected. 'And don't believe for one minute that he can. The arse thinks he's clever.' She knocked those offensive hands away, simultaneously manoeuvring herself away from the custodian. 'Pierce thinks I'll say, "No, I'll take my share".'

He smirked. 'Bright degenerate, aren't you? Get out, Ruth, I'll deal with you in due course.'

Alice remained standing, arms folded, with her back to him. 'And get out yourself,' she said.

'I had you wrong, that I will admit.' She smelt the whiskey on his breath and knew he was close. 'I thought you naïve, innocent, a bit on the gullible side.'

Alice ignored him. She could see their reflections in the windowpane, ghostly images, unreal, dreamlike.

'There I guess I was wrong. You are one calculating, devious, hard bitch.'

'That's your opinion is it, Eddie Pierce? Thank you for the benefit of your wisdom. Now leave me alone.'

He leaned around her, and picked up a length of rope. 'Shame I came along and interrupted, eh?' He held the cord up. 'Spoiled your fun by the look of it.'

'Unless you have something of consequence to say, please leave.'

'Ah, but I have.'

'I don't think so.'

'First, I don't want to fuck you. No, that's a lie. I do want to fuck you, but I accept I probably never will.'

'You have such a romantic way with words. To think, I actually took a shine to you for all of five minutes. Then I realised what a sleazebag you are.'

'I speak my mind—'

'Straight from the sewer.'

'I say what I want. Up front. No blarney. I reckon I'll get a little bit closer to you tonight.

Alice turned, and tired, frustrated, driven to the point of indifference, she laughed in his face.

Expression serious, Pierce delved a trouser pocket. 'I have something that may be of interest to you.' He removed a folded piece of paper, which he held up. 'Have a look. See what you think.'

Puzzled, unsettled by Pierce's complacency, she took it, and a set of numbers neatly printed on the page set her heart pounding. Eyebrows knitted, forehead furrowed, Alice muttered, 'I don't understand.'

'It's a telephone number,' Pierce informed her unnecessarily.

'I know what it is,' she answered, bewildered. 'But how? Where?' Obviously distraught she ran fingers through her hair. 'I don't… this is mad. I'm dreaming, aren't I? This is another of those dreadful nightmares.'

Pierce slowly shook his head. 'You recognise the number then?'

'Of course I do.' She jabbed a finger at her scalp. 'It's engraved in here. It always will be.'

'Frightened, aren't you?' Pierce surmised victoriously.

'Where? Where Pierce? Where did you get this from?'

Chest thrown out the bully folded his arms. 'He's a weed… a bespectacled, balding weed. What hold does he have over you, huh? What does he know?'

Alice trembled. All aspects of health drained from her face. 'He was here?' she asked, incredulous.

'Looking for you in the early hours.'

'What did you tell him?'

'He took some persuading. He insisted he had sound evidence that you were here. You stole from him, didn't you?'

'Is that what he told you?'

'Sort of. Money. A lot of money.'

Alice slumped on the bed, all courage and grit stripped from her in one foul blow. 'I took the evidence of his money, that's all. He only has to go to the bank. There won't be a problem.'

'Then why are you shitting yourself?'

'That's my business. Did you tell him I'm here?'

'I told him you were; that you stayed a day and moved on. He gave me that number and said to ring him if you returned.'

'Why did you do that?'

Pierce smiled. 'And that is my business.'

'What now?' Alice asked, haunted, her glass world falling apart around her.

Pierce leant, reached and pulled her blouse apart. 'Simple, Alice; you take your medicine.'

'I'll not have sex with you, Pierce,' she vowed. 'You try that and I'll have the police on your back so fast you wont know what's hit you.'

Pierce refolded the paper and slipped it back in a pocket. 'No?'

She vigorously shook her head. 'If that's what you intended, then ring him.'

Pierce nodded. 'Okay… no vaginal sex.'

'No sex at all.'

'You have my word I won't fill your cunt. And that's it.'

'And you have my word, Edward Pierce, that if I see a way to destroy you I will.'

'Then we both know where we stand, don't we?' He placed a hand beneath Alice's upper arm and eased her to her feet. 'You won't sit for a week after I'm finished tonight.'

Ruth waited halfway along the corridor. Surprised, but half expecting her, she met Alice, and still naked she walked beside the escorted girl. 'You agreed then?'

Dejected, anxious, Alice nodded. 'Yes, I agreed.'

'You didn't have to.'

'I had to.'

The trio reached Pierce's room, Alice hoping she would wake up at any second. 'I'll see you tomorrow,' Pierce informed Ruth, the man puffed with victory, edgy with excitement. 'And don't think for one minute I'm letting you off. It's just that,' he grinned broadly, 'I'll be too occupied to deal with you tonight.'

Ruth remained, witnessing the closing and locking of Pierce's door. A sly smile played on her lips. Hands squeezed jutting breasts, before traversing ribs and flat belly to apply pressured fingers to her shaven mound. She threw her head back, long blonde tresses brushing her lower back. The girl sighed.

Sandra fled, an inebriated, laughing Geoffrey Hughes just behind. She clutched crimson buttocks in a vain bid to protect them, her bottom so agonisingly sore she couldn't face another slap from that dreadful strap, let alone the twelve Hughes promised. With no penchant for mathematics she had no idea of how many excruciating cracks her butt had endured. She only knew it was a hell of a lot and she couldn't take any more.

The athletic girl leapt onto the settee and over the back, a flushed principal in hot pursuit. She grasped the door handle praying he hadn't locked it. Thrown open, expecting his hand pulling at her hair, or the vicious smack of leather on her tenderised bum, she fled upstairs.

Hughes followed eagerly, eyes glazed and mad, a twisted leer on his lips. The Scot stumbled, missed her footing halfway up, Hughes seizing the opportunity. Sandra squealed to the thunderous clap of leather on a ravaged cheek, the hurt awesome, sickening, but before she could regain her feet Hughes had landed another two.

Clambering, almost on all fours, clueless to her ultimate means of escape, she climbed higher. Hughes followed, the jostle of those burning bum cheeks providing much satisfaction. He tendered another volatile stinger, that leather ripping into her left haunch. It navigated the hip, whip-lashing against the girl's groin. Hand clasping that bitter scald she attained the summit and headed for the bathroom, her intention to seek respite by locking herself in.

Hughes laid a hand to that precious doorknob first. He glared at the Scot, daring her, urging her to try something else. She backed to a corner, blitzed rump hidden, temporarily protected.

Hughes smirked. 'Another eight, Wareholme, and you haven't managed the trick yet.'

Stinging, raw seat kept from him she pleaded. 'Please sir, no more, you've beaten me black and blue already. My arse is throbbing in agony.'

'Throbbing in agony?' The man laughed. 'What you've had tonight is just a prelude, an introduction. You failed. You failed yourself, and worse you failed me. Now, heathen slut, show me your arse.'

Faced screwed in fear she shook her head.

'It's either your backside, Wareholme, or it's your tits.'

The young woman bowed, arms protectively covering her chest, whipped behind pressed to the wall.

Hughes snarled and lifted the strap high. 'You fucking streak of highland piss. Don't you defy me.'

Sandra tensed to the rush of air and flinched as durable leather slapped noisily on upper thigh, but she declined to alter her stance, the defence of her chest paramount.

He levelled a backhander, propelling it forcefully towards her lower abdomen. Sandra could only brace herself. Leather brutally struck, ferociously biting her groin, her pubic mound ignited. 'It's your defiance that landed you here in the first place, you stupid tart.'

Sandra yelped to a second helping, the inferno in her crotch unbearable. Unable to ignore it her hands fell to succour that dreadful burn.

Reason had evaporated with intoxication. The overwhelming desire to inflict misery ruled the agitated, sexually deranged principal. 'I'll no eat this shite!' he roared as leather slammed into vulnerable breasts.

Sandra sank to her knees, sobbing. 'Why don't you just kill me, you bastard? It would be better than this. Anything would be better than this.'

Unsympathetic, Sandra's pathetic situation exciting his libido, Hughes stood over her. 'Arse, Sandra. Stick up your arse. You still have eight to go.'

Two minutes later the Scot crawled into Hughes' bedroom, her bottom feeling as if it had been flayed. He took off his shirt, tossing it to one side. Tacit, he dropped his trousers, carefully folding them before throwing them onto a chair. Eyeing the young woman with ambitious interest he peeled black underpants from his hips, hard cock leaping to the horizontal.

Still wordless the principal stooped, seized Sandra by the hair and lifted. On her knees she faced the man's purpled dome, his thick shaft pulsing. 'Please me, Sandy, and I'll not whip your arse again tonight. Displease me and I'll send you straight to hell.'

He took her by the ears, bloated plum pressed to her lips, the abrupt thrust of hips taking her by surprise. Hughes stuffed her mouth, cock forced to the back of her throat. His hips withdrew that ardent torpedo, only to return with excessive zeal.

'After this I'll have your arsehole, and then your cunt,' Hughes mused, fucking her mouth with selfish vigour. 'And then tomorrow a new life.' He chuckled. 'Or was it a living death?'

Chapter Eight

The light switched on, Alice laid face down ruminating on the two hours spent with Pierce. The pig took his time, drew out the session, mauling her at every opportunity. He took many liberties, but she guessed he would.

The mirror presented an enrapturing posture, a sprawled, chastised body of a young woman. She lay, auburn curls spread upon a pillow, blankets and eiderdown pinned by her weight. Her curious position and the line of sight obscured many intriguing details. One could not, for example, glimpse her perfect breasts, which lay compressed and cushioned beneath her moist torso. One could not descry or revel in the teasing impressions etched upon those acutely feminine spheres.

Alice focused on the fleshy hummocks, wondering what the reflection did to deserve those monstrous stripes. Methodically laid, the pattern quite appealing, those bloated welts rippled the once flawless curves. Perhaps she sinned.

Saliva coated her chin and wet the pillowslip. Spittle seeped from between her burdened lips and the rag forced between. Her voice disabled, she was left only the sighs and moans of the tormented.

Buttock a sea of waxed crimson; eighteen purple ridges lurched uniformly over the summit. Some ten inches long each stretched, tenderised and distended, that haunch indelibly marked to the hip, every stripe a token of exceptional severity.

If one could rise a little, gaze down upon that tortured rump, one would be awarded with the complete picture. Lids settled over emerald eyes, the view captured, etched on the mind. A second hillock joined its persecuted twin, cast beyond and complementing the perfection. It too burned hot and inflamed, that meat scored by the potent slash of a quarter inch thick cane.

Torso ailed by goose bumps, excited shivers racking her body, Alice tallied the score. *'She suffered thirty-six strokes; eighteen from the left, eighteen from the right, and she deserved every brutal slash of rattan on her upturned bum.'*

That fleshy bottom captured in Alice's mind's eye shuddered to a vigorous stroke, her corporeal and heavily marked haunches tightening in accord. She moaned.

Dreamy eyes unveiled, Alice again absorbed her reflection. *'Was it punishment, though? His cane wrapped about my bum with a sickening ferocity. The sting was the worst I have ever experienced.'* Alice wriggled, attempted a more comfortable position. *'But it was what I wanted. It was what I've been yearning for since...'*

She gazed once more at that devastated flank. *'What is it about the marks of punishment? Why are those bloated welts so arousing?'*

Alice managed to lift that caned rump up a few inches. Her hands played and exploited. Lambasted nates strained and quivered. Ropes extracted bizarre responses, her body cloaked in rapture. Fingers stroked the soreness. They encircled the protruding bud. Her movement limited she plunged and withdrew the wicked insert with as much vigour as she could exert.

Mental images streamed through her delirious mind. Sweat dotted her face, wetted her captured breasts and soaked her groin. Breathing ragged, eyes glazed, she sighed and gasped, her crotch burning with the euphoric promise of climax. Alice squealed in rapture, gasped, then slumped.

'God...' she breathed, wearily pulling her hands up a half inch, the explicit bite of rope to her crotch and buttock division exasperatingly delicious.

Curious fingers prodded that shaft, the twinge of post-orgasm almost too much to bear. What did he call the thing? A dido?

No, that wasn't it. She'd had her fanny punished with a belt and stretched with a plastic cock. She shouldn't be feeling like this. She should be devastated. She should be sobbing her heart out. She'd been abused, not just punished.

But she felt so calm. She felt sexually fulfilled for the first time... ever. Pierce took the foulest liberties and she indulged in everything he did.

Alice checked the bedside clock. It was two in the morning. She looked back to the glass, reminding herself of how wide he had parted her legs. The memory of his rough hand there flitted, a depth charge ignited in her tummy.

A chill settled on her sweat-coated body. She shivered. Remorse edged into the void left by ecstasy. What had she done? What had she let Pierce do? She very nearly let him... when he put his erection between her thighs... when she felt the head, that massive plum, her backside burning from that spanking, her sex on fire. She could have taken him. She could have easily begged him.

Perhaps Richard was right. Maybe she was a slut. Maybe she did provoke men, tease them and then disappoint them at the final hurdle. But she did what Pierce demanded. She put up with his wandering hands. She didn't object. Maybe that was it; maybe she gave the wrong impression.

Alice winced. A length of jute encircled her waist, looping and pinning her forearms on route. Tightly bound wrists were anchored to her pubic mound, the remaining lengths of cord crisscrossed before the vaginal insert and again behind. Those then scored the buttock gorge, to tuck beneath the waist rope. There they parted, each subsequently secured to an ankle, legs strained, calves kissing thighs. A tether ran beneath the bed, the ends girding the girl's limbs above the knees. The rope restricted movement, kept her facedown and crudely parted her legs wide.

Another length strangled her breasts. Two loops sank deep into those sweet mounds. Two loops drawn exceedingly tight, one passing through the other. The ends were then secured to her upper arms, knots to the rear. Those limbs were then drawn close, a rope securing, squeezing the breasts between.

The girl was acutely aware of another predicament. Anyone entering the room would have a worm's eye view of Miss Hussey's very private anatomy, and Pierce had deliberately left the door ajar.

Guilt failed to dampen that night's awakening. Sexual tension crept insidiously back. Alice couldn't tear her eyes from that reflection. What had been, what was and what might be, created copious material for the feverish dream. The amalgamation of external pressures and sensations jousted with crazed desire, fermenting peculiar and arousing sensations.

Naked and helpless. Spread and vulnerable. Tied in a sexually explicit fashion, her vagina exposed, displayed and invaded. Erogenous flesh whipped, bound, squeezed and manhandled. Dominated and humiliated. Such was that evening's roller coaster ride. Such was the crude awakening. Pierce provided the key that unlocked her convoluted needs and aspirations.

As Alice squirmed, rubbing her body against the bedclothes, her hands against her sex, she finally realised *why*. Pride had been the obstacle. A mix of dignity, morality and humility stunted her understanding. She *came* because her peculiar appetite inclined her towards immoderate subjection. The act of domination lay open that raw and susceptible quirk.

Her thoughts returned to that evening's carnal events. How she had taken the short walk to Pierce's room, her tummy in knots. Apprehension played on her sex strings as well as her nerves. The sane Alice feared his malice, his strong right arm and the slash of his cane. The deranged side grew increasingly excited, inflamed by the diverse possibilities. Those opposites, good and evil, moral and immoral, clashed and cancelled one another, leaving her open-minded…

Pierce slammed and locked the door, leaving Alice with little doubt. He tossed aside the usual preliminaries, seizing her instead by a handful of blouse, and she offered no vocal remonstration as she was ungraciously thrown over his lap.

The man's heavy breathing and intense manner showed her how the land laid, and the first hefty slap to her skirt-covered backside reinforced her intuition.

Any vestige of dignity soon crumbled, Pierce rapidly inducing a raging inferno. Alice struggled and kicked, her repeated squeals feeding his sadistic appetite. Her blouse parted company with her skirt, a widening gap exposing her naked back. The shirt progressively rose higher, revealing her bra, the sight triggering sexual interest. Pierce discarded civility, choosing to take what he could.

Skirt tugged high, the man laboured upon those scantily covered dunes, the traumatised flesh already spanked to a livid red, and that constantly shuddering corpulence mesmerised him. The heave and jostle of seductive buttocks provoked his libido. The man's penis swelled, attained its glorious mass, and demanded release.

Pierce was not a man to submit to modesty, and lifting Alice with one arm he let the monster loose, Alice glad of the short respite. Lowered again she immediately felt the hot shaft pressing into her naked belly. She accepted she should have been horrified, concerned for her safety, but that brazen, bestial act changed her perspective.

Fires of depravity licked at her core. Inhibitions melted. That indefinable glow heaved and pulsated. Abruptly Alice's disposition changed. Complacency dissipated. Urgency engulfed resignation. Those crippling explosions rained on her backside suddenly became agreeable, still excruciatingly painful but strangely satisfying.

Only one spectre remained to haunt her: Richard, the paradox; the pious man who preached his interpretation of God's law; the saintly crusader who readily jabbed the finger of accusation; who demanded humility and obedience; the man with the tongue that could slash an impressionable girl's pride to the bone. And yet there she lay over Pierce's lap because of him. She had fled to Flint because of him, but she knew he could so easily find her. And knowing him the way she did, he would somehow extricate what had transpired. That had a sobering effect.

Disturbed, her mind in chaos, Alice found wholehearted indulgence impossible. Opposites continued to do battle. Lust raked hot coals in her groin, while guilt demanded unconditional suffering. The only certain factor was those murderous slaps to her tender bottom.

Pierce abruptly ceased. 'So why are you so frightened of this Barker?'

Alice spat her reply in frustration. 'Why are you so interested?' She felt his warmed palm roaming her blistered behind, the lecher openly groping her.

He chuckled. 'That really is some stupid question.' He sank his fingers between her thighs and poked her vagina through the thin gusset. 'It's quite simple. I want this.' He pressed harder, Alice wincing, the finger penetrating.

'I'd stitch it up first,' Alice defied.

'And I can also see us spending quite a lot of evenings just as we are now. I think Barker might be the key to that.'

'Then ask *him*.'

'Now there's an idea. I could ring him. Do you reckon he would pay hard cash to know where you are?'

'He's Ebenezer Scrooge reincarnated. You'd stand more chance of getting blood out of a stone.'

Pierce's fingertips sank beneath her panty elastic. 'First, who is he?'

'Richard Barker.'

Alice jerked to the abrupt loss of her panties. Pierce sighed, his hand gently tapping a buttock. 'You know what I'm getting at.' Her right cheek leapt beneath another impact, the resultant burn sickening. 'Relationship?' Pierce demanded.

'Father confessor,' Alice goaded.

That same area of flesh reeled to another almighty smack. 'You'll tell me eventually.'

Alice gritted her teeth. 'There's nothing to tell. He's just someone from the past that I don't want to see again.'

Pierce massaged the sting. 'Is he the one who caned you?'

He drew a finger over her buttocks. 'You had stripes on your backside that first night. Cane stripes.'

'Look, you've got what you wanted. I'm here. Spank me. Cane me. Tie me up. Whip my tits if you want. But my past is dead, and it's staying that way.'

'You only came here because of Barker.'

'No, that's only part of it. I'll tell you the reason why. I'll also tell you why I acted the way I did that night.' Pierce helped her to her feet, her panties sliding to her ankles. She stood before him cautiously rubbing her stinging behind. 'I'm catholic.'

Pierce nodded.

'I believe in the punishment of sinners. Richard Barker is a catholic. He is also a strict disciplinarian. I sinned, and because I sinned I have to atone. The lash is one accepted method, but it has to be severe. It has to hurt. I have to suffer.'

She flinched, his fingers brushing against her pubic mound.

'I am human, I am cowardly, and much as I knew I had to face my conscience, I kept running. Tonight, when you reminded me of Barker, I finally found the courage.' Alice gazed down at the man. 'So, Mr Pierce, punish me. Absolve my sins.'

He smiled. 'Okay.' The girl's stomach somersaulted. 'But I would still like to know just who this Barker guy is.'

'I thought he was a decent man. Hard, but decent. He's not. He's a lying, deceitful pervert.'

'Whip your tits?'

Alice frowned. 'What?'

'You said not two minutes ago: I can whip your tits.'

'Ah…'

Pierce shrugged. 'That would hurt, I'm sure. And you would certainly suffer.'

'If I said do it, then do it.'

The man rose, tucking his erection back into his trousers. He placed an arm about Alice's shoulder. 'If you want someone to help you purge your soul, then you know where to find me.'

'If you forget about Barker, then maybe.'

'No, not maybe, Alice. I forget about Barker, then I reckon

you would sin roughly about once a fortnight.'

Alice's arms and legs grew numb. Her hands, feet and skin chilled. But still the sexual phantasm pranced enticingly. Graphic pictures and concepts lashed her morality. There in her room, sleep denying her, fleshly desires continued to nag indiscriminately.

She had made her down payment to Pierce, bought his silence for the time being. The man was still curious about Richard, but content to let sleeping dogs lie as long as she appeased his sadistic nature. To begin with she firmly believed she could acquit that sin; that she could suffer intolerably beneath Pierce's rough hand. Fate, however, decided otherwise, and all she managed was to open Pandora's box, to see herself as something far worse than she could ever have imagined.

Pierce caned her all right, with agonising efficiency. But there lacked an ingredient, one that was always present with Richard. To endure pain was not enough. There had to be a certain psychology involved; Barker was an adept, Pierce merely an apprentice.

Pierce tied her over the chair just like he wanted. With her ankles bound to the rear legs, he secured her wrists to the front cross brace. She was still partially dressed at that stage, her blouse and bra intact.

He began on promising form, swishing the cane, the chill of fear ascending Alice's spine. The slash of air, the crisp whistle of rattan slicing the ether spun a foreboding threat – one that twisted the gut and laid a slick of sweat over the waiting victim's body.

Mouth dry, breath short, Alice tensed. Her mind focused, amplifying the sensitivity of those sacrificial buttocks. The sheer dread of that expected blast of fire inspired panic. Doubts, second thoughts, utter dread and terror lambasted the stricken creature. Muscles gave to jitters, skin to goose bumps, palms sweated profusely.

The touch of sleek rattan pressed to hot cheeks. The preparatory, nerve-jingling slide of cane as it moved slowly back and forth intimidated. She screwed her face in anticipation, fists clenched, knuckles white.

Time stood still. The hostile, torturous wand lifted, rose high and hovered. Her heart faltered, thumped. Her pulse bellowed in her ears. One question screamed for an answer: *why do I want this…?*

Alice gazed at her reflection, at those appalling stripes. That first stroke sounded like the approach of the banshee. It hit with unbelievable force, slicing buttocks, pulverising flesh, despatching a tidal wave of raw pain. Alice could have put her finger on that particular welt. She knew exactly where the rod struck. She would not forget in a hurry.

Buttocks involuntarily clenched, her legs turned to jelly. Fire consumed her bottom, an inferno out of control.

Pierce's low voice penetrated the haze of shock. 'Was that penance enough, or would you like to hurt a little more?'

The stripe continued to burn, ten inches of traumatised flesh screaming its surrender. It was some seconds before Alice could voice a reply. They ticked by, the scald refusing to die, but eventually she answered, 'Do your worst, Mr Pierce.'

The man licked a forefinger, and placing it on her left cheek, he traced the flourishing mark to the division, and then to its conclusion. 'Colouring quickly. Won't be long before that one puffs up.'

The ensuing five rigorous cuts proved no easier to deal with, Alice accepting that perhaps she had found her saviour.

Pierce took a mirror from its hook on the wall, and held it so she could see her bottom. That first stroke laid so devastatingly, only ninety seconds before, had begun to lift. 'Do you think God has forgiven you yet?' he enquired sarcastically.

Alice closed her eyes, hands feeling her crotch. Her backside lifted, rocked from side to side, the girl murmuring. She yearned to inspect, touch, feel the evidence of her harsh flogging. She ached to run her hand over those tortured dunes, to savour the corrugation of buttock flesh before those magnificent welts subsided.

A suggestion launched from ingenuous mental catacombs stunned and lit the fuse of yet another orgasm. Alice rejected the concept, the damage already done.

Richard, dominant tyrant. Alice, subjugated innocent. Loveless, passionless, austere and harsh punishment. Richard, cruel and insatiable. Alice, beaten at his whim. She whimpered. She sucked air, sweet breath exhaled on the wings of a sigh. 'Oh God!' she cried softly, the words stifled. She rolled her body to the right, lifting her left shoulder clear of the bed, and gazed at the mirror image. A blast of energy ripped through her lower torso.

The reminder that Pierce was responsible launched another euphoric discharge. Alice sank teeth into the moist rag, expression concentrated. He stripped her. He caned her and tied her like this...

She needed to be fucked. She wouldn't even look to see who it was. It wouldn't matter. Just to feel the excited meat inside her, thrusting, violating, while she was tied, while she couldn't do anything about it...

And then he untied her and she rubbed her stinging bum, those raised welts so obvious to her fingertips. Half naked, massaging her naked buttocks, her fanny right there for him to look at. And he did, brazenly. She had such a weird and wonderful feeling. So vulnerable. So at his mercy. So nervous about what he would do next.

Alice shook her head, erasing the tide of sleep and encroaching demons. She reeled in the memory, seeing it as an act of contrition.

Pierce waited patiently, a short-handled, double-thong whip gripped in a large fist. Alice eyed those dangling leather cords with anxiety. The same old tune played on her nerves; fear and longing.

She loosened the buttons, drew back the curtains, Pierce smirking at the revelation. Smooth, pallid globes pushed up from black cups, those soft cushions trembling magnetically with her every movement.

The blouse slipped from her shoulders, descended her arms, and fell silently to the floor. She posed more than waited. She projected sultry. She exuded irresistible female. Invisible, enchanting pheromones enslaved the unwitting observer. Her innocence hooked the mighty, indefatigable Pierce. The intangible ensnared his reason, erased the few remaining scruples. He gradually lost control.

The way she stood. The manner in which she removed her bra. That damnable perfection. Pierce licked his lips. Those green eyes poured apprehension. Her sulky, full lips stirred the beast.

Her stance cried vulnerable, that body begging attention. Clasp unhitched, the siren guided the straps from her shoulders, delaying the unveiling, twanging Pierce's sex strings.

The man had seen them. He had been treated before. But that held no influence that night. He was like the child before Santa Claus waiting to tear open the goodies. Those feminine charms enslaved his every thought, the man ravenous for action.

The jet-laced undergarment peeled from those fruits, Alice's hands protectively replacing them, and that glimpse, that momentary flash of consummate breasts launched the ensuing madness.

As custodian he owned several sets of handcuffs. He snatched one pair from their slot and advanced on the uncertain redhead. He shackled her wrists, snapping the cold steel with a professional flair. That unexpected spontaneity flustered the girl. She stared stupidly at the gleaming bracelets, failing to assimilate the thick rope being lashed about her waist.

Pierce seized the connecting links, hauling her arms up and over her head, and there he secured the length rising from her waist.

Alice bent, twisted her torso away from him, the urge to protect her exposed breasts overwhelming. She was naked and completely defenceless, so very conscious of her plight. Her skin tingled, flinched before an imaginary assault, her mauled, raw buttocks twitching in anticipation. She pressed her thighs together attempting to conceal the slit of womanhood.

That trepidation, her cowering, served to advance Pierce's urgency, and as his particular pot closed on boiling so his sadistic side became more prevalent. Alice spotted the rapid movement of arm and tried to avoid the worst, but by turning her back on him a solitary breast caught the full force of those flexile twin leads. She doubled, the sting unbearable, her breasts quivering and lurching as she pranced her tortured dance.

The proffering of her thrashed bottom proved irresistible, and tough leather bit left and right cheeks, Alice rearing, staggering forward.

Pierce followed, grinning maliciously. She half turned and sobbed, 'I've had enough, Mr Pierce.' But the man shook his head and let fly another cruel stinger to witness the jerk of stricken breasts again. Alice twisted, contorted, tried to console that whipped flesh with her elbow.

She endured six lashes in all, twelve fine stripes decorating her breasts, and it was immediately after, Pierce fired beyond reason, that he tried his luck. Alice had come to rest before his chest of drawers, and there she bent, grimacing, examining the scarlet trails.

Pierce released his penis, the shaft erect, the purple head bloated. He moved close to the girl, scrutiny of that whipped behind increasing his ardour. Then as she resettled a leg he saw his chance and thrust his cock between her thighs, pressing to her sex lips, an impressive plum protruding beyond her mound.

Alice stared down in disbelief, too stunned to feel shock or horror. Hirsute arms encircled her body, coarse hands engulfing her breasts. Pierce held her tight, erect penis thrust slowly to and fro whilst fingers groped her nipples. 'Bend over backwards for me, Alice, and this could be giving you enormous satisfaction.'

Held against the drawers, Pierce's weight against her, Alice couldn't move. Hands still shackled behind her head she was completely defenceless. 'No thank you, Mr Pierce,' she replied, controlled and polite.

'I'll treat you gently,' he persisted.

Alice wriggled, pushing against the man. 'No.'

'Oh, I like that,' he whispered. 'Your lovely bum hard against my crotch. That's some feeling.'

Ropes seeming to grow ever tighter, Alice squirmed. Her legs ached, her back complained, while rough fibres chafed her breasts. She flexed her muscles, more to savour the bite and pull of ropes than any other reason. And then that last dreadful act, when he realised she meant no. She protested, but it did something unbelievable.

He pushed her back over that armchair, and when he pulled her legs apart and unbuckled his belt she felt breathless with excitement. It was one of the most irresistible, sensual sensations ever. Fear. Adrenaline. Sheer bliss. If he hadn't carried it through she actually believed she would have been disappointed.

When he lifted that leather, that doubled belt, she nearly fainted. Not because she was terrified, but because the surge of pre-climax was so incredible.

That blast! That smart! Right there on her intimate, private part. It stung. It drove a hot nail of bliss right into her pussy. But then he had second thoughts. Alice didn't. Alice wanted it again, and again. It was penance. It should have been the ultimate penance. *'Smite that which offends thee.'* But he put his belt on. He took off the handcuffs. She thought that was it.

He didn't say another word, not until just before he left. Shoved the length of the hallway, still without a stitch on, he threw Alice on her bed. She wondered for a few moments, but thankfully he kept his trousers on, although she didn't know whether she would have said no again.

Quickly and roughly he tied her again, trussed so she couldn't move, with her hands squeezed between her legs, with her arms bound to her breasts, secured with her legs wide apart.

And as a last act of humiliation he pressed that dildo into her, callously pressing and twisting until it would go no further.

'See if that puts a smile on your miserable face,' he said, before leaving her alone to her thoughts.

Chapter Nine

Alice awoke with a start. Instinctively she pulled on her arms, startled by the lack of restriction. She sat up, dazed, and stared about the room. No ropes? She felt between her legs. No dildo? Blankets covered her body; her clothes neatly folded and piled on a chair.

She scratched her head, puzzled. Another dream? No, surely not. It was real. She knew it was real.

She tossed back the covers and turned on her bottom, wincing as she did so. 'God, that's sore!'

She stood, straightened and stretched, then curious she checked her reflection. No, it was no dream. Her breasts were marked, and there were rope impressions around her waist and thighs.

She twisted, aiming her bottom at the mirror. 'Oh, shit!' What a mess. She'd been striped! She wasn't going to be able to sit for a week! Pierce was a brute.

'Ah, there you are,' startled the girl and she turned, arms attempting to hide her embarrassment. Geoffrey Hughes strolled in, and baffled, she stared open-mouthed.

'I take it you decided to give breakfast a miss,' he said, tone sarcastic.

Alice checked the time. 'But it's only half-six, sir,' she defended.

'Really?' Hughes sat on the edge of her bed. 'Watches stop, and yours seems to be in the habit.' He seemed unaffected by her nudity, as if he hadn't noticed.

'But I have my bedside clock as well,' she pointed out.

'Am I to understand that because Alice Hussey has two

timepieces she must be right?'

'I don't understand, sir.'

'I must have every clock in this establishment realigned to Hussey time. Is that it?'

'Mr Hughes, I'm sorry, I've just woken, you have me at a disadvantage. Am I late? Is that it?'

'You are one and a half hours late to be precise. I am beginning to think you are incapable of getting up in the morning.'

'But my clock says…'

'Damn your bloody clock, young lady! The sun doesn't lie! Look out of the window, girl. Can't you see how high in the sky it is?'

Alice picked up her timepiece and listened carefully. 'It hasn't stopped, sir. Therefore it's been altered.'

'What is that supposed to mean?'

'I set it correctly last night, sir, but this morning it's wrong…'

'How did you set it? By what yardstick?'

'My watch, sir.'

Hughes rose. He took three strides and stood directly before Alice, glaring at her. 'But your watch is wrong, you stupid girl.'

'It wasn't last night, sir, of that I'm certain.'

Hughes blinked. He studied Alice. 'You're naked,' he stated.

'Yes, I didn't have a chance to…'

The principal turned his back on her. 'Why didn't you lock your door?'

'I… I thought I had.'

'It would seem we have mischief about, doesn't it?'

'How do you mean, sir?'

'Shadows in the night. Flitting menaces that contrive, plot and seek to upset the status quo.'

'I'm not with you.'

'A pound to a penny it's O'Leary. Or one of her clan. Twenty bottoms, Alice. We'll assume none will admit their complicity, as none will play Judas. So you will flog the lot.'

'But there's no proof, sir!' she protested.

'There rarely is. If we waited for evidence then the devils

175

would run riot. So we assume and we dissuade. That's the way of it. That's how Hope conquers malignancy.'

'But if you're wrong?'

He shrugged indifferently. 'A few warmed backsides, a few stinging stripes, they have probably earned them anyway.'

'You want me to cane them all?'

'Hmmm, cane or strap. Makes no difference. You can birch the lot if you have a mind to.'

'Now sir?'

The man faced Alice. He smiled, amused. 'I should get dressed first. Unless of course you wish to show them how a real young lady takes a thrashing.'

Her face burned and she mentally begged the floor to open and swallow her.

'None of my business, of course; what you get up to in your own time is your affair.' He reached out, laid a hand on her shoulder and urged her away from the window. 'It's not wise to press your naked bottom to the glass though, Alice. There are those below that would take advantage.'

He leaned forward and inspected the marks. 'Ouch. I hope it was worth it, girl. You'll be pretty sore for a few days.'

Embarrassed, she couldn't argue or refute the head's assumption. She wanted to die, to escape the most humiliating episode of her life.

Nonchalant, Hughes strolled to the door. One hand on the jam he studied her again. 'You're a lovely looking lass, with a very desirable body,' he pointed a finger at her, 'and you still have to pay the piper. You have fifteen minutes, Alice. My office in fifteen.'

Alice dressed in three minutes flat. Still flushed she checked her appearance. She looked every part the martinet in her white blouse, black skirt and cardigan. Her panties lay on the bed, her bottom too sore to bear them.

Did Pierce come back? Did he untie her? Why didn't she wake? Did he tinker with her clock and watch, or was it someone else? Perhaps that was Pierce's game, to leave her trussed until someone found her. But if that had happened, then who?

High heels clicked rhythmically, the martinet's stride confident. Hair tied back, Alice fancied she looked the part. Her world had become an unsettled, shifting and sometimes surreal place. At times fantasy merged incomprehensibly with a dark reality. At others reality became fantasy and visa versa. So did Pierce do anything else? Could she be sure of anything? She went to sleep trussed and awoke freed.

Just about anything could happen here. Accepted courtesies had flown out of the window. It reminded her of the book, *Alice through the Looking Glass*. What had she drifted into? Where was it going to end? Maybe she should just get out of there before she did something she'd regret.

Alice strode into the hallway to witness ten young women lined up outside the punishment room, and her confidence faltered. How could she punish those innocent behinds?

Hughes appeared ahead of her, indicating his office. Alice stepped in, the principal closing the door behind them.

'Ten young miscreants, Alice. Half the dorm. I gave them an option. All twenty, or they could draw lots. That way half survive to bend another day, and mark my words they all will, eventually.'

'O'Leary drew a long straw so she has escaped this time, though she isn't off the hook entirely. As far as I am concerned this is your session, so do what you deem just.'

Hughes lit his pipe. 'I'm not even going to oversee. Your brief is to offer no clemency, to use the strength in your arm, and to brook no insolence, dumb or otherwise. Should any of those ten give you the excuse, then double their stripes.'

'Did they admit to anything?'

'Alice, you could catch one of them with their hand in your pocket and she would emphatically deny she was even in the vicinity.'

'How many am I expected to give each, sir?' Alice enquired, unsure.

'If I had not accepted your explanation, Alice, I would have, had my wrist been capable, provided your bottom with some eighteen very unpleasant shocks.' He shrugged. 'So?'

Alice pulled a face. 'Eighteen?'

Hughes smiled callously. 'And if I thought for one minute that was ineffective, then I would have continued until such a time... well, I expect you get the picture.'

Alice nodded.

'Select your weapon, Miss Hussey. Go whip your backsides. Give them hell.' Alice selected a thinnish rattan, but Hughes frowned. 'You are supposed to pain, not tickle.'

Alice bent the rod, Hughes leant against his desk, legs crossed and spread before him. 'Supple, sir, and heavy for its size. A good spring to the length.' She cut the air with it. 'It will leave a lasting impression, sir, and it will whip all the buttock, not just a few inches.'

Hughes held a finger up. 'Ah yes, I understand your reasoning. By the way, how is your bottom now?'

She blushed and stared at the floor, shamed. 'Sore, sir.'

'One other thing, Alice.'

'Yes sir?' she responded, subdued.

'I would be interested in any of that bunch who might show a certain resilience.'

'Sorry, I don't understand.'

Hughes smiled. 'One that might sigh instead of yelp.'

'Oh,' she whispered.

'I think perhaps you might notice such.'

'What would happen to such a girl?'

Hughes sucked on his pipe, thoughtful. 'I believe that every person has a threshold. Even a girl who can endure, say, a rigorous over the knee spanking followed by three-dozen strokes of the cane from someone like Pierce. Even she can only take so much.'

Alice absently played with the cane, turning it in her hands. 'I have heard, tales and rumour, you understand, that some...' She held up a finger, 'but there again it may have only been one, grows more frenzied by the lash.'

Lips puckered, Hughes dwelt on the suggestion. 'So far I have always found that threshold. There has never been a female that didn't eventually beg me to stop. Some took longer than others, I will admit. The odd one hung on for an interminable time, but eventually every single one of them capitulated. If you hit even the hardiest individual with a cricket bat, then they will quickly crumble. These spirited young maids have stamina for the marathon but not for martyrdom.'

'I have ten bums waiting on me, sir,' Alice pointed out.

'Then let them wait. I love a controversy. Tell me more about this whisper. What was she famous for? Or perhaps it was infamy.'

'The story is that she is a stranger to herself. There is a white side and there is a black side. Neither will recognise the other. They loathe what each stands for, and she is therefore torn. The dark side manipulates and influences. The dark side leads the light to desperate situations. The dark side inveigles, it corrupts. When it retires it leaves the light to face the consequences, to live with the results of that dark passion.'

'And what is this dark passion exactly?'

'She's not sure. There are glimpses. There are moments. But there is no assurance. But it's suggested, when the frenzy takes her and the dark overwhelms the light. When all righteous protests and moral objections are totally eclipsed, then she can give herself wholeheartedly to the lash.'

'Lash, as in whip?'

Alice nodded.

'Food for thought.' Hughes rubbed his jaw. 'I appreciate it is only rumour, but you have heard it, I haven't. How do you think this woman would have reacted to an audience?'

Alice shook her head. 'I don't know.'

Hughes shrugged. 'Just a thought, that's all. I wondered if perhaps exhibitionism was linked in any way.'

'Like I said…'

'You don't know.'

Her back to him, fingers about the handle, Hughes added, 'I

have heard a rumour, too. The right woman could make some very serious money if she were inclined to exhibitionism.'

'Punished before an audience, you mean?'

'No Alice, punished before a camera.'

The click of heels heralded her approach, the waiting girls sceptical, Alice cogitating on her chat with Hughes. He knew what happened last night, but how? Did Pierce give him a full report? Worse, he knew what she was, but then she suspected he had for some time. What now? What next? Did she go along with it, or pretend she wasn't what she was? She wanted what he might have to offer, but she didn't want it. Was that contrary?

Was she losing sight of what was right, wandering blindly into licentiousness? But she wasn't, was she? She could see it coming. So what did that make her? She wanted to go there, then maybe the demons would let her be.

Alice aimed at the girl nearest, cutting her hip with a light stroke. 'You first, in you go.'

Scowling, rubbing her flank as if it hurt, the young brunette ambled reluctantly in.

What was he on about, punished before a camera? Surely principals of government establishments weren't involved in such things? Did he mean Snap? Was Snap working in a similar field to Jay?

Alice met the iced stare of that first victim. 'Name?' she demanded.

'Janet Brooks,' the girl replied defiantly.

'Miss,' Alice corrected.

'Okay; Miss Janet Brooks.'

The young woman tested her, and Alice guessed she might be the hard nut of the pack, placed at the front of the line for good reason. It was a simple matter of win or lose. Alice pushed the tip of the cane beneath the girl's hand, and guided both until the arm posed horizontal. 'Palm uppermost, please,' she requested.

Frowning, a trifle anxious, Janet complied. Alice moved and

struck with lightning speed, that whippy rattan slashing the inmate's hand with a sickening crack. Janet tried desperately to conceal her horror, the arm still level, but pain and tears appeared in her eyes.

'Well?' Alice asked.

'Well what?' Janet managed bravely.

Alice caned that stinging palm a second time. 'This will go on and on, Janet,' she promised. 'It's not my hand. I don't care how much it hurts.'

Brooks' arm fell, and she bit her bottom lip. 'Shit, that hurts!'

'Lift your dress, then stand there and bend over, hands on the bench.' Alice indicated a spot some three feet from the apparatus she had become so obsessed with, then observed the ritual unveiling of the intimate target, Janet's ample bottom becoming exposed. Alice's pulse began to race as Brooks adopted the position, her partly covered behind tightening, proffering a highly sensual objective.

Alice wiped the palm of her right hand on her skirt, then placed the rod to those sacrificial cheeks. She lifted the cane and dealt a potent cut to the crease of thighs and buttocks. She noted with satisfaction the girl rock on her heels and the dip of her head as Janet dealt with the blast of pain.

The young woman's panties offered no protection as Alice's rattan sliced and slashed, Brooks' bottom leaping and trembling with every bitter stroke. The seventh induced a sudden lift of a leg, the young woman grunting with the intensity of that excruciating cut. By the twelfth the girl openly whimpered, her bottom etched, welts burgeoning puffy and sore.

'Ask the next to come in on your way out, please Brooks,' Alice instructed.

Arm aching, fingers cramped, Alice knocked on Hughes' door. One hundred and thirty-eight strokes had taken their toll. One hundred and forty, if she counted the two on Brooks' hand. Alice rapped again, and understood the theory of overindulgence to cure a compulsive disorder. She had caned fat bums, skinny bums, squat bums and the decidedly unattractive bum, and that appealing slap and quiver of bottom flesh no longer held any great attraction for her.

With no reply she tried the door. The office was empty, but Alice nosed inside to replace the cane. She detected the sound of running water, and noticed the shower door stood ajar. A wicked impulse gripped her, Alice's curiosity proving too great. Cautiously she tiptoed to the door, ears pricked, listening for the slightest clue.

Carefully she peered around the door jam, noting Hughes' clothes piled on a stool. Eyes large, she scrutinised the cubicle, the naked form of the principal a haze behind the curtain. Alice shivered, the thrill of audacity seizing her. She smiled, eyes sparkling as Hughes' squared backside encountered the plastic, revealing more than she should have seen.

The girl's eyes widened further, Alice clamping a hand over her mouth as Hughes turned, the misted shadow of his pubic 'V' discernible. Alice squinted, focused on that intimate quarter, trying to make out his genitals. He swayed closer, Alice freezing, the man's face so close to the curtain.

He seemed not to spot her, Alice's gaze descending, attention gripped by the blurred revelation of an impressive portion. She retreated, not daring to push her luck. She crept quietly out into the hallway, carefully closing the door.

Chapter Ten

Time passed quickly, ten days lost in a flurry of activity and new experiences. Alice slept better, the confusing dreams and nightmares having lapsed. Her confidence steadily grew, Mavis beginning to see her as a competitor. Hughes adopted the charming, courteous facade, and said no more about either the pictures or a possible punishment. Alice settled into a daily routine, happy to stay, content to forget her past.

Hughes called upon her regularly, either to assist him personally or to take care of a miscreant or two. She became adept at administering the cane, provoking a dissuasive smart in those errant girls' behinds. Whether she caned, strapped or birched, they always left with tears in their eyes and hands gripping traumatised cheeks. Alice became feared.

'Alice, do you know where to find Dr Doodney?'

The girl nodded. 'I believe so, Mr Hughes.'

'Ground floor, back of the building. It's marked *psychology*. There are a couple of letters here for her. They were addressed to me but they are more pertinent to Sheila.'

Alice picked up the missives, and carefully refolding them she settled both back in their envelopes. 'I won't be long, sir.'

'I thought we had settled on Geoffrey.'

'That's the informal term, sir,' she pointed out, leaving.

Hughes watched that alluring young woman go, the jiggle of her delectable behind as beguiling as ever, then expression determined he whispered, 'Oh, you will dance to my tune, and soon, Hussey. And you will prove the most pleasant, satisfying course on the menu. Oh yes indeed.'

183

Sheila Doodney occupied two rooms, one her office, the second a consulting space. Alice knocked lightly on the office door and waited for a reply. Thirty silent seconds passed so she rapped again. A third knock a half minute later still raised no reply, so she tried the handle. The office unlocked and apparently devoid of human life, Alice crossed the room and dropped the letters on Sheila's desk.

In no immediate hurry to return to Hughes, especially to that unpredictable mood, Alice dallied. She occupied her time by reading the numerous wall charts and notices pinned to a board. She lingered also in the hope Sheila might return. Alice had taken a shine to the woman, and genuinely felt she could trust her. A few words at that time she thought would not go amiss.

A handful of letters remained strewn on the desk, as if scattered by a draught. Alice scanned them, disinterested, but a handwritten one, its corner protruding, caught her eye. The writing was familiar, and angry, fearful, she snatched at it, the neatly scribed address nigh on stopping her heart.

'No,' she whispered. 'No!'

Alice read, a very determined Richard Barker didn't ask, he demanded answers. The wording proved polite, beyond reproach, but within the context lay the barbed wire and threats.

It was originally addressed to Geoffrey Hughes, the principal's reply scrawled across the bottom. *See to this please, Sheila. The man is obviously besotted by his own importance. Have you ever heard of an Alice Hussey? I haven't. Also, use your contacts to try to find out just who this guy is. My understanding is Alice doesn't have any living relatives.*

A feeling of unease crept over her. She replaced the letter. Was Hughes trying to protect her? She didn't understand. Why hide the fact she was there? Why didn't he just tell Richard to get lost? She wasn't a child, and even if she was, Richard would have no jurisdiction over her.

Alice paced, arms folded, expression worried. Best he didn't know she was there, though. He would only cause trouble. Calling himself her uncle! The cheek of it! Demanding to know if she was there or not. Who did he think he was? Why did he even begin to think she might go back to him? What was he up to?

Alice detected voices, two she recognised. She braced herself to explain her presence, but the pair went directly next-door. Curious, Alice pried. She moved close to the frosted glass panel door, cautious not to present a shadow.

'How many sessions have you had, girl? More than most I can assure you. And you always give me the same twaddle-laden tripe. I am beginning to think you're beyond redemption. That you sneer at and snub any conscientious attempt to help you.'

'Perhaps you ain't no good at yer job. Have you thought about that?' The voice was unmistakably that of O'Leary.

A tensed silence ensued, both parties contemplating the next move.

'I have a doctorate, Ruth. I have worked with the criminal fraternity for ten years. You, on the other hand, have wasted your life thus far, in an attempt for an easy ride. All you have ever considered is a buck for a fuck, because that doesn't cost you any effort.'

'I'll give yer a fuck for a quid, miss. See that tongue? Long, ain't it? It can please some very interesting places.'

'Why did you reset Miss Hussey's clocks?'

Alice listened more intently.

'Did I? Supposed to be innocent until proven guilty, yer know.'

'Who else could it be?'

'Don't know. But I suppose it must be me. I mean, there's only another one hundred and eighteen gels up there. But I will tell yer one thing. It weren't Sandy Wareholme, cos she's disappeared. Evaporated, like.'

'Not that it's any of your business, Ruth, but Sandra has returned to prison. Hope wasn't her calling.'

'It ain't mine neither.'

'Oh, you're not going anywhere, young woman. You, we will straighten out. Eventually.'

'So what's it to be? Lie on the couch? Tell yer all about me troubled past? I could tell yer how I was used and abused. I could tell yer all about me childhood, like I didn't have one. Yer knows, dumped by those gits that called themselves parents, and dragged through thirty homes. I could tell yer 'ow me only decent relative was blown to bloody bits by a nazi bomb. But yer don't really care, do yer? All yer wants is a result for a bit of fucking paper. Well, Dr Sheila Doodney, fuck you and yer brainwashin'. Fuck Hope. And fuck yer golden future.'

So far so good, thought Alice sarcastically, but what next?

'Perhaps I should open your mind to possibilities, Ruth. Perhaps we should commence a therapy that generally makes the patient more receptive.'

'Yer ain't sticking no drugs in me.'

'No? I thought you above all else would have leapt at that idea.'

'I ain't no junkie. Junkie's get taken advantage of. No one takes advantage of Ruth O'Leary.'

'I wasn't contemplating drugs. No, something a little more basic. Something fundamentally primitive. A remedy that generally inhibits pride and makes the mind more persuadable.'

'That's one mean looking strap you got there, doc.'

'All the better to instruct you on better manners, don't you think?'

'I thought this was to be therapy. Yer knows, open me mind to that better life.'

'Oh no, Ruth, this part is to reprimand you for your deplorable lack of respect. The ensuing caning will be to open your mind.'

'Good old physical violence, eh? Works every time, don't it?'

'Not always, Ruth, but I have to admit to a certain job satisfaction. If the criminal doesn't respond to discussion, then I can always whip their butts. That seems to eradicate the frustration I used to feel. Good, ain't it, gel?'

'Yer thinks it will have any effect on me? I got the most whipped arse in the place.'

'Your arse has never been seriously whipped, Ruth. Oh, Pierce has teased it. Mr Hughes has smacked it. But it has never been subjected to a long and agonising ordeal.'

Alice detected the change of tone in O'Leary. No longer the brash loudmouth. 'How many was yer thinking of giving me, doc?'

'I recall a hard young woman in another institute some years ago. She constantly caused trouble, and after an insurrection was put down, and this particular young woman named as ringleader, she was subjected to sixty strokes of the strap on her bare flesh. That young woman never so much as caused a whiff of trouble after that.'

'Yer ain't gonna give me sixty with that, are yer?' Ruth asked anxiously.

'Aren't I? Strange, I thought I was.'

'What if I was to own up and say I was sorry, and then lie on your couch and answer every one of yer questions?'

'A change in attitude! Miraculous! And you haven't even felt the remorseless bite of this strap. I really don't want to disappoint me, Ruth. I have been so looking forward to beating your loathsome backside to a pulp. Take your pinafore off, there's an obedient lamb.'

Alice leant against the partition wall, ear close to the door, listening intently. The conversation aroused her, sparked a sexual tornado where reason went to the wall and lust became paramount.

'Underwear, O'Leary. Every stitch.'

Alice closed her eyes, imagined herself in Ruth's place, naked, exposed and vulnerable, that wonderful sensation of impotency cloaking her, awareness sharpening, her flesh becoming super-sensitive.

The girl's hand wandered, touching, igniting, accelerating her ardour. Her breasts tingled, nipples so erect, so receptive. Goose pimples flourished, their effects stimulating.

'That's just fine, Ruth. Now lay facedown on the couch.'

Misty-eyed, delirium sweeping over her, Alice moaned. She lifted the hem of her skirt, fingers caressing, petting her sex.

'Put this underneath your hips. Good. That's perfect. Now, in case you decide you can't take it.'

'You ain't gonna tie me down.'

'Oh, I certainly am.'

Alice eavesdropped on the grunts, both of exertion and discomfort. Her back hard to the wall, legs parted and angled forward, she slipped a hand inside her panties.

'Christ, any tighter and me ankle bones'll break.'

A loud slap, open hand hitting bottom flesh, resounded. 'Save your complaints for the strap.'

'Uh. Uh. You're cutting me bleedin' legs in half.'

'When I am finished your backside will be immobilised. A perfectly presented sitting duck. And girl, I am going to whip it mercilessly.'

'That rope's burning me waist, yer cow!'

Alice jerked to another loud and explosive slap.

'Handcuffs?' Ruth exclaimed.

'Oh yes, Ruth, handcuffs. Now kiss the couch.'

Alice detected the sound of ratchets, two sets clicking consecutively.

'Well that's you well and truly scuppered. You can grasp the legs if you want. After a half dozen I think you might just have to.'

Alice listened intently for that first explosive crack of unforgiving leather on naked buttocks. The sexual tension accumulated, built to a giddy crescendo, and a few seconds later that kinky yearning was appeased. There was nothing quite as dramatic as broad leather striking generous human corpulence. Nothing quite so gratifying as an almighty slap on a firm, well rounded bottom.

'Jesus!' sounded, the recipient shocked.

Alice moaned again, her hand feverishly playing inside her panties.

A second, Ruth whimpering, Alice ascending to a plane of dizzy euphoria. She pressed her bottom against a wood panel, rolled her hips, imagined her cheeks receiving those disabling strokes.

The drubbing proceeded, O'Leary becoming more vociferous in her response, Alice spiralling ever deeper into sexual oblivion. Her fingers sank within her vaginal opening, prodding and rubbing. Her mind floated on an ocean of sadistic intolerance, Ruth's plaintiff cries feeding her bizarre craving.

The tally mounted, every lash pure hell to those tormented dunes, the strength of delivery not receding. Alice visualised the state, the deep discoloration, the sheer intensity of that crimson. She dwelt on the heat exuded, those captured haunches burning fiercely.

Her thoughts drifted to Ruth. She sounded agonised, but had she surmounted the magical barrier? Did every one of those detonations add their raging scald to a mountain of ecstasy? Did Ruth yell to camouflage the truth? Did she long for, crave the visit of pounding leather? Did the fires of sexual climax burn hot in her core?

Perhaps, just perhaps Hughes or Doodney would catch Alice there. Catch her listening, with her hands stuck in her panties. What would they do? What would be their reaction? Would she find herself in Ruth's place? Would they thrash her naked backside with merciless abandon? Would they lash and whip, flog and spank her to a rosy crimson sheen?

Alice gasped, pulled her hands free and her skirt down. 'I really am going to have to do something about this,' she whispered.

Panting, she crept to the door and left, left Ruth to that bumblistering flogging, and Sheila to her consoling physical therapy.

Alice answered an urgent call, thoroughly washing her hands afterwards. They were all at it, and if she had any sense she'd get the hell out of there. She looked at her reflection. 'You're not horrified or appalled, are you, Alice?' she said to herself. 'And you don't want to leave, do you?' What was wrong with her? Six months ago she never gave a thought to masochism, except maybe with regards to Kate, but she didn't even understand that!

'So what's happened? What has changed you so much? You had ideals once. You had ambition. You held unshakeable beliefs. Now, all you crave is sex. You're a sad little creature, Alice Hussey, and you deserve what you get.'

That evening morbid curiosity got the better of Alice. She waited for Ruth, and on the pretext of discussing their fateful meeting a week and a half earlier, she beckoned her to her room.

'Let's get one thing straight, gel. I ain't getting into no trouble. Me bum can't take no more today.'

Relieved she didn't have to pry, Alice enquired. 'Another hiding?'

'A humdinger, Al. Me arse is black and blue. And don't you go losing it, but yer could hang yer fucking hockey sticks on the welts.'

Alice grinned and Ruth knelt, then lay facedown on Alice's bed. 'Don't mind, do yer gel?'

Alice shook her head. 'Who whopped you Ruth? And why?'

'Don't matter who or why really. It happened and I doubt if I'll be able to sit on it for two or three days. But of course I will. I'll have to. That's part of the punishment, see. Make you sit on a real hard chair for hours. Oh, you can squirm if you wants another licking.'

'Can I look?'

'Oh, you fucking queer perv.'

'No, just concerned.'

'Come on, Al. You is a queer perv and you knows it. Yer was all over me like a rash, and it weren't no concern then. It were lust, the same as with me. Now tell me it weren't.'

Alice knelt, and very cautiously she lifted Ruth's skirt. 'I'm not sure what I am, but I do know I'm not a lesbian. Not completely.'

'Yer likes a dick up yer tunnel, does yer? Don't we all. The trouble is dicks come expensive in here. Look at poor old Sandy. Reckon she got herself shafted and then moved somewhere, where she couldn't tell tales.'

'God, the state of your bum! What did they hit you with, a baseball bat?'

'Nah, it were a demon strap. I lost count, but it were somewhere around three dozen before she gave up.'

'She? As in Sheila Doodney?'

'Yer's quick, ain't yer. Next yer'll be telling me yer was stood outside.'

'Looks like she caned you, too.'

'Hmm, but by then I'd gone numb.'

'Did any of it…?'

'Turn me on? Yeah, it always does. Especially now, with your cool hands all over me hot arse. Now that I do like. And if yer was to stick a couple of fingers between me legs I wouldn't complain.'

'I don't think that would be wise, Ruth.'

O'Leary smiled. 'Did Pierce cane yer last time?'

'Yes, he did.'

'He'll keep his mouth shut though, if yer divvies up.'

'I believe he has.'

'You must have bedazzled him that night, cos he never did get back to me.'

Alice eased Ruth's skirt back. 'Best get off to your dorm. What did Sheila thrash you for, anyway?'

'Pissing with your clocks, besides giving her some mouth.'

'Was it you?'

'Nah. Why would I? And I don't reckon it were any of the gels, neither.'

'Who then?'

'In this place nothing is what it seems, and no one can be trusted, Al. Someone wanted you late on duty. Someone wanted to either see you thrashed, or have an excuse to do it themselves.'

Alice shrugged. 'Then it could have been just about anyone.'

'Ain't that the bleedin' truth.'

Alice strolled the length of the hallway to Ruth's dormitory, and hugged the girl before saying goodnight, then Ambling back, deep in thought, she failed to hear Pierce open his door. Her pondering was abruptly shattered as her blouse was seized from behind, the fabric pulled tight to her breasts. 'Nearly time for that second payment,' he reminded her, boozy breath on her cheek.

She wriggled, the lecher's hand groping her buttock. 'Let me go, Pierce,' she warned. 'And get your dirty paw off my backside.'

'Want to make it tonight? Get it done with?'

'I said let me go, Pierce.'

'What's going on, Eddie?' Hughes asked, appearing at the end of the hallway.

Pierce relaxed his grip, his face reddening. 'Just a bit of fun, Geoff. That's all it was.'

'Looked more serious than that to me.'

Pierce released Alice, the girl quickly straightening her blouse. 'No Geoff, like I said, a bit of fun, that's all,' the bully bumbled.

'Go and pack your stuff, Eddie,' Hughes instructed.

'What? Are you sacking me?'

Hughes shook his head. 'What, over a bit of fun? Of course not, Eddie. No, I think you deserve better than that pokey flat, with all those criminals to keep your eye on. How can you possibly get a good night's sleep? I want to give you the suite next to Sheila's offices. More room there. A bit of well deserved peace and quiet. You can go to bed knowing nothing will wake you.'

'What about the riffraff? Who's going to keep an eye on them?'

'I was rather hoping Alice would. She has proved herself an excellent disciplinarian. What say you, Alice?'

The principal's diplomacy impressed her. Hughes demoted Pierce, effectively removed him from the dormitories, and made it sound like an improvement. 'Yes, thank you, sir. I'm sure I can cope,' she accepted.

'Settled then. See you're in your new home by Sunday, please, Eddie. No point in delaying matters.'

Scowling, grumbling, the custodian pushed past Hughes and disappeared into his rooms.

'I don't know what Pierce thought he was doing,' Alice said, still a little flustered by the assault, thankful for Hughes' calm and timely intervention.

'Don't you? I thought that was quite obvious. The man was in a state of arousal. Another two minutes and your eyes would have been popping.'

Hughes guided Alice to his office and closed the door. He sat behind his desk, and indicated for Alice to sit on the chair before it.

'I did nothing to encourage him,' she stated defensively.

'That is a matter of opinion,' he countered, hurting her with his unexpected barb. 'I run a tight ship here, Alice. I generally know or hear of everything that goes on in Hope. People talk. Walls have ears. Not much passes unmissed, and I think you gave Eddie the come on without realising it. That's why I didn't sack him.'

'I didn't mean to.'

'Alice, you are an exceedingly attractive, might I say beautiful young woman. You have the body of a goddess. You are highly desirable, and you emanate a certain innocence which I'm afraid merely enhances the attraction.'

'Do you find me desirable?' Alice asked, spilling naivety.

'Yes, I do.'

'I see.'

'Does that offend you?'

'No, not at all, I'm flattered.'

'However, just because I find you engaging that doesn't mean I'll abuse my position. One should exercise control, demonstrate a certain professional detachment.'

'Yes, of course.'

Hughes pondered the girl before him for a few quiet seconds. 'Yes, you really do have a delightful figure. I've not seen better. Did you think about that suggestion I made? You know, the film.'

'How do you know this photographer?' Alice enquired.

'Army.'

'Is he above board?'

'Hardly. He makes soft porn movies.'

'Soft porn?'

'As opposed to hard porn.'

'Is that a contact a man of your standing should have?'

Hughes leaned forward, his elbows on his desk. 'That sounds snobbish to me. Why shouldn't I know him? Why shouldn't he do what he does? This is the last chance saloon for many. Half of those girls will go back on the streets. Barely any of them will find a decent job. They are what they are. My job, the Hope charter is to keep them out of prison. So if a few of them find lucrative work taking off their clothes, then surely that's better than laying flat on their backs.'

'But I'm not one of them, am I?'

'Oh, I see, you're destined for great things are you?'

'I didn't mean that.'

Hughes sat back again, scrutinising her. 'I'm offering you the chance to kill several birds with one stone. It will be exciting. You're a girl who strikes me as liking a bit of a thrill. It will prove infinitely satisfying. You understand my meaning? And it will offer a damn good income.'

Their eyes locked. 'What would I have to do?'

'He has to fill at least forty minutes of film. You can do several sessions if you want. That really depends on how much you can take in one sitting. It's for real. There's no trickery involved. And the more severe it is, the more copies are likely to be sold.'

'You say this man is trustworthy.'

'I'd stake my honour on it.'

'I don't know, Mr Hughes. It doesn't seem right.'

'I'm not going to talk you into it. It's your choice. Meet the man. See what he has to offer. Chat about expectations. Do a test run. Whatever you want, Alice.'

194

Chapter Eleven

'Personally, I think she is one very confused young lady. What have your chats unearthed? Anything positive?'

'Alice has steered clear of me for a week or more. I don't think your bright idea of sending her down to witness O'Leary's smacking helped. She probably sees me as a sadistic tyrant now.'

'How was I to know? Anyway, we know what she is. All we have to do is draw it to the surface and boil the pot. The girl is being driven mad by something she can't come to terms with. Arouse her enough and she won't be able to help herself.'

Hughes tapped his pipe on a glass ashtray. 'You chatted with her that night at my house.'

'I told you after what transpired. Alice is undoubtedly a masochist, but she is also devout and responsible. There is a serious conflict of interests. To her it is Satan versus God Almighty. I don't think she will agree unless she's convinced she won't burn in purgatory for it, or she can be persuaded that life is life, and one has to make the best of any opportunity.'

'Shame, really. She could make us a fortune. She is sex on legs. I get the horn just thinking about her.'

'Well, you'll have to persuade her she's not being used.'

'Or…' he mused, baiting the women to enquire further.

'Or what?'

'Or do it without her knowing.'

'How can you manage that?'

Hughes laughed. 'Oh, it's so simple. All I have to do is snap my fingers, and I won't have to pay her a penny.'

'Like I said, Alice, you don't have to do this. I was wrong to suggest it in the first place.'

'Mr Hughes, I've thought long and hard about it. I've been thrashed so many times these last few months, for what I can only state is for other people's pleasure, so why shouldn't I be selfish? Why shouldn't I make the most of what I have, while I can? And why shouldn't I be paid for it?'

'I wish I hadn't said anything.' Hughes glanced skyward.

'I'm glad you did. I knew someone else in the trade, so to speak. I would have done it for him, but like you are trying to, he talked me out of it. I understand why. I know you are just doing what you think is best for me.

'This is the way to Snap's house, isn't it?'

'Snap's part of it. He has a partner. A professional filmmaker and actor.'

Ten minutes later Hughes drew the car to a halt on the familiar drive. 'We can still turn around and go home, Alice.'

'Thanks, but let's go and talk.'

Alice shook Davies' hand. 'And this is my partner in crime, so to speak, John James.'

Much younger than Snap, John took Alice's hand. Keen blue eyes probed her, examined and approved. 'You will certainly do, young lady. Oh yes, you will do.' He spoke to Snap. 'It would be sacrilege not to have this Aphrodite recorded for posterity.'

John clasped her hand with both of his. 'You will stun your audience, Alice. Fans will pay a fortune for a lock of your hair.' He bent to her ear and whispered, 'And even more if it's a pubic lock.'

Alice laughed. 'Not a chance there, I'm afraid.'

'Ah, smooth as a baby's bot, I presume.'

'Um, I'd like to know more about the deal,' Alice pressed.

'Quite. A businesswoman I see. We will pay you a fee initially, for your time and,' John grinned, 'suffering.'

'It's won't be a huge amount, more a recognition of your

potential,' Snap continued. 'Let's say, ten pounds.'

'And is that it?'

'No, of course not. You'll be due royalties. Ten percent of sales.'

'How much will that be?'

'Impossible to say. There are a number of factors to take into account. The main one being how far you're prepared to go.'

'In what respect?' Alice asked, feeling a little anxious. 'It sounds like you're talking sex.'

'Both,' said John. 'Look, sit down. I'll explain. Wine?'

Alice nodded and the man poured two glasses, handing one to Alice. 'I don't know how much has been explained to you. I would prefer the film to be forty minutes minimum, and I'd like it to be one scenario. So allowing for the verbal chastisement, you know, the lead in and reasoning, and the stripping and bondage, there will be approximately thirty minutes left to fill. Obviously the punter will buy for the content, and that content should be mostly implement on flesh. Do you see what I'm getting at?'

Alice nodded. 'One long thrashing, I assume.'

'Good. You understand.'

'And the sex; what do you expect from me?'

'The further you are willing to go the better. It's as simple as that.'

'I'm not.' She smiled disarmingly. 'I might do the punishment bit, but no more.'

John shook his head ruefully. 'Shame. Most films finish with vaginal, oral, or anal sex. How about being intimately touched?'

Alice abruptly stood up. She fastened her jacket. 'It's been nice talking to you, Mr James. Do you script these sessions?'

'Loosely. A broad concept. Some dialogue, yes.'

'Send me something. Let me read it, and then I'll give you a decision.'

Hughes drove Alice back to Hope. 'Going to give it a miss?'

'Don't know.'

'It all sounds a bit tacky, I suppose.'

'It's not that, Mr Hughes. I just don't know if it's me. I don't want to go into detail, but I think what's inside my head is sacrosanct. I am what I am, but it doesn't mean I want it exploited.'

'I understand that. Forget I ever mentioned it.'

'No, I *will* think about doing it, but if I do it will be on my terms.'

'You could always write your own script.'

Alice smiled.

'Then it would encompass precisely what you want.'

'And tell the world my innermost thoughts.'

'I'm beginning to think you're obsessed with this girl.'

'Is that the green-eyed monster talking?'

'No, it's a professional analyst's opinion.'

'Maybe I'm wrong, or perhaps it's merely the challenge, but I feel… no, I'm convinced that Miss Hussey can provide a lucrative income.'

'Geoff, she's not an inmate. You can't do with her what you have with the others.'

'I can with the right angle. I suppose it would be easier if she was willing, but she seems to be a bit of a righteous bitch. Oh, it's all there, Sheila. She has the bias. She's an orphan. She's completely alone in the world. She's naïve, trusting and wears that simple innocence. She's ripe for plucking.'

Hughes rubbed his eyes. 'Peter Carmichael spotted her a few days ago. Do you know what he said?'

Sheila shook her head, interested.

'Provide me with her for a weekend and I will donate two hundred to the Hope fund.'

'He always did have more money than sense.'

Hughes eased his frame from the armchair and ambled toward Sheila. 'They say money is the root of all evil. Personally, I think it's obsession. Or perhaps compulsion.' He picked up a length of broom handle and spun it cheerleader style. 'We are free spirits so it's said, but are we? I'm convinced we are victims of our own cerebral chemistry, that we are left with little choice in some matters.'

Hughes lifted one of a puzzled Sheila's arms, and slid the pole the length of her sleeve. 'Especially sexual inclinations.' He pushed the handle deeper, the end chafing her back. 'See this as an experiment. Level your other arm.'

Bemused, the doctor raised her limb, Hughes sliding the shaft until it protruded from the opposite sleeve. 'You trust me, don't you Sheila?'

'You know I do.'

Hughes stepped back, hands on hips, scrutinising her stance. 'Good. Quite defenceless, aren't you?'

'I can still kick and bite.'

'Of course you can. Now as I was saying. What provokes us? Why do we do the most outrageous of things? Drugged, is the answer.'

'What's brought this on? And what's the point of me having this broom handle shoved in my shirt?'

'I was just trying to explain why I am going to sexually assault you, that's all.'

Sheila laughed nervously. 'Nice one, Geoff. Now if you don't mind I'm tired.'

'Testosterone is a powerful coercion. It seems to overwhelm accepted moral decency. It persuades the rational to be irrational. It rids the mind of virtuous objection. Or perhaps it's a case of primitive instinct set free.'

He stood directly before Sheila, his formidable strength of character irresistible. The man moved before she could react, his hands ripping her blouse apart. She stared dumbfounded, mouth agape, disbelieving.

'Nice tits, Sheila,' he remarked crudely, scrutinising them. 'What's the subliminal message? You know, no bra.'

'You pig!' she gasped. 'How *dare* you?'

Hughes laughed. 'Oh, I dare. I've had the yearning – no, compulsion – to do that for a long time. See, irrational. Not responsible for my actions. Unless you have a more educated reason?

'No?' Geoff cupped a breast and fondled it. 'A small titty, but still a very pretty titty.'

Sheila brought a knee up in a wild attempt to crush his balls, but Hughes caught the limb, fingers gripping the thigh. 'Firm... you are in rather fine fettle for a bird of thirty-five.'

'You will regret this, mister! I swear you will rue the moment...'

'Perhaps I will, in the cold light of day. That moment of madness.' His hand ran the length of her thigh, settling close to her panties. 'And there again, maybe not.'

'Okay, you've had your feel, now what?'

'This.' Hughes stooped, thrust both hands high up her skirt and grabbed the elastic of her underwear, and in one swift movement the skimpy cotton panties fell to her ankles.

He straightened, and with supreme arrogance stared into her eyes. 'How do you feel, Sheila? Vulnerable?'

The doctor spat in his face.

'Personally I feel... I feel... can you guess how I feel, doctor?'

'Like a bully?'

Hughes' arm dived beneath her skirt again, hand lifting the hem, fingers pushing between her thighs. 'No, like this.'

The woman tried in vain to cross her legs, Hughes groping her vagina. 'You must have an analysis, doc. It's well known psychologists are cold and calculating. So give me your prognosis.'

Hatred in her face, Sheila refused capitulation. 'I would assume you are overworked, that the pressure of running this place has dented your reason.'

Hughes withdrew his hand. 'No, that's absolute crap.' He picked a short cane off a table, then strolling around her, cane bent, twisted and flexed between his fists, he enlightened her. 'I was born callous, indifferent and brutal. The war offered me as much in satisfaction as it did in horror. I suspect it also accentuated a mean streak. Making people suffer extends enormous enjoyment to me. I get one hell of a sexual kick from domination and,' he struck her bottom with a solid stroke, Sheila squealing and rising to tiptoe, 'inflicting pain.'

'You bastard! That hurt.'

'Put it down to experience. Now you know what those girls suffer at your vindictive hands.'

'They deserve it. I don't.'

'Don't you? Are you sure? If you did an Alice and confessed your sins, would you walk away without so much as a Holy Mary?'

'Shit! That still stings.'

'Then have another.' Sheila gasped as that rattan thudded ferociously against her skirt-covered buttocks. 'Now, answer the question.'

'I'm not a catholic. I'm not even religious.'

Hughes pressed the rod against her naked belly. 'Have you sinned?'

'You wouldn't. Not there.'

'One. Two. Three.'

'I...'

Sheila doubled, outstretched arms unable to comfort. She danced from foot to foot, writhing.

'Too late,' Hughes announced.

'I don't understand. Why are you doing this? I thought we were partners.'

'We are. Partners. We do everything together. Laugh. Cry. Make money. Hurt one another. Have sex.'

Sheila straightened, and wincing she stated adamantly, 'Oh no, we are definitely not having sex.'

'No? Then you have a problem. Red stripes. Welts. Those reactive marks of punishment inflame my libido. Unless I vent the pressure I will just keep on inflicting them.'

'What can I say? How can I stop you from doing this?'

Hughes pointed the cane at her chest. 'Tell you what, Sheila, you can return the favour next week if you want.'

'I don't want! My arms are aching. Take this broom handle out, for Christ's sake!'

'Oh dear, profanity. That has to be worth, what? What would you say taking the Lord's name in vain should cost you?'

Sheila chewed her lower lip, eyes brimming with tears, and she simply shook her head in dismay.

'How about three strokes to the titties?'

'No, no, please Geoff, don't.'

'But Sheila,' he mocked, 'what you gonna do when you get to hell? If you can't take three lashes to the tits you're going to find purgatory pretty intolerable, aren't you?'

'Look, Geoff, why don't we just talk about this? I'm sure I can help…'

Hughes roared. 'Help? I don't want help. I'm having the time of my life. In fact, I don't know why I didn't do this sooner.'

Sheila tried to evade the slash of cane. She screwed her face in horror as the rod bit and ignited a breast. She bent, breasts suspended, and Hughes arced low, catching both as they swayed.

Sheila showed him her back, her bottom thrust out, body in a semi-crouch. Two dynamic strokes, one to the left and one to the right cheek urged her forward. Hughes followed, an arrogant smirk demonstrating his pleasure.

She met with the wall, the woman desperately pressing her stinging breasts to the cold paintwork. Geoff grabbed her by the hair and yanked her head back. 'One more for Christ, doc.'

'Breasts are delicate organs,' she protested. 'You could—'

The slap of flexile rod cutting those supple knolls stopped her mid-sentence. The woman twisted and turned, executed a frantic dance, the stripes on her breasts a fiery red.

'Tits are ninety percent fat. Pleasantly presented fat, but fat all the same.'

'How would you like me to cane your balls?' she hissed.

'Hardly the same thing.' Hughes grinned. 'But we could draw equivalents.'

Sheila eyed him with horror. 'No. No. You're not hitting me there.'

'And how can you stop me?'

She tugged on her sleeves, pressuring the fabric, the wooden pole digging painfully into her shoulders. 'Damn!' She snatched, jerked her arms in frustration. 'Please, let me go.'

Hughes clamped a hand to her breast, fingers probing the stinging meat. 'Could be a long night. There's your arse to cover.' He swished the cane, Sheila jerking. 'Then your thighs; back and front.' He ran a fingernail down her belly. 'This… and you already know how much that hurts.' He sank his hand beneath Sheila's waistband, fingers locating the jumble of pubic curls. 'And here; that I will enjoy. You may find it interesting too.' One finger slid between her legs. 'And of course, here.'

'What do you want from me, Geoff?' she panted desperately.

'Ever heard of Papillon?'

'Of course I have.'

'He witnessed a Negro being whipped all day and all night. The guards took it in turns. Endlessly lashing him for hours on end. Could be you.'

'What do you *want*?' she pleaded, anger, frustration and fear intermingled.

'You don't get it, do you? I have what I want. He threw his arms wide. This place. The Hope. One hundred and twenty girls to do with much as I please. I have a magnificent specimen of young womanhood who is settling deeper and deeper in the mire of gullibility. I have a stupid secretary who is so devoted and terrified of me she will do nigh on anything to keep me happy.'

Hughes unfastened Sheila's skirt before urging it over her trim hips. 'If I told Mavis to run naked to Flint High Street and back, she probably would.'

The skirt shimmered down to join her panties on the floor. 'And I have Pierce. The muscle, should I ever need it. Now there's a fiercely loyal aide. Thick as two short planks, but loyal.'

Hughes ran a hand over her naked buttocks, inspecting the substance and marks on an exquisitely prominent bottom. 'I also have you. A comrade in arms. You just need to understand your place in the pecking order, that's all. Once you realise that

I am god, then all will be well again.'

'Fine, I accept that. I always have. So I don't understand why you have to prove it now, like this.'

'No, Sheila, you are just saying that. You seem to think you are my equal. You talk to me as if you are. You advise me as if you are. And you even have the audacity to criticise me.'

Sheila heard the telltale swish of incoming cane. Her buttocks flexed apprehensively, the woman thrusting her hips forward in a vain attempt to diffuse the impact. Hughes smiled, satisfied at her manic jig, her bottom severely stung.

'So what have I got to suffer before you accept I know my place?'

'Your bum appears quite impervious to the strokes so far. Must be quite a fit bum. It's definitely a nice bum. Pretty well-rounded; nicely plump; very feminine, I would say.'

'The sort you like to beat, I assume.'

'Not that bothered, Sheila. A bum is a bum, and can be the source of the utmost discomfort. That's what matters. Though I do admit to a certain appreciation of the way yours quivers.'

The doctor's backside trembled to another act of brute violence. 'I'll give you a clue. Attitude persuades.'

'I've said I accept my place. What more do you want?'

'Stick your bum out.'

Sheila grimaced and offered that snug behind, knowing she would get striped anyway.

Hughes caned it three times in quick succession. 'Attitude, doctor. You're an intelligent woman. Think it through.'

Her bottom stinging fitfully, she offered, 'I'm *sorry* if I didn't show due respect. I will in future.'

Her attempt at appeasement was met with abrupt hostility, her marked posterior blasted by another three slashes. 'Perhaps abasement might mean something to you.'

'Oh, you want me to crawl.'

'I want you to kneel. Kneel before me.'

Sheila faced him, then fell to her knees. 'Will this do?'

'Not really, but it's a start.'

She watched concerned as the man unfastened and dropped his trousers, underpants quickly following, her uneasiness met by Hughes' erect shaft. 'You don't expect me to…'

'Hmmm, I do. How expert are you? Can you ease back the foreskin with your teeth? I would like you to. Ease it, that is.'

'You're *asking* me now?'

'No, just being polite.' Hughes flexed the rattan as a warning.

'And what if I say, go ahead and whip the shit out of me?'

'The pleasure would all be mine. Same ending, though.'

Her backside still smarted, Sheila unsure of how many stripes she all ready sported, she scrutinised his cock, the plum inches from her mouth. 'And if I do it? Will that be it?'

'I won't pain you any more, if that's what you mean.'

'Look Geoff, I haven't, you know, for a long time. I've been celibate for nigh on—'

Hughes seized her by the ears and forced his bulbous tip between her lips. 'Now, suck me,' he growled.

His erection overfilled her mouth, stuffed it to capacity, Sheila barely able to contend with the massive poker.

'Suck hard, and swallow when the time *comes*,' he demanded. 'Ah, that's it.' Hughes threw his head back and sighed. 'Suck me, and dwell on this magnificent specimen penetrating, sinking, cramming your tight, embracing cunt.'

Hughes thrust, several inches of that thick shaft immersed before he withdrew, the stem wet with saliva.

Mouth wide, lips stretched to excess, Sheila's expression was unreadable. She struggled, barely coped with that prodigious dome. Then as Hughes drew back for another plunge the woman sank her teeth into his pride.

Eyes wild, Hughes staring like a madman, he lifted her by her ears, his erection sliding clear, and forcing her to tiptoe he promised, 'You will pay dearly for that. And then I'll shove it where there are no teeth.'

He dragged her to the table, picking a rectangular leather paddle from a shelf en route. He forced her over the surface, her breasts flattened, bottom positioned for a vertical assault. A slap reverberated about the room, Sheila's buttocks lurching, flesh ignited.

'Do your worst, you tyrant. I'm glad I bit your loathsome cock. Next time I'll bite it right... ow!'

Hughes laid into her, that hefty paddle lively in flight, slamming into her butt with alacrity. Those posterior cheeks shuddered almost continuously, the battered flesh barely stilled before another explosion set them flying again. Hughes set a pattern, the upper reaches of the far haunch, followed by the lower corpulence of the nearest. And then the far lower, succeeded by the near upper. Every three to four seconds that ravaged behind met with the destructive energy of four millimetres of uncompromising leather. Every four heartbeats a flank heaved beneath twenty-one square inches of pounding hide.

The woman's buttocks speedily reacted, burning red. They deepened to crimson, the once silken, pallid haunches burnished, bruised and mottled. Sheila's body jerked with every detonation, her backside beaten raw. Eyes squeezed tightly closed, open mouth distorted, she laid her forehead against the table.

The guttural cries had subsided, her body virtually inert. Little moved except for the jerk of her torso and that leaping bottom. She sucked air, moaned and sighed, those being the only signs of response.

Hughes, still naked below the waist, his cock in a state of high arousal, laid the paddle on those lambasted dunes. Wordlessly he parted her legs, and stepping closer he thrust, his length sliding deep into her vagina. Sheila tensed, then sighed contentedly.

Hughes began with a measured prod, the momentum aggressive. Focussing on that thrashed butt, the savagery expended and the pitch of unsettled cheeks both stimulated. Hughes fucked, Sheila very much plundered. Minutes passed, the man breathing hard, his pace constant, that sexual well filled and stretched.

Sheila eventually tensed, groaned, then gasped, a series of whimpers spilling into the silence.

Pulling clear, seed thwarted, Hughes slid her further onto the table. Cane back in his hand he stood to one side of those levelled buttocks, gauging a stroke. He noted the anticipatory gathering and tightening of thighs, the pull on flank muscles and consequential dimpling of haunches.

The rod wavered aloft, then swept down with precise and devastating strength. The tip lashed, slashed and arced, the solid *thwip* of rattan on bare arse highly rewarding. Sheila twitched, jaw clenched, expression pained.

Hughes levied a second, the cane bouncing on tightened behind. Utilising every ounce of his considerable strength he thrashed that rump again and again. Repeatedly the quiet was ruptured by the shriek of cane, the thump of connecting missile and a gurgle from the punished.

Fourteen volatile strokes later Sheila's thigh muscles drew rigid, those limbs held tightly together, her blitzed, striped, marred bum inflexible.

Hughes stripped off his shirt and tie, tossing them over a chair. Naked, he drew the pole from Sheila's blouse, dropping it to the floor. He rolled her onto her back, the woman torpid. Legs lifted to the vertical, Hughes rested her ankles on his shoulders. His excited cock touched, provoked her inviting gates of womanhood. Pressure parted the folds, hard meat sliding effortlessly in. Eyes still closed Sheila's face twitched, her only recognition.

Hughes pumped, he rode her indiscriminately, penis thrusting at a rapid pace. Her breasts danced, shook and trembled, the woman's body constantly jarred by Hughes' energetic lunges.

A few minutes later the man's rhythm eased. He bent, threaded his arms beneath her back and lifted. Sheila met him, hands raised, fingers clutching locks of his hair. Expression determined she pressed her mouth to his, lips labouring, tongue probing.

Her thighs wrapped about his waist, calves pressed to his arse, ankles crossing. His hands supported hot, welted, sore buttocks. Fingers clawed at raw flesh. Breasts met pectorals, the pressure flattening them. Hughes persisted, wrapped in woman, his hips jerking, cock plumbing her depths.

Hughes knelt, the pair still engaged in fervent kissing. He squatted, lay back, Sheila managing to retain his dick. She stared down at him, gaze malicious, a sneer lifting a lip. Her teeth met, lips bared, the enamel white. Her hands swept up his torso, settling on the pectorals. Fingernails sank and gouged his flesh.

She rose, his slick pole gleaming, its exposure short. Sheila plunged, his shaft cramming and stretching her burrow, the manner most satisfying.

Galvanised by her antics, Hughes lay; content to wallow in that sexual manipulation. The constant suck of pussy juices emphasised the act, focussed his attention on that union, his rigid stem ramming between her legs. He savoured the uninterrupted bounce and sway of breast flesh, those orbs etched by the cane. He revelled in the twist and prance of her body, the rise and drop of hips, the feel of her bum slapping his thighs.

Sweat beaded, trickled, meandered the length of her throat. Perspiration accumulated and dribbled between those lurching breasts. Moisture lay slick on her belly and heavy between the driven legs. She panted constantly, her mind away, seeking consummation.

The swell of orgasm crawled electrifyingly through his groin, expanding with disabling strength. Each lunge by the energetic Sheila accentuated it further, Hughes seizing her breasts, squeezing them remorselessly in those seconds of undisputed ecstasy.

His balls went into spasm, cock jerking, pumping seed, the squirts felt by the heaving Sheila. Knowing she would lose her prod she reached down and wrapped moist fingers about the shaft. She held it, squeezed it, and drove her hips onto it with furious abandon.

She squatted, Hughes' withering penis unable to appease her further. She replaced the flaccid meat with four fingers and thrust again and again, the thumb rubbing madly at the nub.

She gasped. She whimpered, then collapsed on top of Hughes.

Some five minutes passed before either spoke. 'I wonder what Alice would say if she knew what a freak you are,' Hughes remarked casually.

'Is that the pot calling the kettle black?'

'Could be. You know, if you were a bit younger I could hire you out.' Hughes winced as Sheila sank her teeth into his chest. 'You can certainly take a licking, I'll say that for you.'

'And you can be so demonstrative. Sometimes I'm not sure if you're playing for real. Like tonight; that sends shivers through my fanny. When I begin to believe it, well that's when everything goes haywire. A rather ecstatic haywire, I might add.'

'You're a good fuck, Sheila. One of the best.'

'And you, sweetheart, are the perfect bastard.'

'Nice of you to say so.'

'So what have you planned for Alice?'

'Alice?' Hughes sighed. 'I am going to give her what she wants. What she hasn't the grit to ask for. I've grown weary of her running in circles. It's time for my wrist to heal and show her what she is.'

'If you go too far she might turn tail and run.'

'I have come to believe she can take whatever I choose to dish out. The daft bitch hankers for a religious flogging. She thinks that will put her to rights, but she hasn't a clue. She has no understanding of her bias whatsoever. She just doesn't realise that sadomasochism is just like coke. The bigger the dose the higher the lift, and the more you need next time. I reckon she's more corruptible than you.

'But there again, she has the most delicious bum; a bum I will take to the limits of endurance and beyond. She'll claw her way through the pain barrier and then we will have one highly aroused young woman, ready to do just about anything.'

'Just about anything?'

'Are you and O'Leary still pleasing each other?'

'Point taken.'

'And Alice? Are you interested in her?'

'She's a very attractive girl. Why, do you think she's bisexual?'

'It's a definite possibility.'

'Well there's an interesting eventuality.' She rolled from Hughes' naked body and lay on her side stroking his chest. 'Geoff?'

'Yeah?'

'My bum's cooled down, and so has something else.'

Slowly his cock took strength. It filled, expanded, rose from its slumbers. 'Go and get the paddle.'

Chapter Twelve

Geoffrey Hughes, although a determined and ruthless man, was also a creature of fancy. Alice was to him the cream on the cake, an ultimate pleasure, and once he had consumed that nectar he would find his life wanting again; or rather, his perverted needs. So Hughes kept putting the day of reckoning off, thereby continually savouring the thrill of anticipation.

Alice said no more about the film idea. She concluded there was time aplenty, and would only proceed when sure of her feelings. Her new responsibilities, which she took seriously, occupied her almost fulltime. She lapsed into a routine, content for the moment to stay at Hope.

Pierce moved out on the designated Sunday, adopting the ground floor rooms for his new home. His pride already mauled, the man suffered another blow when Hughes relieved him of the top floor keys, and his access to all those wanton young women.

Another ten days drifted by, Hughes exerting his charm, Alice cautiously placing her trust in him. They chatted often and she accepted his increasing closeness; an arm around her waist and regular pats on her bottom.

The inmates bowed to Alice's discipline, the heartened young woman cracking the odd hard nut. Uncertainty, regret and commiseration melted, and a calculating and confident disciplinarian emerged from the cocoon of uncertainty. Alice welted bums with aplomb. She thrashed miscreants without concern for their suffering, and afterwards she enjoyed a feeling of well-being.

Even Hope adhered to Sunday as a day of rest. The inmates

were generally confined to quarters, with certain parts of the building and the quadrangle available for recreational purposes. With Pierce keeping his beady eye on those that occupied the lower floors, Alice was left responsible for the upper.

Late on what proved to be a balmy early October afternoon, a combination of heat and exhaustion took its toll. Alice lay on her bed with the intention of grabbing forty winks.

The young woman fell to a heavy sleep, dreams flitting inconsequentially, the insanity of that inconceivable world paradoxically quite acceptable. Through the haze of a summer's steamy woodland a hand caressed, Alice trying to determine who touched her. Confusing, panicky seconds lumbered ponderously, the girl unable to comprehend. Then Jay's welcome features filled the void, Alice subjected to crushing pangs of homesickness.

Smiling, she stirred, arms stretching. The touch became more tangible, fingers stroking her belly, the sensation calming, reminiscent of early childhood years.

Her father replaced Jay, his voice soft, distant. 'Feeling sick, Alice? Never mind. Daddy will ease it. Daddy will take the sick away.'

Alice clasped the man's wrist and held it. 'But you're not my daddy, are you?' she accused. 'You lied. You lied! So who is my father? You *must* know.'

Reality probed the mists, consciousness surfacing. Her eyelids sprang open, focus blurred with sleep. Her lips parted, mouth dry, her question lost to torpor.

'What the devil is going on, Alice?' Hughes demanded, having prodded her awake.

'I... I... I must have dropped off.' Alice sat bolt upright, her head spinning with the premature movement.

Hughes pointed out into the corridor. 'They need constant and vigilant observation, and I need someone I can trust. Have I made a mistake giving you the responsibility?'

Alice stared stupidly, dumbfounded.

'They were running amok. Just as well I popped over, isn't

it?'

The girl battled to clear the fog of sleep, excuse beyond her.

'Well, have the courtesy to answer me, young lady.'

'I'm sorry. I only laid down for five minutes.'

'About two hours ago. It's not good enough, is it?'

'No sir. I really am sorry.'

Hughes shook his head. 'Sorry doesn't cut the mustard. I've heard that word from you too often. Do you require twelve hours a day sleep? Is that it? Because if you do you're no good to me.'

'No, honestly.' Alice rubbed her eyes. 'I've no excuse. I apologise, sir. I'll try to make sure it doesn't happen again.'

'And in turn, I shall provide you with an incentive.'

Her jaw dropped, Alice whispering, 'Oh.' Apprehension tightened her stomach, the man's bearing intimidating, inspiring a stirring dread.

'Be outside my study at eight. And don't be late.'

'Yes sir, of course.' Hughes stepped towards the door. 'Can I ask what to expect?' she chanced, not sure if she wanted to know.

Hughes held the door open. 'Do you really need to ask that?'

Alice stared at her feet. 'I guess not. I suppose I've had it coming.'

'See it as paying your debts, as well as a very good reason not to let me down again.'

She watched him leave, still not certain. Would he flog her, or had he some other devious notion?

Alice opened a window, and leaning out, elbows resting on the sill, she assembled her thoughts, fears and aspirations. This could be the culmination of what they'd been dancing around for weeks. Maybe he just needed the excuse; after all, what was a chastisement worth if it wasn't done for real.

But she couldn't even be sure that's what he had in mind. How did she really feel about this? How did she really, honestly feel about a severe thrashing?

She studied the moisture on her palms. Scared? Yes scared.

Commonsense told her she was crazy. Was it just the fantasy that appealed? Would the reality be horrendous? Would she be kicking and screaming and begging him to stop?

How many? With what? In what fashion? Dressed or undressed? Would he strap her down over that wicked seat? She pressed fingers to the front of her skirt, an abrupt burst of sexual energy requiring attention.

'What if I was late?' she whispered. 'What would he really do? Or should I see his warning as more of a suggestion?'

Alice idly stepped towards the mirror, and there she studied her reflection. She wore a beige summer dress, the thin cotton hugging her body, emphasising every inch of a voluptuous figure. Beneath, she filled white silk and lace panties and a matching half-cup bra. Chocolate stockings were supported by a delicate cream suspender belt.

'Where are you, conscience?' she asked quietly. 'You used to hound me night and day? What's up? Given in?'

Hope had fallen strangely quiet. Gone was the disorderly background rumble. The silence disturbed. It was eerily foreboding. Suddenly Alice felt very alone. Ice swathed her body, her buttocks twitching apprehensively. Nausea seized her stomach, launching the girl to the toilet, where she knelt and heaved.

Hot and sticky she returned to her room, stomach acidic and burning. She gazed at the dispirited girl in the mirror, admitting, 'Oh hell, I don't want to do this.'

Alice slumped on her bed, shoulders hunched. 'Half an hour, and I feel more like the condemned than a girl about to fulfil a dream.'

She dabbed at her mouth and face with a moist cloth. 'Why am I so uneasy? Why do I have this terrible sense of dread? Perhaps it will change when I get there.'

Her eyes fell on her holdall, an urge descending for her to run. She could go back to Katy. They would all be pleased to see her.

'Go on, run, Alice Hussey. Flee your destiny. Just as you are

about to face the trial you have begged for, you lose courage.
It's no more than I expected. You are an aimless babbling brook.
Plenty to say, pretty to look at, but with no depth. You are
puerile and superficial.'

'Oh, you're back then? So what are you saying? Go through
with it?'

'Have the courage to demand a true punishment. Offer your
worthless body to the judgement and wrath of God. Turn away
from lechery. Spurn those malign inclinations you covet and
disguise, and renounce that scoundrel's wily attempts at
seduction. Life is a trial, heaven is the reward for mortal
hardship. Sin and repent and you will find your place waiting.
Sin with indifference and you will find purgatory.'

'And what if I sin and sin and then eventually repent? What
then, clever clogs?'

'Then you must reap what you sow.'

As if electrocuted Alice dropped a small bottle of perfume,
having just wet a finger with the scent. Dark mental clouds
parted, the defensive veil of confusion shattered. Truth tore
open old psychological wounds, lay raw her vulnerability. A
multitude of horrors pounded her stunned mind, guilt and regret
piling high against the doors of integrity.

Alice unbuttoned her dress and slipped it from her shoulders.
She released that delicate brassiere and dropped it to the floor.
Seductive panties, suspender and stockings quickly followed.
She refastened the dress and adjusted the hem before again
gazing at her reflection.

'Okay girl, wear the mask so he can't see your fear. Get this
done with once and for all. Pay your debts, and then get the hell
out of here, and leave this abominable place behind.'

Alice gazed upward. 'I'll pay for my sins. I'll suffer in your
name. Please forgive me for what I have done.'

Hand raised, fist clenched, Alice took a last deep breath before
knocking. Nerves riotous, resolve crumbling, she fought
desperately with her convictions.

The knuckles rapped without her consent, Hughes' voice replying, somewhere far and distant. Mechanically she turned the handle and opened the door.

Hughes studied her. 'You seem a little distracted, Alice. A touch nervous?'

Back straight, shoulders back, hands meeting at her front, she answered with honesty and determination. 'I am. But that is only because I don't know what you intend.'

'Elements, Alice. Necessary elements in keeping my flock under control. They wait, unknowing. The tension builds to an unbearable height, and when their time comes they are beyond self-control. It's as if apprehension removes willpower.'

Hughes closed the distance. He studied her unabashed. 'And how do you feel? Anxious?'

'Yes,' the young woman admitted. 'But there is a specific reason.'

Hughes cupped a hand to her buttock, squeezing the flesh there. 'You aren't wearing any knickers.'

'No sir, I'm not wearing any underwear at all.'

'Is there an explanation for such flagrancy?'

Alice frowned. 'I don't understand. You can't actually see anything.'

Hughes slapped her bum cheek, the flat of his hand stunningly painful. 'I *can* see.' The same hand that ignited the sting in her behind grabbed her breast. 'I can see, but I'm not sure what I'm supposed to think, or do.'

He peered into her eyes, his face two inches from hers. 'Well, Miss Hussey, what am I supposed to think? Is this an attempted seduction to divert me from the business in hand?'

'No,' she replied, controlled. 'That is precisely why I took them off; because they were seductive.'

Hughes scratched his head. 'How can underwear be seductive under a dress?'

'I assumed...' she began, her face warming.

'You assumed. You assumed what, exactly? Hmm? You assumed that I required your attendance to have you remove

216

your dress. You then *assumed* that your irresistible body enhanced with saucy bra and knickers would prove too much for this depraved lecher. Is that it?'

'No.'

'What then? You must have a reason.'

'I want no misunderstandings,' she blurted.

'Misunderstandings? I can assure you, Miss Hussey, there will be no misunderstandings.'

Insignificance fell upon her weary shoulders. Alice felt belittled, small, humiliated, but defiantly she decided to vent her decision. 'I'll make it plain, Mr Hughes.'

He sneered. 'Please do. We want no misunderstandings.'

Alice hovered on the edge of an embarrassing void. She had no idea of the principal's intent. To trespass on uncertain ground could prove calamitous, place ideas where there were none. 'I assume you are going to use corporal punishment.'

'That's plain speak indeed, young lady. And you are yet again assuming. But before I reveal my reasons for asking you to come here, please would you do me the courtesy of explaining why you chose to arrive without, let's say, foundations.'

'I may have given out the wrong signals. Oh, I seem to have made a complete ass of myself.' Her face gave to the burn of utter embarrassment. 'I'm sorry, sir. If I have presumed incorrectly, then I apologise.'

Hughes smiled, the turn of lips chilled. He reached back and picked a cane from his desk. He flexed it, the rod yielding little. 'You were correct. I am going to cane you. I am going to provide you with six painful reasons not to be presumptuous. Then I shall leave you for ten minutes to massage the smart, and contemplate this. Vanity according to your religion is a sin. To believe yourself irresistible is vain. You seem to be under the illusion that I demanded your attendance for some sexual motive. Not so.

'I believe you have the right qualities. That you can do very well here at Hope. But there seem to be some psychological undercurrents impeding such advancement. You know what I

217

refer to?'

She nodded. 'I think so.

'Attendance. Punctuality. Respect and courtesy. You either lack or need to improve. I also suspect you may be taking advantage of certain situations. This preoccupation you have with sin and absolution seems to push you toward deliberate confrontations. It's almost as if you wish me to punish you for some obscure event, that has nothing to do with Hope.

'If you cannot get on top of that, then I suggest you either see a priest or sort something out with me. If flogging you eases your conscience and in turn benefits your ability to work, then I can readily make myself available.'

Alice listened. Alice burned with humiliation. Alice fidgeted and died a dozen deaths.

'As from tomorrow I shall watch you like a hawk. Lateness will bring about a swift and grievous reply. A lack of respect or courtesy will be remedied with a painful interlude over my knee. And if you fail to consult a priest, then I shall arrange a confessional with Dr Doodney, who will instigate the appropriate remedy.

'Have you any comment?'

Alice shook her head. She hadn't expected the verbal assault, and remained somewhat taken aback.

'Very well,' he said, striding past her. 'Follow me.'

Alice walked in his wake, eyes glued to the cane he clasped. Over and over she visualised that impacting, lashing her flexed backside. Numbness consumed nerves, Alice accepting her lot, her mind refusing to acknowledge the promise of excruciating agony. She knew in her heart that Hughes would cane her with gusto. She knew she had unsettled him; did she dare to think she had in fact disappointed him?

The door to the punishment room swung wide, Alice following Hughes. She stopped, cast a glance about the austere cell. She had lorded it there, caning so many over the previous few weeks. She noted Hughes pointing with the tip of the cane, indicating where she was to stand. There she would wait in utter dread

218

until he issued the order to bend.

Alice contemplated the small window set high in the wall, the glass misted with dust, time and cobwebs. She tried not to think about how naked her bottom felt, the gossamer thin dress tendering barely any protection. She could cut and run. She could turn her back on Hope, Hughes and the cold savagery she had dished out for weeks. But a tenuous thread kept her there.

'Bend over and touch your toes.'

She closed her eyes and doubled, fingertips pressed to shoes. The sacrifice, the tendering of her bottom for the rigorous slash of cane, both frightened and excited. The bum quailed at the prospect of being viciously stung, but the spirit longed to feel the untenable bite. Her soul still sought an excruciating torment, and preferably the worst Hughes could administer.

She sensed the touch, the press, the slide of hard cane. Her heart pounded; pulse racing as the switch departed. Seconds would pass before its bitter return, all flesh before it pulverised, stung with unbelievable force.

She tensed to the abrupt shriek of approaching cane, lurched to its uncompromising impact. The thud of rattan hitting stretched buttocks ricocheted off the bare walls, a ferocious burn consuming those traumatised spheres.

The stroke hurt. It ignited an unbearable swath of stricken flesh. Her fingers curled to tightened fists. She bit hard, upper teeth grinding on lower, her face screwed in distress.

Hughes understood what he had provoked. He knew exactly how much the lash pained the girl. He also knew the stripe would burn intolerably for some minutes.

He eyed those flanks, libido excited by the torturous stripe that burgeoned unseen. Alice didn't squeal. She failed to whimper. Both were essential ingredients for the sadistic Geoffrey Hughes.

He powered the second stroke towards expectant buttocks. The cane whipped ferociously, burrowing greedily into scalded flanks. Hughes listened for the expected squeal; Alice's gasp the only treat.

Hughes wiped the sweat from a palm, then re-gripped the rod. He swished it back and forth, focussing his mind on the next stroke, his gaze not straying from that gently swaying bottom.

Two stripes burning intensely Hughes delivered the third, lower buttock flesh launched with the explosive connection. Alice whimpered. Hughes smiled.

'Why do I long for this?' she questioned, knowing the answer, a strange satisfaction sating the lust.

The fourth sliced, erogenous flesh shuddering, the excruciating hurt magnified further. The girl's legs shook, her stance increasingly untenable. Molten lava seemed to burn deep into her flesh, her backside torched, the whole aglow.

Hughes savoured his task, meting out excess, Alice's bum reeling to shock after shock. The fifth reaped its havoc; the ultimate stroke ten seconds later, just that.

'Rise,' he ordered.

Alice struggled, flayed buttocks screaming at the transition. She straightened, offering a telltale wince and grunt.

Hughes hung the cane, a cord wound around the handle offering a loop. He studied the stooped figure of the whipped Alice, and unable to resist the gibe he asked, 'Has God forgiven you yet?'

Grit not having fled, she replied calm and collected. 'If it would cleanse my soul, I would undergo ten times that.'

Hughes smirked. 'Is that so? No, I don't believe any callow girl could endure that.'

'I didn't say anything about enduring, sir.'

Hughes unfastened the six buttons fastening her dress. He pulled the fabric apart, baring her back. Licking his lips he ran a finger the length of her spine. 'Nice unspoilt skin, Alice. Skin that would soon ripple and swell under the bite of a quirt.'

Breathing ragged, she closed her eyes. 'Is that what you intend, sir?'

'Maybe. Maybe not.' He urged the material from her shoulders and tugged it down, baring her breasts, which trembled with the release, Alice reeling to their abrupt exposure. 'Let's say that the next hour will be full of surprises. Whatever you expect might not happen. What you don't expect probably will. One thing that is certain though, is that it will be an extremely uncomfortable passing of time.'

Her wrists still gripped by buttoned cuffs, Hughes led her to that bench. She stood anxiously before it, the recollection of her humiliating experiment careering back.

Hughes whispered, 'Struggle, Alice. Fight back. You don't really want to be strapped down on that, do you? You don't want to be held very tightly in a most unladylike fashion, do you?'

'I'll do what you tell me,' she replied, attempting to sound unfazed.

'You'll be held in such a fashion that nothing will remain private. Your bared breasts will hang precariously over the far edge. Your upper arms will be pinioned to your body, your wrists gripped and held by those straps near the top. Your thighs will be forced and held apart, and the belt across the lower back is pulled so tight it forces the bottom up and out, thereby stretching the flesh and increasing the sensitivity.'

'You want me to resist so you can increase the punishment, I presume?'

'No, Alice, not at all. I want you to resist because that would increase my enjoyment.'

Alice glanced sideways, the memory of that mirror returning. She viewed the reflection with interest, her breasts bared, the whipping stool about to become a reality. She had dreamed of, longed for the moment, but for whatever reason she faced an anticlimax.

She heard the fateful instruction, 'Lay over the stool please, Alice.'

She shook her head. 'No, sir, I don't think I will.'

'I will ask you again. Lay over the stool, please.'

Again she declined. Alice had reasons beyond Hughes' fetish. She had come so far. The final hurdle could not be of her choosing. She had to be forced, and then anything that occurred later would be beyond her responsibility.

The girl lasted fifteen seconds, but then Hughes' superior strength forced her down, Alice pushing against the stool proving no match. She collapsed, her belly settling to the dished support.

Hughes buckled the belt across her back to keep her from rising. He followed that with her wrists, each coerced into position and then fettered by the straps. Already moist with sweat, the perspiration flowed more conspicuously. Her palms proved quite greasy as Hughes tightened the leather, not satisfied until the worn hide bit hard.

The man lingered there awhile, ogling the drape of luxurious bosom, Alice's breasts suspended and vulnerable.

Skirt torn, ripped to the waist, Hughes levered a leg to one side, wrapping a strap about it above the knee. Alice winced as he yanked it tight, leather cutting into the soft flesh of her thigh. The other found its place, the girl's legs separated, her sex concealed by the hem of her skirt.

Hughes then tightened the strap over her waist, wrenching on it until her belly pressed uncomfortably to the slats of the support. He fully exposed her hips, the cotton of her dress rent about the waist.

Posture far from relaxed or comfortable, Alice focussed on the floor. Her bare feet rested on the cold tiles, knees bent, calves slightly angled. The forward edge of the dished body support already probed her groin, the slats delving and sticking to her belly and ribcage.

The restraint of arms held her in an untenable position, and placed a strain on her shoulders and back. She could not rest, but had to fight to keep her torso horizontal and her head up.

Hughes inspected her. He lifted the skirt and examined the marks. She felt his fingers roam her bottom, gauging the thrust of bloated welts. 'These will keep you from sitting for a day or two, Alice. A reminder of your poor manners and sloth.'

'Yes sir,' she offered, wishing he would get on with whatever he had in mind.

The man folded the torn fabric back over her etched cheeks. 'Ten minutes to reflect, Alice, and then we shall get on with serving your misery.' The man left.

The young woman wriggled, fidgeted, tried to improve her position. The sway and jiggle of hanging breasts persuaded her to peruse that reflection, the image sending waves of sensual electricity through her body. She had never witnessed such a helpless victim. The vision of a scantily covered self strapped so sacrificially to an apparatus turned her insides to jelly.

She could clearly discern her bared and perilously placed breasts. She shivered to the exposed upper back, and what would in time be an unveiled bottom. Alice flexed her legs, testing the straps that pinned her thighs. Every fetter held. Every shackle gripped her tightly and remorselessly. For her there would be no escape, no let up until Hughes released her. The grip and bite of stained and well-used leather, in addition to her feeling of total defencelessness, lit the fuel for an eventual climax, and Alice launched into the intriguing journey to an ecstatic end.

Chapter Thirteen

A good ten minutes passed despairingly, the girl's body and mind tormented by her exacting position. Alice settled as Hughes, she assumed, returned. She didn't want to give him the satisfaction of seeing her struggle, so she waited for the man to speak or begin hostilities.

As the tensed seconds stole by abnormalities subconsciously aroused suspicion, Alice mentally questioning who stood directly behind her. A full half-minute had elapsed without word or deed. There was a discordant if vaguely familiar smell in the room, and the entrance was not heralded by the usual click of Hughes' leather soles on the floor.

Alice's hackles rose. A disproportionate fear gripped her. She made an attempt to see, her heart already informed, her mind dropping into freefall. Panic consumed her, the girl frantically snatching at her bonds, her partially naked body writhing in desperate straits.

'Are we that well tuned that you sense who I am?' The voice confirmed her worse nightmare.

'No!' she hissed, struggling like a girl possessed. 'No, it can't be. It's impossible.'

'Obviously not. I'm here. And so are you, Alice. Fettered and spread like some seventeenth-century harlot. Very appropriate under the circumstances.'

'What are you doing here? Where's Mr Hughes?'

Richard Barker strolled around his trapped prey. 'It must seem baffling to the gullible. How can your dear uncle suddenly materialise at the most inopportune moment possible? Extremely embarrassing for you, I don't doubt.'

'You've no right to be here. Does Mr Hughes know?'

'Oh yes, Mr Hughes is fully aware of my presence. I have an hour in which to persuade you on the error of your ways.'

'Why would he let you do that?'

'He had no choice.'

'You came before, didn't you? You saw Pierce and he told you to piss off. So why have you come back?'

'Your expensive education seems to have achieved little, Alice. You talk like the gutter snipe you have become.' The onerous man slipped off his jacket and hung it on a hook.

He loosened the cuffs and rolled his shirtsleeves up. 'First there is the matter of attacking me with a knife. But fair's fair, I shall elucidate the chain of events, as I educate you on respect for sharp objects and your betters.'

'No,' she whispered, terrified as Richard armed himself with a twelve inch taws.

He stood beside her, rubbing an area of skin below her shoulder blade. 'If you wish to play with villains, then you should forget the word trust.' The split end of that durable implement slapped painfully against her back.

Alice winced.

'You alienated Pierce, it would seem. He certainly wasn't a happy man when he rang me. I think the appropriate word might be revenge. Much like I shall be exacting.'

Alice gasped to a second, the slap of leather on naked back louder. 'S-so Pierce t-told you I was here?'

'That's what I said.'

Alice jerked to another volatile lash.

'He also informed on *you*, I'm afraid.' Face twisted with contempt Barker increased his strength, the taws ripping into the soft flesh of her back.

'Informed? Th-there was nothing to inform about.'

He moved casually to her other side. 'No? It would seem, from what Mr Pierce told me, that you have sunk even lower. That the episode with the pusillanimous Malcolm was merely a prelude to more depraved acts.'

225

Alice sucked air as the taws ravaged another strip of sensitive flesh. 'I don't know what he told you, but he's lying.'

'An old soldier, a sergeant major, lying? No, I think not. It is you that tries to conceal the truth. And I have to wonder why. Why do you feel you have to lie to me?'

Alice's upper back recoiled beneath another swingeing slap. The marks of that leather's assault coloured, narrow bands of scarlet traversing the once fair skin. The young woman gave up on escape, realising the pointlessness of the exercise. She would remain there until Richard decided otherwise. She would suffer his excesses until the man had vented his anger.

'If I was nothing to you, as you would have me believe, then why lie? What advantage does it provide?'

'Because you're a savage bastard, that's why!' She immediately regretted the outburst.

'Am I, indeed? Savage bastard?' Barker nodded his head, feigning deep thought. 'Because I have the temerity to take my niece to task for outrageous acts of perversion, I am a savage bastard? Because I care for her soul. Because, above all else, I don't wish her to end her life in the bosom of Satan; ergo, savage bastard. You see precisely what you want to see.'

'You're not my uncle. How dare you pretend?'

'We lack a piece of paper. Morally I am your uncle and guardian. Your father left me the challenge of guidance. And in that, Alice, I will not fail. One way or another you will learn right from wrong. You have turned your back on God, and now it seems I am the only one to educate you on the error of your ways.'

He ran his hand over her back, the flesh discoloured, hot and sore. 'The moment I grant you responsibility of choice you leap into the abyss of wickedness like some desperate junkie. But still I care. I will not forsake you, Alice. No matter what depraved path you follow, I will be there to pick up the pieces.'

'But you are nothing to do with me,' she protested hopelessly. 'Nothing. I will be eighteen very soon. I'm my own woman. I'll do what I please. Are you listening, non-uncle? Is this sinking into your sick head? You are nothing to do with me, and even if you were, I choose, not you.'

'And you are possessed. It is the devil that screams at me, not my Alice. Not my sweet and devout Alice.'

Alice laughed. Frustration boiled. She wanted to attack the imbecile, tear his eyes out with her claws. She yearned to rip the skin off his bespectacled, ugly face. But Hughes had betrayed her. He had left her strapped down as a sacrifice to the loony Barker.

And then as Richard exchanged the taws for a cruel strap, the awful penny dropped. Call it feminine intuition, the gelling of numerous facts, or a case of understand your man. Alice glared at the mirror, and eyes hostile, expression loathing, she mouthed, 'You deceitful bastard.'

Richard parted the torn dress, baring that welted posterior. He examined the stripes, fingertips scrutinising the dilation. 'Confess, Alice. Give me your confession now. I will absolve you. And then I shall remove you from this den of iniquity, and safely deliver you to Heptonstall.'

'I have nothing to confess, and you are no priest.' Alice lowered her head, knowing what lay in store, determined to hold her ground.

'That is the devil talking. You must find the courage to usurp him, Alice. We must beat this demon from you. Then, and only then, you will be able to accept your sins.'

'Hokum!'

'I beg your pardon?'

'I said hokum, Richard. You make it up as you go along. All you want to do is beat me. Beat me and get an eyeful as you do it. Why don't *you* confess? You're a withered, middle-aged, sadistic pervert. I'm the only woman available, and that's why you've got your damned claws in. That's why you follow me everywhere.'

'I have no interest in your body!' Barker powered that hostile implement at expectant buttocks, the leather ripping into and scalding the taut cheeks. Alice clenched her fists, bit hard, and squeezed her eyes tight.

'It is your soul I wish to save. You sin of the flesh, then you suffer with the flesh.' Her backside heaved before a second, the almighty crack slamming sharply off the walls.

Alice wailed. 'Ahh… what has Pierce told you?'

'Filth! Sordid, outrageous filth!' Her buttock flesh was launched by another strenuous lash.

'He did that to me!'

A vertical swing slapped the upper heights, Alice's bum set ablaze. 'You permitted the outrage. In fact I believe you instigated it. But you have to confess. You have to tell me, not I, you.

'Have you found what you were looking for, Alice? Does the pain in your rear match what you envisaged?' The girl's bum leapt and shuddered beneath the savage onslaught, Barker determined to break her, to force her into confession. 'Why don't you tell me, Alice? Why not get it over with? Go on, explain about the night you were tied and shafted. Tell the father confessor all about that. Especially how many orgasms you had to endure.'

The inferno exceeded the intolerable, Alice dipping into a living hell. Her bottom screamed its protest, that delightful rump stinging intolerably.

Mind blitzed by the shocks and jolts of those immense blasts of pain, she could not make the final connection. Why did Hughes permit Richard the outrage. 'Okay,' she sobbed. 'Okay, I'll confess, if you tell me why Mr Hughes let you in here.'

'Deals? You try to broker deals? You are in no position to barter, whore.'

'Please.'

Richard laid the strap on those tortured haunches. Her bum burning, the flesh heated, scarlet and distressed, he calmly agreed. 'It really is quite simple. I am not blinkered by naivety, nor a desire for the unholy. I see what stands before me. Hughes is a rascal. The man is an outright villain. Such crumble before the might of righteousness. Hughes crumbled before me. I, unlike you, was in a position to do a deal. I have offered my silence for the chance to save you. I won't involve the authorities, provided I am given the opportunity to open your eyes.

'I don't expect any thanks from you. Not yet. But once the necessary is done, and my Alice is returned to me, then in time I will expect your eternal gratitude. We will conduct this business to its satisfactory conclusion. Once I am content that the devil has been dissuaded, and that you are back on the road to redemption, then and only then, I will release you. You will pack your bags, and we will leave this evil place for the hallowed halls of Heptonstall.'

'I still don't understand. How can you blackmail Mr Hughes, when he hasn't done anything wrong?'

'Blackmail? There is no blackmail. There is an understanding. An adult means to an end. And as for doing nothing wrong, then I suggest you look more closely. This is no more than a penitentiary. The damnable place and its wretched inhabitants have been written off. Hughes does as he pleases.'

'He tries to find a new and better life for the girls.'

'You stupid girl. Hughes is a tyrant. He sells them, and he will sell you too.'

'I don't believe you.'

'I knew you were here from the day Miss Lake rang me. She was concerned. She thought perhaps I hadn't taken my responsibility seriously. I came here the same day, and that Pierce fellow told me you had been and gone.

'I asked myself, why lie? Because people lie when they have something to hide. I laid my suspicions at your benefactor's door, and what his employees turned up proved extremely worrying.'

'So why don't you call in the police?'

'I am only interested in your welfare. The others here are damned anyway. They have trodden the path of wickedness for too long. They are beyond salvation. They are the devil's children. Perhaps what Hughes provides is God's judgement. It is not for me to say, and I will not meddle in divine intervention.'

Alice knew there was no point in arguing. All she could do was plot her own escape. She had to be rid of Barker once and for all.

'Your confession, Alice?'

She took a deep breath, intent on revealing all, on shocking the pious Richard. She had no idea what Pierce had told him, and if she missed anything she would pay a costly price. 'I have given my body to the devil. I am his tool. I am guilty of many debauched acts. I have succumbed to sins of the flesh. Satan turns the whip to ecstatic pleasure. He makes the bite of rope consummately irresistible.'

'Go on. There's more.'

'I have succumbed to the sexual advances of others.'

'And something else?'

'I have indulged in sexual gratification with a plastic tool.'

'Thoughts? What thoughts run through that diseased mind?'

Alice desperately tried to conjure something that would satisfy the ogre. 'Endless sexual depravation. Things that please my master, Satan.'

Richard stroked her bottom, his hand bathing in the fires of extreme discipline. 'I am going to whip you, Alice. But it won't be purification. No, it will be the severest punishment you have ever undergone. I will not be flogging you in order to save your soul, I will be hopefully teaching you a lesson never to be forgot. Do not presume me to be a fool.'

'But I...'

'You have just said what you think I want to hear. Satan drives you? Balderdash. It is you that is inherently wicked.' Richard seized her by the hair and pulled her head back. He glared into her face. 'You! Devious! Cunning! A filthy whore! But I have the answer, nonetheless. I will break you, Alice. I will reduce you to a shambling wreck. You will be only too happy to jump to my command.'

Barker scoffed. 'Satan turns the whip to ecstatic pleasure. He makes the bite of rope consummately irresistible. That is not Satan. That is your perverse preference. Bad blood. Your mother's blood. She had a taste for the lash, too, and I understand she got more than she bargained for once they locked her up.'

Alice watched in abject terror as Richard selected a quirt from the implements cupboard. 'I think you will not find this whipping to your taste. Even delinquent whores have their limit. And perhaps while we're occupied we might make the concept of sexual intercourse a little less beguiling.'

Alice winced to the touch of those twin tails, Barker draping them on her buttocks. Ambling forward he dragged them the length of her body. 'Not much left to the imagination, is there? Typical. It's what I have come to expect. Alice Hussey, half naked, her bosom hanging out.'

'I didn't choose this,' she protested.

'No? Why don't I believe you?'

Richard paused by her shoulders. 'This *is* quite an ingenious contrivance.' He leant, spoke quietly in her ear. 'It mounts and exhibits you in the most provocative manner. Even your bosom dangles, exposed and naked. Expectant, begging attention in a way.'

The tails of that whip dangled from her shoulder, the thick leather thongs swinging close to her chest, unnerving her. 'What sort of attention would they appreciate, Alice?'

'Have a feel, if that's what you're after. I can't do much about it, can I? Go on, help yourself. Fondle my tits, *Uncle* Richard.'

Barker straightened. 'If I give any consideration to those fat swellings then it will be with this. He took two steps towards her rear, then lifting an arm high he brought a formidable lash to bear, the girl's left buttock taking the full force. The thongs cut vertically, whipping flesh from loin to thigh. Alice stiffened, a sickening hurt penetrated, turning her stomach.

'Perhaps I simply don't understand. We are, after all, generations apart. So, explain to me, why have you discarded all your morals?'

Alice panted. Nerves wrought, her mind dwelt in turmoil. Sweat beaded from her brow and dribbled annoyingly over her eyebrows and nose. She had sought divine punishment, a penance severe enough to acquit her conscience. That she seemed to have been granted, but her feelings troubled her. The whip's retribution proved harsh, excessively so, but her body and mind failed to shy from its fitful smart.

Richard lashed her again. The hiss of those speeding thongs, the virulent bite of unforgiving leather, and the subsequent caustic burn, all contributed their effect. They augmented a sensation of immense contentment.

'Answer me,' the man demanded, whipping her again.

Alice hung her head, gasping. The coercive punch of impropriety fed a chronic obsession and stirred a relentless avalanche of erogenous stimulation. Her immodest posture, the grip of sweat-soaked straps, the vulgar promotion of tits, arse and fanny, and the stretch and thrust of those fleshy buttocks nurtured her weakness. The fact she was pinned, captured, held immobilised and subject to the withering bite of Barker's scourge, enhanced the inner furore. She was dinner on a plate, and served purely for the delectation of others. She would find no absolution there.

Six times that twin-tailed flesh-biter ravaged the meat of her left flank. There the fires raged, the whole buttock torched and burning. Preoccupied with his torturous recreation, Alice was certain Richard revelled in every second.

The hurt bordered on excruciating, a wall of raw heat continually surging though her loins. Alice had often pondered on the why and wherefore, deliberating on the extremities of corporal punishment. Richard provided her with part of the answer, maybe the ultimate in severity, a whipping never to be surpassed. Alice suffered it, surprising herself by her ability to endure.

She avoided the mirror. She deliberately averted her gaze, for she knew what lay behind. But the draw became too much. Aware of possible repercussions she joined the game, witnessing the demented Richard whipping her backside with furious abandon. The harsh, graphic presentation crowned the bubbling cauldron deep in her stomach. Tentacles of delicious energy encircled, squeezed, and encouraged orgasm. The grim, regular beat of thongs ripping into fired bottom flesh stressed the predicament. The jolt of stung body, and the subsequent tremble of breasts amplified the bawdy consequence. Her face grimaced, lips parted, teeth ground, the picture before her spiralling her ever closer to unconscionable consummation.

The marks of the whip mauled and stained her bottom, the visible cheek welted and etched. Stripes flourished, thrust from her heated flesh. Barker persevered, trouncing her bottom, the flesh constantly aquiver, stung to a rapturous flush.

A tally lay beyond Alice, the bitter acid consuming every ounce of her being. The thwip and thump of tails whipping numbed corpulence mesmerised. She hovered on the edge, entranced by the deepening colour of her own behind, and the accumulation of livid marks raised by that excessive flogging.

Eyes glazed, Richard backed off. Sweat rained on his face, soiled his shirt and soaked his hands. Panting he took time to survey the devastation. 'Just the beginning, Alice,' he whispered. 'That is merely a taste.'

Her bottom stung, prickled, burned in a most exasperating fashion, Alice strung from the tenterhooks of eroticism. She wanted, yearned for more. Whatever liberties Richard evoked would only serve her needs. A licentious quagmire sucked her ever deeper, Alice plumbing the depths of wanton depravity. Richard inspired the sexual frenzy more than anyone else. He ignited the muddle of emotive eruptions more efficiently than Hughes or Jay ever could. Richard dominated with ruthless, uncaring efficiency. He aimed to hurt, to cut to her very soul with his vindictive sadism. Richard met her deficiency with ruthless proficiency.

Alice sought to provoke. She refused to see, turned her mind from the possibility, wallowing in the frantic sexual thrill instead. 'Why?' she probed. 'Why are you doing this? If it's because you enjoy it then just say so. For a fee you can have the pleasure on a regular basis.'

'What did you say?' Richard demanded, teeth clenched.

'Ten pounds. How's that? Ten pounds to satisfy yourself.'

'Have all my remonstrations been in vain? You lay there…
God Almighty! You are incorrigible. You are beyond saving.
You are rotten to the core.'

'At last!' she spat. 'Now it's sunk in, so leave me alone!'

Richard jabbed a forefinger at her. 'I have an hour with you,
whore. I have used less than half that. In the time remaining I
will justify this visit. You *will* regret and beg forgiveness.'

Alice looked over her shoulder and glared. 'You *paid*. You
have *paid* for *this*.'

'No…'

'Yes you have. God, look at the *devout* punter. You're pathetic.'

'I haven't paid. I have purely negotiated one hour in which to
bring you to your senses.'

'I don't believe you, but you'd better get a hurry on. You
don't want to miss out on anything. A few minutes could make
all the difference.'

'How dare you? How dare you insinuate?'

'Oh, I dare. I know you. I am well versed in your conniving
ways. Have you paid for the privilege of having me as well? Is
this to be the lead in to teaching me another lesson? Are you
hard, Richard? Is your cock rubbing against your trousers?'

'You filthy-mouthed bitch!'

'Yes, and it will suck you off for a consideration.' Alice held
her mouth open.

Face flushed Richard growled. 'You are pushing your luck. I
warn you. You have changed beyond all recognition. You were
the bad penny, but now…'

'Now I see you with my eyes wide open. I see you for what
you are. Come on *uncle*, you're wasting time. There's bits of me
you haven't thrashed yet.' Alice pushed up, her back arching
magnificently, her breasts clear of the support. She jiggled them,
quivering enticingly. 'Don't you fancy these?'

Stunned, seeming to have lost the advantage, the man turned
his back on her. She listened to his restrained breathing, Richard

trying to regain control.

'I had forgotten how abusive you can be,' he admitted. 'I came here with the intention of saving you. And I will admit, revenge. That was wrong. The good Lord preaches forgiveness. I should forgive you. But what you did was reprehensible. No man should suffer the wiles and vagaries of a lascivious Jezebel. No man should be subjected to and ensnared by the seductive technique of a designing Lolita.'

'You what?' Alice gasped at the man's sheer audacity.

'I am flesh. I am human. I have red blood coursing through my veins. Even a staunch disciple like me can wither before such temptation. And you *are* desirable. You hold the trick of enchantment. It is only after the madness has lifted that one can see the wrong, the damage done.'

'I see.' Alice sighed. 'So, are you enchanted tonight? Will you be losing your mind again? Will you be ruing sexual coition in the morning?'

'Maybe I am wrong about *something*. Perhaps the devil does reside in you. Perhaps he and that filthy mouth should be silenced.'

'What's it to be, *uncle*? Gag or penis?'

Richard spun on his heels, the abruptness stunning Alice. He snatched the tie from his neck and held it out. 'This, you smart-mouthed bitch.' Enraged, he wrapped it about her jaw, pulling it tight, the silk sinking painfully deep into the corners of her mouth.

'And as you seem so keen, after I have finished with this,' he showed her the quirt, 'you can pay for your brazen effrontery.' Barker strode angrily to the door. He checked in the hallway before closing and locking it.

Back he marched, quirt held ready, and positioned directly behind the girl he proceeded to lash her thighs, the whip alternately raking the inner and outer of each limb. Impassioned, he worked his way down, stripes proliferating, her legs whipped indiscriminately.

Alice struggled to survive. The pain proved unbelievably

horrendous. Richard withheld nothing, the girl beside herself with despair. She chewed his tie, tears spilling, her gut contracting. Tears ran, wetting her lips, dribbling down her chin. She wriggled, she writhed, she squealed and grunted. Hands yanked at her bonds, biceps bulging, her shoulders twisting this way and that. The wide strap across her waist chafed and probed, the skin beneath wet and sore. She kicked with her calves, feet scrabbling in thin air.

Then the hell ceased, the jubilant Barker adjusting his position. Alice waited, anticipated, heart in mouth. She grimaced as his hand probed between her legs, feeling her vaginal lips. She winced to the insertion, a finger sliding deep.

'Wet,' Richard announced with glee. 'You are wet. So again we see the depths you readily sink to. What is it? Are you anticipating? Is your salacious mind unable to think of anything else? If you expect with such passion, then perhaps it would be unfair not to fulfil that insatiable lust. Perhaps, though, you should be paid in advance.' Two tough leather thongs bit ferociously. They struck with shocking force. They sliced her vulva before cutting into her shaven pubic mound.

Alice gurgled. Eyes thrown wide she howled. Her body lurched, straps cutting deep into struggling flesh. Barker watched her antics with satisfaction. He revelled in the restricted roll of hips, the limited waggle of welt-smothered tail. Pleased with her pained reaction he repeated the savagery, Alice jerking, contorting in desperation.

Two more he delivered to that sensitive arch, the tails biting agonisingly. 'Is that payment enough?' he asked sarcastically.

Thighs trembling, Alice nodded frantically. She had no intention of extending that particular misery. She felt the knot loosen, the tension on her gag easing. Barker tugged the wet rag from her mouth before making an issue of undoing his flies. She tried to look away, but Richard wound her hair about a fist and pulled her head back.

'A consideration, you said,' he reminded her. His fingers delved inside trousers, found and extricated the excited six-inch shaft. Alice watched the plum pop clear of its stretched foreskin. 'Consider,' Barker whispered. 'Consider this lesson.'

Alice gave to the thrust. She knew it would be pointless to resist. The man's rigid penis sank ingloriously, pushed until her throat ceased its passage. 'Tempt and you shall be given. Remember that, Alice. Now, how does the filthy mouth feel? A trifle stuffed?'

Richard gazed down on that flayed bottom, the crisscrossed welts triggering another animal reaction. His hips retreated then lunged, his talon-like fingers clamping her head, his cock forced deep.

'See where your arrogance has got you? See where conceit and cowardice have brought you?' Sneering, he forcibly fucked the girl's mouth, hips delivering a rapid and irresistible rhythm. 'You run. You aspire. You connive, cheat and whore. But where does it get you?'

The combination of whipped bottom and lip-squeezed erection proved too much, and too quickly for his liking his balls loosed their prolific wad, creaming Alice's mouth, the rapidly deflating penis leaving its trail of slick come.

Panting, eyes staring wildly at the ceiling, Barker stepped back, Alice stupidly watching the cock retire. Semen dribbled from her mouth, trickled down her chin and throat. She retched, then spat the residue clear.

'It gets you precisely where you'd rather not be. But you won't see that, will you? How many times have you been punished by my hand? How many times have you fallen foul of the Lord's justice?'

Cock and balls still exposed, and hanging impotently from his trouser fly, Richard used the quirt to excruciating effect. Those two twenty-inch thongs lashed Alice's sweet breasts, slashing viciously, biting effectively, stinging remorselessly.

Richard followed the blur of careering thongs. He staggered to the satisfying slap of leather on vulnerable flesh, and took sustenance from the shocked lurch of stung fruits.

'Yes, Alice, the Lord's justice. From him you cannot hide.

From him you cannot conceal your sins.'

Pain ripped through those succulent orbs, leather ravaging the sleek flesh, and Alice noted with horror the revitalisation of the man's penis, the ponderous lift of waking cock.

'You can run, you can hide, and you can sin. But I *will* find you. And I pledge before God Almighty that you will suffer his judgement.'

Richard whipped her breasts again as he moved to her rear. 'Again and again I have to prove your insignificance. I have to demonstrate your lack of worth.'

Alice winced to the violence delivered between her legs, her vagina brutally stung.

'You are nothing. I look at you, and I spit on you.' A globule of saliva struck her between the buttocks. 'And this proves I can do whatever God commands. Whatever he deems fit and just.

'Don't you wonder at the sequence of events, Alice? How you came to this? How at the precisely right moment you're delivered to me, stripped and readied for the Lord's ordained scourging?'

A trace of a smile flickered as Alice felt the intrusion, the insertion of hard cock, her sex surrendering, Richard's sexual plunge stretching her. 'You have been delivered unto me. It is my portentous calling to save your miserable soul, and I will save it with or without your cooperation.'

Alice hung her head, damp, auburn tresses licking about her face. *I ask for penance and absolution and you send him. What is the message, God? What am I supposed to think? You work in mysterious ways? Well, you couldn't have spun a more ambiguous message than this. This tells me to go to hell. Your Church, your creed, your disciples are all cold and harsh. They preach mercy and offer none. They leave no room for compassion. They whip the flesh in the name of the gospel, and reap the rewards of sexual gratification.'

'Is my soul in there, Richard?' she muttered sarcastically. 'Does your cock commune directly with my spirit?'

The quirt's stinging tails replied, lashing about a shoulder, whipping her right breast. A couple of seconds later her left breast shuddered, a raging burn ignited. 'A bridle, bit and reins and the picture would be complete,' Richard mused. 'The master rides his nag.'

He increased his momentum, his cock plunging, withdrawing to lunge again. 'Giddyup, hussy,' he urged, laying two more strokes to those vulnerable breasts, and Alice screamed with the frustration of it.

'You refuse to see this as it is,' Richard continued. 'All those damned eyes perceive is a middle-aged man enthralled by youth and sadistic pleasure. That is the easy path. There you don't have to delve your conscience. On that trail everything fits with your distorted view.'

Alice jerked to the fierce slice of slashing leather, her breasts etched in scarlet welts. 'You won't accept I treat you for what you are, for what you have become. You act the tart; I treat you like a tart. Does the mist of conscious deceit thin? Can you comprehend what you are?' The girl's left breast heaved, thongs biting around the nipple. 'Can you, girl?' Her right twitched, leather cords snaking about and beneath it. 'I can ride you all day. I can whip you all night. I can continue to regard you as a piece of live meat, whose only purpose is to provide carnal satisfaction. Or you can open your eyes, Alice. You can behold the lowly creature that fools itself more than anyone else.'

Gasping, mind hell-bent on escape, Alice reminded him, 'Your hour's up. Was I worth what you paid?'

Richard withdrew, buttoned his flies and hung the quirt back on its hook. 'It doesn't end here, Alice. You have chosen an unrighteous path—'

'I have chosen *my* path.'

'You act and sound like the guttersnipe you have become. I barely recognise you. I shall take you back to Southport with me tonight. There we will straighten this out. There we will rediscover Alice Hussey.'

'No, Richard, I don't think so.'

'You will have no choice in the matter. Hughes will do what I demand. He will not sacrifice this lucrative business for the likes of you.'

'So you would barter over one hundred girls' futures for the opportunity to enslave me? That sounds like your idea of ethical behaviour.'

'Don't you even begin to attempt to teach me right from wrong. I know exactly how you came to be strapped to that bench. I know precisely what you hoped for.' He pointed a trembling finger at Alice. 'I could have administered a lot worse. I could have made you wish you had never been born. But it is the lesson not the pain that is important. And that education we will continue in Southport.'

'And what happened to Heptonstall?'

'You arrogant, impudent brat. You are not fit as you are, to grace the halls of that noble college. You would only bring the name of Hussey into disrepute. First, we must make a lady out this sow's ear.'

'You've whipped most of me. There's not much left.'

'I will have you ready by Christmas. Maybe sooner. In the meantime you can study at home.'

'I hope you've had that rotten shed re-felted. I don't fancy that much in winter.'

'There is no point in continuing this. Not in your current state of conceit. I shall have Hughes release you, and then we must pack.' Richard unlocked the door and left.

'Why pack?' Alice bellowed after him. 'You'll only have me burn it all later.'

A blanket about her shoulders, Alice nursed her whipped body. Every movement, every chafe of dress set her flesh to stinging. She couldn't fasten the buttons, so the fabric hung loose, the blanket protecting what little modesty she retained.

Richard oozed arrogance. Hands on hips, chest puffed, he laid down his demands. 'You will release Alice from any obligation, sir. You will pay her what you owe and permit her to

240

leave your employ this night.'

Hughes sat behind his desk exuding an equal amount of swagger, except he remained relaxed, confident. 'Have you asked Alice what she wants to do?'

'The girl is not capable of making responsible decisions. She has proved that beyond doubt.'

'She is mature enough. Alice, do you want to go with Mr Barker?'

'I'd sooner boil in oil, sir.'

'Don't prevaricate, girl. Tell the man straight.'

Alice yielded to a slight smile.

'I have explained the situation, sir,' Barker resumed, anger colouring his face. 'Either I take Alice tonight or I ring the police.'

Hughes tapped his pipe on the ashtray. 'Do you really think I give a shit? I report directly to the Home Office. I carry the same weight as a Chief Constable. Firstly, the authorities would most likely take you to be a simple-minded soul, and at worst carry out a preliminary investigation.'

Alice thought she could see the bloat hissing out of the loathsome Barker.

'I have no worries on that account, whatever you may or may not believe. However, I try to offer consideration where it is due, or appears due. You came here as Alice's uncle. I therefore extended the privilege of a meeting with what I assumed was your niece.' Hughes grinned. 'Some meeting. What a debauched score you notched up there, sir.'

Barker scowled.

'He demanded you were strapped down partly naked, Alice. Mr Barker insisted on that.' Hughes shrugged. 'I suppose I shouldn't have agreed, but it did suit my purpose.'

'What purpose?' Richard demanded, perplexed.

'I have the complete hour on film.' Hughes beamed. 'Glorious eight millimetre black and white. A sort of screen test for Alice, and…' he raised his eyebrows, 'something to send to Southport and a certain Arab employer of yours, should you not take the hint and fuck off.'

'I don't believe you,' Barker challenged.

'I'll have a copy made and sent on. You can spend many future hours reminiscing and wanking yourself silly watching it.'

'How dare you!'

Hughes stood. He lit his pipe. 'Go and play with the nursery brats, they're about your level. Now if you don't mind, goodnight.'

'You're bluffing.'

'Eddie, show Mr Barker the two-way mirror and the set up on his way out, please.'

Alice cautiously placed her tender bottom on a soft cushion. She winced.

'Sore?' Hughes enquired, knowing the answer.

'I knew what you were up to, sir,' she said quietly. 'I guessed just after Richard came in.'

'Very astute of you.'

'I suppose you'll keep the film, just in case?'

'Oh, we'll keep it, Alice. Don't you worry about that.'

'You said screen test to Richard,' Alice reminded him, confused.

Hughes shrugged. 'Snap will develop the film. We'll send a copy to Barker and you can watch the other. See what you think.'

Alice frowned. 'I don't know if I would want to see it.'

'Pound against your penny you will. Alice, I know what you are. I understand completely.' He leant forward, smiling. 'Take a long cold shower. Watch the film, and I bet you here and now a finger dipped between your legs would come out wet.'

Alice blushed. 'Sir, that's so crude!'

'It's the truth.'

'Did he pay?'

'Who, Richard?' Hughes chuckled. 'I only wish I had thought of that. He might have. The cretin was desperate.'

'Why did you let him in? Why did you strip me and strap me

242

down? When he started whipping me why didn't you stop him? When he took those disgusting liberties, why did you let it go on?'

'I suppose…'

'Don't lie. You know he proposed no threat.'

Hughes toyed with his pipe. 'As I was about to say, Alice, I suppose he came along at the right moment. We wanted reality, and it soon became apparent by the weasel's attitude that was what he was offering.'

'What are you saying?'

He smiled. 'We were going to do the film anyway.'

'Why?'

'Oh, you really are the most stunning and naïve young lady I have ever met.'

The penny dropped. 'You bastard!' she squealed.

'So many say, but usually after I've striped their backsides.'

'I may not be able to do anything about what you have, but I certainly will not be starring in another,' she vowed indignantly.

'I think you'll change your mind, Alice.'

'I won't.'

'While you work for me you'll do exactly what I say. And from now on you'll bend over precisely when I tell you to.'

'What?'

'I really envied Richard tonight. Having the pleasure of whipping you like that. Still, give it a week or two, eh?'

'What makes you think I'm going to stay?'

Hughes sighed. 'Your reprehensible behaviour along with that pious guilty conscience I suppose. A girl on the streets?' He shook his head.

'I can get another job.'

'Not a good one. Not without a reference.'

'I don't need you for that, you pig.'

Hughes pointed a finger in her direction. 'Six of the best for that insult. So, without a reference from me you will need one from Miss Lake, though after she has seen the film? What will she think? How could she endorse a girl who has sex with her

243

uncle?'

'I'll go to the authorities myself,' she threatened. 'And he isn't my uncle!'

'Another six, on the bare bottom this time. What will you tell them? You know nothing. At least dear *Uncle* Richard had some evidence. And there again you have been assaulting my inmates for several weeks now.'

'I haven't,' she protested meekly, feeling crushed by this twist.

'You have been beating them with a cane.'

'You told me to.'

'Did I?'

Alice trembled with rage and fear. Suddenly she felt very alone.

'Not one of those canings had been entered in the punishment book. Not only would you be disgraced, but probably prosecuted. You might even be sent back here as an inmate. Oh, I would like that, Alice. I would like that very much.'

'The girls would…'

'Don't expect too much from those disloyal, cowardly strumpets. All they care about is their own hides. And they know very well I would strip those, should they fail me.'

'I…I…I…'

'Take a shower, Alice. Wash that sweat off your body. All is not lost. You will come to see that in due course. Life at Hope could prove highly profitable as well as extremely interesting. I for one understand you. I can satisfy the demons that drive you mad. You'll find if you tow the line that I am an equitable and honourable man. So, play ball and enjoy the rewards.'

Hughes smiled warmly. 'Go on, Alice. Use my shower. You'll feel a lot better after.'

To be continued…

More exciting titles available from Chimera

***

All **Chimera** titles are available from your local bookshop or newsagent, or direct from our mail order department. Please send your order with your credit card details, a cheque or postal order (made payable to *Chimera Publishing Ltd*) to: **Chimera Publishing Ltd., Readers' Services, PO Box 152, Waterlooville, Hants, PO8 9FS**. Or call our **24 hour telephone/fax credit card hotline: +44 (0)23 92 646062** (Visa, Mastercard, Switch, JCB and Solo only).

UK & BFPO - Aimed delivery within three working days.
    ·   A delivery charge of £3.00.
    ·   An item charge of £0.20 per item, up to a maximum of five items.
For example, a customer ordering two items for delivery within the UK will be charged £3.00 delivery + £0.40 items charge, totalling a delivery charge of £3.40. The maximum delivery cost for a UK customer is £4.00. Therefore if you order more than five items for delivery within the UK you will not be charged more than a total of £4.00 for delivery.

Western Europe - Aimed delivery within five to ten working days.
    ·   A delivery charge of £3.00.
    ·   An item charge of £1.25 per item.
For example, a customer ordering two items for delivery to W. Europe, will be charged £3.00 delivery + £2.50 items charge, totalling a delivery charge of £5.50.

USA - Aimed delivery within twelve to fifteen working days.
    ·   A delivery charge of £3.00.
    ·   An item charge of £2.00 per item.
For example, a customer ordering two items for delivery to the USA, will be charged £3.00 delivery + £4.00 item charge, totalling a delivery charge of £7.00.

Rest of the World - Aimed delivery within fifteen to twenty-two working days.
    ·   A delivery charge of £3.00.
    ·   An item charge of £2.75 per item.
For example, a customer ordering two items for delivery to the ROW, will be charged £3.00 delivery + £5.50 item charge, totalling a delivery charge of £8.50.

For a copy of our free catalogue please write to

Chimera Publishing Ltd
Readers' Services
PO Box 152
Waterlooville
Hants
PO8 9FS

or email us at
info@chimerabooks.co.uk

or purchase from our range of superbly erotic titles at
www.chimerabooks.co.uk

*Titles £5.99. **£7.99. **All others £6.99**

The full range of our wonderfully erotic titles are now
available as downloadable ebooks at our website

www.chimerabooks.co.uk

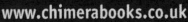

If you've not yet read the first two episodes of Alice's tormented teenage life, *Alice – Promise of Heaven. Promise of Hell* and *Alice – Shadows of Perdition*, you can obtain them from our Readers' Services, or from **www.chimerabooks.co.uk**.

Alice – Promise of Heaven. Promise of Hell
by
Surreal

This is the first in a biographical series, in 1950's Lancashire. Her parents killed in a freak accident, naïve sixteen-year-old Alice falls to the custody of the austere Richard Barker, the girl's only relative. Tyrannical and scheming, the pious Barker ensures the innocent girl's stay is not a happy one.

Kate Howell, precocious schoolmate and intimate, offers the exquisite Alice the means of escape. But life is never that simple.

Embracing opposing ideals the pair begin the journey of life - a trek that takes the vulnerable Alice directly into the arms of an older man.

The trials of Alice is a story of harsh discipline, lust and infatuation - of sexual confusion, carnal exploration, and the coming to terms with curious cravings.

1-903931-27-4 • £6.99

Alice – Shadows of Perdition
by
Surreal

Having escaped the clutches of the overbearing and pious Uncle Richard, Alice settled with the Howells, and although welcomed and cosseted, her feelings toward Jonathan cannot be suppressed. For all the attacks on her conscience she again attempts a seduction, reasoning the woman might succeed where the callow girl failed.

Oblivious of her sexual magnetism, Alice stumbles through the week, her only concern to protect that irresistible rear, but it transpires that Jonathan is not the only one with designs upon her delectable seat and beguiling figure. In an effort to deliver Katy from the wily and incorrigible Harris, she entraps herself, discovering his arm to be one to avoid.

Seeking the results from Carters, she meets again with the unpredictable Richard, and nothing would have prepared her for the bitter reception, or for the awful secret he harbours.

This powerful mix of tenderness, passion and austerity will take you into a candid and plausible world of the provocative...

1-903931-47-9 ● £6.99

Chimera Publishing Ltd

PO Box 152
Waterlooville
Hants
PO8 9FS

www.chimerabooks.co.uk
info@chimerabooks.co.uk
www.chimera-connections.com

***

Sales and Distribution in the USA and Canada

Client Distribution Services, Inc
193 Edwards Drive
Jackson
TN 38301
USA

***

Sales and Distribution in Australia

Dennis Jones & Associates Pty Ltd
19a Michellan Ct
Bayswater
Victoria
Australia 3153